BEYOND THE CHAIN

BEYOND THE CHAIN

MAYA MIDDLEMISS

ISBN: 978-9949-01-256-5

Published by

BLOCK
SPARKS

Cover design & interior formatting:
Mark Thomas / Coverness.com

A Note From The Author

Though fiction, *Beyond the Chain* is based on real world experiences of cryptocurrency purchasing and use, and present blockchain technologies.

To add a broader understanding of these subjects the story contains a limited number of informational endnotes, which are entirely optional extras to the narrative itself. These endnotes are denoted by use of a small superscript number in the text (eg ^{2}). These endnotes are located at the very end of the book.

Furthermore, as the world of crypto and blockchain moves very quickly, up-to-date references and further information will be maintained at
https://www.blocksparks.io/beyond-the-chain-book-reader-resources/

- Maya Middlemiss

CHAPTER ONE

Carrie had eaten nothing during the journey away from home. Her stomach was churning, but she knew it was a mixture of adrenaline and excitement rather than hunger. Not fear, she was beyond fear now and looking determinedly towards the future. In the past she had never travelled further from home than a couple of hours on the bus, but her life was changing at such a rapid pace. Things were going to be different.

As the plane took off, she left the final remnants of the old Carrie behind her. Glancing back down at the flat Stansted landscapes, she almost gasped as they broke through the clouds into the sunlight that was always just there waiting, even in the murky September afternoon. That was the first point at which she started to relax and unclench a little bit, release the knot in her stomach and the physical tension in her shoulders. She was away. She'd always been a nervous flyer, but so much of the fear and tension she felt now was tied up in memories of other journeys in the past, and a sense of breaking so many taboos by travelling alone.

Above her were blue skies, and the rest of her life lay ahead.

She felt lightheaded and giddy. She had told no one, except for Mrs Shah, with whom she'd left her front door key, and all she had said to her was that she would be going away for a couple of weeks. The decision had been made quite hastily, as she was dealing with the countdown to her son Alex's considerably better-planned travels, but once she had decided to take this trip, there was no possibility of reconsidering. It was obvious that she had to go, as soon as she could make it happen.

She'd packed sensible clothing, layers and practical shoes, having no real idea what to expect or plan for. Within minutes of landing, she realized her smart gilt-framed holiday suitcase felt all wrong for her present journey, which was so unlike any she'd known before. As she wheeled it away from the belt towards the exit at Athens airport, she remembered shopping with Alex just a couple of weeks ago, for all his travel gear. If only she'd been thinking more clearly, she could have been buying two of everything – rucksacks, sleeping bags, first aid kits. No one would have believed that Carrie too would take herself off with her world on her back, days after her eighteen-year-old son had done the same thing. Until she'd made up her mind in the last few days, she'd kept her plans to herself.

Carrie grabbed a stuffed pitta while she waited for the bus to the port. Chewing mechanically despite not really feeling hungry, she reminded herself that the next few days might be hard, travelling over land and sea. No one else would be looking out for her, reminding her to eat and take care of herself – but then again no one would be telling her when to eat or how much or whether or not they approved. Already this industrial landscape outside of Athens airport looked nothing like the Greece she remembered from her family holidays, it was hard to believe this was the same country. Those trips had been all retsina, suntan lotion, and good hotels -- Mark hadn't stinted, when it came to his time in the sun, she'd give him that, he had been generous in some ways. But from now on Carrie had to conserve the small amount of cash she'd been able to put together and make it last, which meant buses, ferries and street food. A whole new world.

She wondered what Alex was eating now, in South Sudan. She'd had one brief email to confirm he'd arrived safely at the project and was lodging with a local family near the school where he'd be volunteering. He'd be eating African food, travelling on far more basic buses than this one, surely – and having the time of his life. She knew it'd be tough for him too at times, her special boy hadn't always had things easy in life, but her pride and love for him welled up suddenly in her throat as she pictured his final wave and smile at the departure gate just a few days ago. Her brave boy.

Besides, even Alex's great adventure was nothing compared to Samar's journey. What her friend had been through must be unimaginable. Carrie couldn't wait to find her and make sure she was OK. It wouldn't be long now.

It was late when Carrie finally boarded the ferry and realised she'd be spending the night on hard, non-reclining seating. She'd never booked independent travel before, and it had been complicated and unfamiliar, especially while trying to keep spending to a minimum. Well, she would just have to manage. It was nothing, the lack of luxury, compared to the circumstances of others.

Everyone around her seemed to be in large family groups, speaking a range of languages, looking like they all somehow belonged together in this world, while she felt that hers had been completely transformed. Did she stand out and look different, alone or vulnerable? 'He's not here, he doesn't know where you are,' she muttered to herself over and over. Carrie had never been afraid of anyone in her life before she met Mark, and during the course of their marriage she had retreated into a tiny enclosure of self-doubt and claustrophobic limitations, where nothing was worth the risk of provoking Mark's violent anger. It had been easier to stay frozen and safe by not asking questions or making choices for herself; to let her world get smaller and smaller. Now she was reaching deep down for inner resources she had buried far away, and finding they were still there to draw upon.

She looked at an elderly Greek couple, sharing something hot from a flask, co-operatively holding each other's cups and bags and looking after each other almost without words. The man fussed, arranging a shabby blanket around his partner tenderly as they settled down for the night on what was obviously a routine journey together. Other groups were families, some with young children, speaking very fast and loud, in the way Carrie always seemed to feel people talked when she didn't understand the language. She smiled. She felt safe in the anonymity and unfamiliarity of the strange circumstances in which she found herself.

Despite the long day, Carrie didn't feel sleepy just yet. She went out on deck and found a seat. She snuggled into her jacket and watched the bright lights and container ships of Piraeus fade into the gloom of the horizon. In the morning she'd arrive at the island, and the last leg of her journey to search for and finally meet the woman she could honestly describe as her first real friend.

But first, she needed to finish her email to Alex. She imagined her words being read aloud to him by the horrible speech synthesiser app voice that they'd laughed at so much at first – but which had helped him get through his A Levels despite his dyslexia. He would have to rely on that far less in the basic environment of the African villages, she reflected, though his reading had improved immensely in the past few years.

She hoped he'd find enough data for the app to read this message out anyway, because there was such a lot to explain, about everything that had happened within the few days since he'd departed, even though she'd been making plans in her head even before she took him to Heathrow. She'd promised him she would be OK, if he would be OK, but had told the details of her plan to no one at all, not even Samar – at least so far as she knew, her reply had still not been read. Alex had been so afraid of leaving Carrie behind to cope with everything that awaited her, but he'd trusted her too, enough to get on his plane and let her sort things out her own way. Hopefully, he'd feel a lot more reassured once he read the message.

CHAPTER TWO

It had all begun with messages. It felt like a lifetime ago, although in fact it was just over three years past.

<hr>

MomsBoard private message:

Dear Carrie,

Sorry it took so long to reply to your PM, I am so glad you got in touch – it does sound like our sons have similar kinds of learning difficulties. And the same age too…

I know exactly what you mean, about feeling like you're almost under false pretences in this community, where some people seem to suffer so proudly through their children's varying limitations. I feel just the same as you, that my Jamal's intelligence and imagination sometimes feels like a benefit of his dyslexia – that it's like a gift for him, to be the way he is and so different to the other boys. He sees things in a unique way, it's just the ordinary people who don't understand. So I am glad my post resonated with you even if some of the other mums were so dismissive. It's not about how 'bad' you are or your situation, or how it compares to someone else's – surely it's about what you do with it, what you make of your life?

Of course it's tough for Jamal at school, but we are luckier than most in our country, as my husband works for the government and I work in the hospital, so we have excellent schooling. He has computers with special filters and software to help him take notes, and read things, and also the most amazing memory. It's not quite a school for 'normal' people, some of his teachers are rather exceptional, and I know how privileged that makes us.

But I don't know anyone else whose child has these learning problems in the same way, so I was so pleased to find the MomsBoard community. Even though I won't mention the creative aspects of dyslexia in the main group again – what is it with this competitive suffering? If they could see the children I see in the hospital, victims of conflict, patiently waiting for treatment and medicines and their families people have nothing... I am generalising, I know, but I think most of the parents on

*the forum are from liberal western countries like yours,
they don't know their sheer good fortune of birth.*

*Anyway, that's why it was so good to hear from you,
and I'd love to know more about Alex and his education.
What does he find helpful and inspiring, how do you
help him as a mum? We can learn from each other and
help each other, I hope.*

Good to know you,

Samar

....

Carrie smiled as she read the message, from the stranger she had defended in a parenting forum over a week ago. Funny how she could be this valiant anonymous warrior online, whereas at home she seemed to lose less and less agency. What would she do without the internet, where she could be whoever she wanted, whenever she dared? But this Samar sounded like a lovely mum who saw the same potential in her son as Carrie did in her own Alex, even though their lives seemed very different.

Carrie logged carefully out of the parenting website. Mark didn't like her using the computer, and she knew that he looked at the websites she visited. If he could find a reason to pick fault, ask nasty questions, and stop her from doing something, then he would do so – but it was just a site where people talked about their children with different learning disabilities and needs. Tried to help each other. Even he couldn't find a problem with that, could he? She only wanted to find the best support for Alex.

'What on earth do you know about his education, you're not a teacher, you've got no idea!' She could imagine the conversation.

Carrie had given in to pressure a few years ago to give up her teaching assistant job because Alex had left the primary school, and Mark couldn't understand that she had loved being in the classroom and working with the other kids. Especially the ones who were struggling, with their lessons and with how to behave. 'I pay enough bloody taxes for them to have special classes for disruptive kids, not untrained helpers who think they know everything, just because they have one "special" child of their own'.

Just one, yes. Carrie's eyes stung momentarily as she thought about the sister Alex should have had. She would have been in junior school now – but her beautiful baby girl had been born too soon at twenty weeks. Carrie had been on her own when it happened, although she was sure that Mark had been there not long before. Her pregnancy had ended abruptly in shock and grief, in a nightmare rush of blood, terror and hatred towards her own body for casting out her tiny, tiny baby when she was unready for the world.

There were times when Carrie wondered if the depression and withdrawal that had followed had affected Alex's development in his pre-school years. She had trouble remembering those days of medication and madness. Would he have learned to read and somehow his mind grown differently if she had been emotionally available and there for him? Certainly, Mark's reaction to the loss of baby Grace had been the beginning of the end of trust and of love: when they should have grieved together, all he had to express was anger. He hadn't even wanted to hold the baby, and seemed to resent paying for the service and the small memorial.

Carrie blinked, trying not to let her thoughts go down pathways that ended in a dark, cold numbness. Guilt didn't help, and there was no mention in anything she'd read to suggest that her lack of reading and playing with her son could have caused a learning disability by itself. All she could do anything about was the future, not the past. She was still taking the medication, reporting dutifully to the doctor who she knew reported to Mark. It was easier just to go along with what they both wanted, and keep doing her best for her boy, the boy she loved more than anything else in the world.

Alex would be home soon, and he'd need the computer, he'd need his mum to help with homework too. He was so smart and had such an incredible memory, it had actually delayed his diagnosis for a time – if he was read a story he could repeat it to his teachers word for word after one listening so they thought he was reading it, and when he could get a grip on the facts and what was expected of him, then his numeracy was way ahead of his key stage. As was his storytelling – it was a shame they did less creative writing in senior school, he had such a gift!

Mark had promised that Alex could have his own laptop for his birthday, so she wasn't going to argue or make a fuss, or be responsible for anything which could spoil that. Having his own computer would be transformational for Alex! Instead, Carrie quietly investigated applications and programmes they could get that would help him master it, enabling him to use it for all his studies and projects. Mark had agreed, the birthday was coming up soon, and Carrie knew it was exactly what Alex needed. All she had to do was not rock the boat and mess things up – and she had learned that lesson well by then.

MomsBoard private message:

Hi Carrie,

Wow, the laptop and the language software sound amazing! Thank you for sending me the lovely picture of Alex's birthday party, what a wonderful handsome young man. He looked so happy with all his friends, I could see you were so proud of him. Fifteen years is an important coming-of-age time, we have this to look forward to with our Jamal in the summer, and it's so strange to see our little boys transforming into men. I did laugh when you told me about him wanting a razor, to shave so optimistically at nothing – boys are just the same, across all cultures!

Jamal loves computers too. He doesn't have his own laptop, but he has built a computer in the basement at home, salvaging bits from all over the place. It doesn't even look like a computer as it's just in an open box, but he will spend hours down there, adding new bits and getting so excited if someone can get him this or that special part for it! It's become a bit obsessive, but I am happy for him. Some of his friends are getting interested in politics, even religion, and others are getting interested in girls – all differently dangerous subjects. So I prefer that he is fidgeting around with his chips and boards and whatever. I am sure he is going to invent something amazing one day. Or does every mother believe this about their sons?

It is odd because he is not great with numbers in school; he doesn't do well with sequencing and remembering things in order. But he can find connections between things, read maps, see the patterns in anything. He just can't remember the list of things like rivers and chiefs that they expect them to repeat in exams, completely useless things. Which king was the son of this one and father of that one. He says to me, 'Mum, we have computers to remember lists of things now, there's no point in using up people's brains to store all this data. We aren't hard drives!' He's so funny. And he knows his brain is different to other peoples' brains, he just isn't bothered by it.

I remember when he was quite little, not even four years old, and there was a dreadful confusion when he was with my stupid niece at the park and she let him wander off. I was pregnant and unwell and maybe hadn't been giving him so much attention just then. So he just walked home, from the other side of the town, she didn't even realise for at least fifteen minutes. And just when we were screaming at each other on the phone about what had happened and when she had last seen him, he knocked on the door and came in! Then I was screaming at him too because I was in such a shock, and he just shrugged his little shoulders and said he'd missed me and wanted to come home. We had hardly ever walked to the park even then, we always took the car – so he hadn't even done the journey on foot very often. And at three he just made his way home to me because he felt like it, through busy city streets!

It was really around that time, or afterwards when I was home with the baby, that we started to notice he saw things differently to the way other boys did – though it's hard when it's with your first isn't it, to know what's normal? All the mothers around here are so competitive about their little princes: Hamid is the first to talk, Aman the first to play the piano or something... None of these mothers have a job, and they all have servants to do everything at home too, so there's nothing for them to do all day except say things like, 'Oh, is Jamal not reading properly yet? My little Sofia can write the Koran backwards in Cantonese, while composing a four-part concerto!'

I was glad when I could go back to work. I am a radiographer in the main city hospital, and it is interesting and useful work – we sometimes help the doctors make lifesaving decisions and diagnoses, because we can read the plates better than they can. I was university educated in Damascus with expert English language teachers as well as scientific training. Oh god, I sound like one of those dreadful competitive mothers now, I know it!

But I am proud of the work I do, and did not go back to it until we had found a school where Jamal could thrive and develop at his own pace, following the things he is fascinated by. For a long time, it was insects and dinosaurs, and now it's computers! But always about organising and fitting and sorting things out, so they make sense to him, even if they make little sense to anybody else, or he doesn't think it's worth explaining.

When did you first notice that Alex was different to other boys? I don't know if it's the same in your culture, but here there is a lot of shame here, associated with disability and difference. People even lie about it, or cover it up, but my husband supported me in being open about our son's needs and making sure he got the help that could let him progress. In the past in our country, and maybe in other parts today outside of the cities where things are very backward, there were a lot of cousin marriages and things like that. So that's what people say to be unkind, if they think there is something wrong with your baby...

They judge that you are backward and tribal and that you essentially brought down this fate on yourself. Our country, our region, has been through such a lot, so many uprisings. There is a lack of trust here and people are quick to divide and turn on each other, even in the affluent and so-called educated middle classes. Like me they are all hoping the next generation will be able to leave and travel to other countries, they pour everything into their precious little princes for this reason.

I make my friends and my community sound like such awful people, for this I must apologise. Some of them are very nice! Just I don't always feel like I have so much in common with them, and it's easier to talk to colleagues at work – even male colleagues, though that's difficult in our religion sometimes – or to you online, in another country!

....

Carrie was enjoying Samar's friendship too, it felt like they had a lot in common with their boys. And she wanted to ask about the baby as well, whether he or she had any learning difficulties? How old was her second child? She didn't want to cause offence though, especially after Samar had said about what people thought was likely to be the cause of such troubles. While they clearly had many things in common, it was obvious that in other ways their lives and cultures were incredibly different, and it was difficult to cross that divide with written words in some ways, even when there was nothing but fascination and curiosity to motivate it.

Once again she carefully logged off the family computer, which Mark didn't really know she used during the day. She wondered about Samar's husband, her home, and how she got online to MomsBoard. Most of the other users seemed to be British or American, how had Samar found them? She must have been really isolated, with her dyslexic boy and her strange friends.

What a sad and judgemental society in which to live in, she caught herself thinking – then stopped herself to reflect on the irony. As if her life was so much better! She seemed to have fewer and fewer friends of her own, because she'd really focussed herself on being there for Alex, and the extra help he needed. Carrie wasn't bright enough to have her own career or regular interests, as Mark kept reminding her – after all, she couldn't even manage to balance the family finances and have quality meals on the table at the end of the month without overdrawing, if he didn't keep an eye on everything for them. She didn't have a lot in common with the other mums at the school either, who either had careers or more interesting and lives and families.

Carrie had lost contact with a lot of friends when they had moved to Nottinghamshire for Mark's job, many years ago. Since giving birth to Alex and being so unwell, she'd not really been in the mood to get to know new people, so she hadn't formed close connections when she was a new mum. Then, her job at the school had let her be close to other children – the ones she wasn't going to have – but she hadn't really got to know the other teachers and parents as friends. That never would have worked, Mark could be so… odd and unpredictable.

Her friend Donna, who'd worked at the school, had even implied there was something weird about Mark! Just because Carrie had rearranged a coffee morning when he was unexpectedly going to be home one day. Donna had made out she hadn't got the text and come round anyway, freaking out when Carrie didn't want to let her in the house, but Mark was *working,* so of course he'd have got angry if they'd disturbed him. She didn't mean to be rude keeping her friend on the doorstep, but no she could hardly go out instead could she, with nothing properly arranged? No, Donna would just have to go now and they'd do something another time.

Donna had tried to get Carrie out on her own a few times after that, and to talk to her at school, but Carrie felt a strange mixture of shame and defensiveness, and above all a burning need to keep her home life and her work in the school completely separated. No dinner parties and weekend picnics for the Paige family. A dinner party, with her and Mark? Carrie shook her head in horror, imagining the controlling, gradually escalating voice, as he drank more wine, and finally the yelling and singling out, perhaps the crockery smashing – and the cringing fear of what would happen when everyone went home to their normal, peaceful lives, in which she vaguely imagined people could converse and exist without fear. It was better not to provoke him.

Not long after that he'd pressured her into giving up the job at the school, anyway. She'd ended up leaving more abruptly than she'd intended, as somebody had thought or told someone else that maybe she was leaving because she was pregnant, and that was too painful to talk about, even to deny it. So, there were no leaving parties or cards or exchanging of phone numbers, Carrie had just tiptoed sideways out of the room. Like always. It had made her stressed and sad to leave though, so Dr Edwards had increased her medication again until those feelings went away. After that she didn't remember being stressed or sad at all.

Thank goodness for her books, to be able to retreat into a story on her Kindle – the only nice thing Mark had ever given her, and it had been a joy to find that most of the classical literature she adored was available freely for download. Thank goodness too for the online world, and places like the MomsBoard group. No one there would judge her for not having a job, or for what was going on in her life. They couldn't see into her marriage or her home and make judgements. She could just be the only thing she cared about being: a loving and concerned mother.

She had been part of a different forum site about pregnancy and miscarriage support years ago, but for some reason Mark had found out and didn't approve of all that wallowing and not getting over it. So these days she was careful to keep her browsing discreet and quiet. It had helped her to make a friend in another country, who was never going to turn up on the doorstep or ask difficult questions or try to see into private parts of her life; never going to ask questions that were difficult or painful, or about things Carrie simply couldn't remember clearly.

It hadn't always been like this. Carrie passed the photo in the hall, of their wedding day. She'd had it framed years ago, after reading somewhere that being surrounded by memories of happier times was the best way to connect with the past in a relationship that had changed somewhere along the way. She must have thought that'd be a good idea at the time, to recapture and reconnect with the two people in the photograph somehow.

Of course they'd both changed, it had been nearly two decades ago. She'd gained weight, let her hair go back to its natural mousy brown, worn in a mid-length mumsy style. It had looked good when it was long enough to style in a beautiful wedding up-do, but that was hardly practical for everyday life decades later. She'd rather have it short, but Mark wouldn't like of that, and it wasn't worth winding him up over. If the dark circles and frown lines around her eyes which made her seem older sometimes than her early forties and a lifetime distant from the smiling young bride in the photo also worried Mark, he didn't mention it.

Mark hadn't changed so much physically, just the hairline and waistline, despite the regular squash games at the weekends. But the man he had been – so passionate and inspiring – where had he gone? They used to talk about all the things he cared about, from his anger and estrangement from his own family, to his dreams for financial independence and early retirement… Well, she reflected, they lived pretty well materially. Looking around the extended semi-detached suburban home they shared on the outskirts of Nottingham, she compared it with the cramped terrace house she'd grown up in, and had to agree she'd 'done alright for herself'. She wished her mother could have seen and enjoyed the spacious living room, study and kitchen. Her beautiful grandson… Mark never had any problem spending money on living well or creating a home that reflected his professional ambitions and values, even though nobody ever visited to see it.

They probably had a nicer house than her friend Samar, in that distant hot country she lived in, and they never had to worry about having enough money to spend. Carrie didn't even need to work. She was very fortunate to be in that position, as Mark often reminded her. It felt like Mark, though, would rather be at work than at home with her and Alex. At least –she'd not really thought about this before – she hoped he was happier there, because all she ever saw at home was his frustration and a sense of barely-concealed anger.

*

The new academic year brought new challenges as Alex got older, but the laptop really helped. He was making good progress with his lessons, and although the football he loved took up a lot of time, he did seem to really understand the importance of getting good marks. He was a popular, attractive boy, and that got him a long way when it came to winning the patient support of friends and teachers, but he did realise he needed the grades too, and was making a lot of effort.

Carrie knew that he *could* read, when he really focused his attention, instead of having music playing or the TV on in the background. She couldn't bear to nag or be controlling, well aware that Alex got enough of that kind of parenting from his father, and she did her best to focus on what he was good at and doing well with, both at school and everywhere else. She tried to nurture his wonderful memory and imagination, and encourage him to think of things he had to learn as a whole shape or pattern - one he could sometimes see better than she could..

Having discussed their boys' challenges further with her online friend, Carrie decided to talk more to Alex about how he remembered things for exams, as it was something Jamal was still continually struggling with, in different ways to Alex, even though they both bore the same medical label. Jamal's last set of exams had apparently gone really badly, and it was affecting his progression at a school which sounded ever so rigorous academically. Samar was frustrated and upset, and didn't know how to help him, so Carrie wanted to help her friend support her son through his challenges.

She knew Alex would relate to everything Jamal was going through at school, with all his struggles. But he must have had a different kind of memory, related to his dyslexia, that made him so good with lists and memorising information, because Alex had no problem with that kind of thing – once he'd managed to read the list properly in the first place, he was really good at remembering it. Carrie wondered if it was something photographic, as though he could call an image of the words on a page and somehow focus in on the details? Her own memory was terrible, even before her illness and the years of taking pills. But she'd not been able to find out any genetic connection between her own memory and Alex's learning disability.

'It isn't like that Mum, I don't learn it using the words, I see it differently instead. Like a whole interconnected thing, instead of a list. Has your friend's son tried that?' Alex was curious and interested. He really wanted to help the boy he'd never met, whose mum had been online friends with his mum for months now.

'I don't know,' Carrie admitted. 'She said he has a hard time learning lists of things, which he needs for exams.' Carrie was making a lasagna for dinner, and Alex was working at his laptop at the kitchen table, glad of any excuse to get diverted from his history homework. He still loved the machine he'd been thrilled to receive for his birthday in the spring, but even with all the voice recognition and text conversion apps they had discovered, some subjects remained hard for him, even though his naturally good memory helped him a lot.

'Oh yeah, that's horrible, when you just have to learn a list of facts, I'm lucky that we don't have to do that very often. At least not now. Mrs McKenzie said they had to learn everything that way when she was at school, she loves telling us about how they beat her fingers with a ruler when they made a mistake in the times tables and things. I don't think I'd have been very successful at her school.' Alex grinned and stretched, and like always, Carrie's heart melted at his disarming good looks. Every day she saw more glimpses of the young man her boy was growing into, and she reflected that that smile would make up for a lot when it came to his struggles with words and reading. She wiped the granite worktop and glanced at the simmering sauce, turning the heat on the halogen hob down to low, before joining Alex at the kitchen table where the three of them usually ate their meals, and that she and her son regularly hung out together between the end of school and Mark getting home from work.

'Who was that English teacher you had last year, who made you learn lists of plays and books?' she asked him. 'The one you liked? I know you're not in his form anymore, but he gave you some useful tricks, didn't he? I remember you saying that you'd managed to learn some things through some kind of memory pattern, at least long enough for the exam.' Because Jamal was surely right, Carrie thought, nobody had to store stuff like that their head long term. It's not even what computers were invented for after all, information like that could surely live easily enough on *paper?*

'Yes, Mr Norton. He was cool! But the funny thing was, although it was a weird way of memorising, it really worked. I mean, it was like, a year ago, and he helped me with the list of Dickens novels, do you remember?'

Carrie did remember. She loved Dickens, and she couldn't understand why Alex's syllabus seemed to put so much weight on memorising a list of novels in order of publication, instead of simply enjoying them for their wonderful storytelling and characterisation. Alex didn't seem too bothered though; it wasn't his preferred style of literature. He did far better with audiobooks – reading Victorian literature would have been very hard work for him. She remembered reading some of Bleak House aloud to him, and the two of them had watched the BBC drama, the one with Scully in it, though Alex hadn't seemed to enjoy it much as his mum did.

'It's so weird, Mum, because I haven't thought about it since that exam – which would have been June, summer before last. I honestly haven't given it a thought and I can't remember anything about the stories – sorry, I know you love them but they're really not my scene. I don't know who the main characters are, even, unless they're in the titles. But I can still remember: The Pickwick Papers, Oliver Twist, Nicholas Nickleby, The Old Curiosity Shop, Barnaby Rudge…!'

Carrie's mouth dropped open slightly. This was a boy who could not remember where his trainers were most of the time, or what days he had to take which homework and textbooks in.

'How on earth do you know that?' She wasn't sure about the order, but it amazed her he could remember the titles of any Dickens novels at all. She wished she still had her mother's beautiful leather-bound hardbacks, what on earth had happened to those? What had happened to any of her mother's things? It was a side effect of the medication she'd been on for so long, that Carrie's thoughts could easily slide away into reveries like this, especially when something triggered a buried memory from long ago. But she was determined to focus on this conversation and stay present with it.

'Well, it's sort of a trick, I guess. Anyone can learn how to do it.'

Alex was keen to explain more. 'You have to know the first one, there's no trick for that, you just have to remember it, and because it was for an exam I could remember it had the word "paper" in it. That was the only reason for having to learn that list in the first place! So that was the start of it, one called something like paper, and that meant The Pickwick Papers.' Alex turned away from his new laptop altogether and pushed it closed, so he could talk with his preferred broad and expressive hand gestures. He really communicated with his whole body – perhaps that helped make up for the struggles he had with words.

'Then he told me to make a really strong picture, joining this up to the next thing I needed to remember, which was Oliver Twist. The funny thing was I found it easier to think about things which were nothing to do with the stories, or even the films – just the words. In fact, if I thought about the films or the people or something, that was sort of confusing, probably as they all seemed really similar to me, with all those dreary dresses and things.

'So I thought about twisting paper. Just chose a word from each book title, a unique or unusual word, to join them up tightly in a single image. Mr Norton said make it really strong and vivid in my mind. So I thought about a bright yellow Moebius strip.'

'A what?' Carrie didn't remember that from Dickens.

'You know, an infinite loop, like when you get a strip of paper and twist it and then join the ends together. So it's continuous and only has one surface. Never mind, Mum, it's a maths thing! I imagined one of those but made of really bright fluorescent yellow like a Post-It Note or highlighter colour. And it's the same colour on both sides, well obviously, because really there's only one side anyway. I made it, like, really eye-burning acid yellow. Obviously, just in my head, I didn't actually make it.'

Carrie must have continued to look baffled, because Alex rushed on, trying to help make it make sense for her.

'Just remember that picture, of a bright yellow paper with a twist in it. If it's easier just think of a paper with any kind of twist, like this one–' He grabbed a Post-It Note from the pile of blocks he kept in his folder. The different colours helped him to make notes and organise his ideas. Alex scrunched a post-it into a strip then twisted it firmly, fanning the ends out into a butterfly. 'But it's supposed to be in your mind's eye, right? You can't make a physical thing each time, that wouldn't really be doable. Though I don't know, maybe it'd be a really powerful way of remembering some things.'

Carrie turned the butterfly of paper over in her hand, trying to make it relate to The Pickwick Papers and Oliver Twist in her mind. A Twist, made of Paper… OK, she'd go with that for now.

Alex was keen to move on.

'Then I had to join Oliver Twist to Nicholas Nickleby. I only needed to think about one word in each title that would make me remember the whole book name. So I...' Alex stopped, looking sheepish suddenly, his enthusiasm stopped in its tracks. His voice did that strange octave-jumping thing that was starting to happen a lot lately, and he changed the subject abruptly.

'Mum, do you remember that little shit from Juniors, Daniel Edgely? The really whiny one who was always telling tales and sneaking around trying to get people in trouble?'

'Alex!' Carrie was secretly a bit proud that her teenage son sometimes spoke to her using words he'd use with his mates, rather than how he'd talk to his teachers, but she did worry about his father hearing him using language like that as she couldn't imagine the rage Mark would get into if he heard him. Not to mention if he heard her not correcting him either.

'Well, he was!' Alex said, defended. 'And he got Ashok into mega trouble once, telling on him about copying Simon's homework. It wasn't even his fault, he just forgot his book and he didn't have time to do it properly, he was going to get a rocket off Miss Baker, anyway. But it was even worse when she knew he copied.'

Carrie remained confused. They surely hadn't been doing Dickens in Juniors. And Miss Baker, she could have sworn, was maths.

'So anyway,' Alex continued in a guilty rush, 'Me and Ashok, we, er, took Daniel's Twister, outside the sweet shop, that afternoon, to sort of teach him a lesson, about not telling on people. Well, I distracted him, and Ash grabbed it. Um, he nicked it, you could say.

Mum, don't do that look, it was like, three years ago, and we were just kids messing around. And I did feel horrible even though Daniel was snivelling tail-telling little… Well, he deserved it. Anyway. I was an accessory to the theft of an ice lolly, and it was a strong memory, as I never did anything like that again before or after. And I did feel bad about it. I used the feeling bad as part of the memory-glue (that was my word for it, not Mr Norton's). It was by Patel's shop near the bus stop, with all the adverts in the window and the coloured canopy. And I was able to use that memory to really stickily join together the ideas of Oliver TWIST, and Nicholas NICKleby'. Alex grabbed a Post-It Note then, and wrote down in order in his unique meticulous-yet-clumsy capital letters: PAPER, TWIST, NICK.

Carrie didn't know whether to be amused, impressed, or shocked. Her son, a thief, and possibly a bully as well? Yet somehow this all helped him to remember the work of Charles Dickens? It was really bizarre, but she was willing to stick with it and see what else would be revealed.

Alex rushed hastily on, not liking the look on his mother's face. 'So that was the first three, in order: The Pickwick Papers, Oliver Twist, Nicholas Nickleby. And then next was The Old Curiosity Shop – another shop, but the important thing was the order – so I had to get right away from the memory of Patel's newsagents and that shop and the idea of nicking things, as it would have really muddled up the sequence.'

'Don't tell me you nicked from Mr Patel?' said Carrie, aghast, feeling like she was still missing something fundamental about the bigger picture, but troubled and distracted by some of these emerging details.

'No, not ever! I never would. I always liked Mr Patel. It was outside on the pavement, and it wasn't even me took the lolly, it was Ashok, and he just grabbed it while I pretended to… Look, it doesn't even matter. I wish I never even told you. But it's part of the explanation.

'I was saying, I needed a totally new way to join up Nicholas Nickleby and the Old Curiosity Shop, I didn't even know what a Curiosity Shop was – thank god we didn't have to read that one, it sounds even worse than that book with all the lawyers in it. But I did know a nickel was an American coin, so I thought about some kind of old antique shop or junk shop, with a big box of ancient coins in the window, and one of them said on it that it was a nickel. I don't even know what an actual nickel looks like, but it didn't really matter. I made a strong mental picture of it just like Mr Norton said to: the shop interior was all dark and the treasure chest of coins was sort of in a spotlight, with a big shiny nickel on top, I knew it was a nickel because it had a big label on it saying what it was.

'So – The Pickwick Papers, Oliver Twist, Nicholas Nickleby, then The Old Curiosity Shop,' he declared decisively. 'You only have to remember each link, not more than two things at a time. Because when you remember them, they each sort of trigger the next one along. Like Nicholas Nickleby doesn't even matter when you're thinking about the twisted paper. It's best if you don't even remember it then, because you have to do it in order, properly. Like a chain. You have to have the links in order.

'Then I had to remember Barnaby Rudge, and I dunno what a Rudge is.'

'It's not a thing, it's a name,' Carries said, smiling. 'The name of the main character. Poor Barnaby lived through some terrible times, and some awful things happened to him, none of it was his fault. He ended up in Newgate Prison, and he–'

'Sounds like all those Dickens books Mum!' Alex grinned. 'That's the thing, all the actual stories and the people in them felt the same to me, so I could never remember anything interesting, or distinct about them. But it doesn't matter, all I needed was the word, and I knew Barnaby was a name. I'd never heard Rudge as a name and that would have been much harder to associate with for a memory. But Barnaby? Well, I did have to think hard at the time, but do you remember that DVD we had when I was little, with all the programmes from your era? You know, Dangermouse and The Clangers and–'

'Barnaby the Bear!' Carrie burst out. 'How on earth did you remember that? That was from the seventies or eighties or something! And you're right, it was another era. Television pre-history!'

'But that DVD Mum, sometimes you must have put it on a loop or something, maybe when you were ill when I was little, as I remember every word of some of those cartoons. And that lion made of plants that used to utterly creep me out. I wasn't even specially fond of Barnaby Bear, but it was the only connection I could think of with that name. And I think it had a bandage on its head for some reason? I don't know if it was some kind of hat, but I remember a white thing on its head.

'So, I had already used 'shop' in the last link the chain, then it seemed better to try to link the word 'curiosity' if I could this time. Link 'curiosity' and this Barnaby, and all I'd got to work with was Barnaby the Bear. I decided that it *was* a bandage on his head and made a story about it, thinking about the saying "curiosity killed the cat". I imagined the bear chasing a cat to see where it was going and it went under the coffee-table in the living room – yes, our living room at home – and the bear banged its head hard. Had to wear a bandage. In my mind it was like a little children's cartoon, a drawn one like the ones on that DVD instead of a modern animation. Sometimes it's easier to remember something like a video, not a still picture. Though usually I do still pictures.'

Carrie was starting to piece it together now. 'So you used one thing to remind you of the next thing?'

'Well, sort of. It's more like, there's all the things, they just are. What you have to do is link them. If each thing is in its place in the chain, it sort of points you to the next one, each thing is the link between two others. It couldn't fit in anywhere else.'

That made it sound like he'd not just remembered a bunch of Dickens' novels, he'd actually remembered them in order.

Carrie reached for the laptop, and smiled inwardly at the irony of using Google to investigate the oeuvre of a Victorian novelist. But her smile froze one click later, when she realised that Alex – her seriously dyslexic though very creative teenage son – had just accurately recalled the exact titles of Dickens' first five novels, in the correct order. As memorised for an exam over fifteen months previously. She stared back at Alex, who grinned proudly.

'Mr Norton says it's a trick which was invented by the Greeks or Romans or someone like that, thousands of years ago, even before they had writing. I don't remember,' he grinned. 'Anyway, they used all sorts of things, like thinking about a journey they were used to walking and all the things they saw in a building or a place. Some of them even invented rooms just for arranging memories in, but that must have been harder than starting with an actual place that you already knew.

'I remember thinking, before they could write anything and read it, it was like the whole of humankind had dyslexia. They had to use their minds to store things, and actually it was possible to do it.'

Carrie was stunned. So there was a way, to use your head like a disk in a computer, and write stuff in it – and retrieve it later?

'Sometimes magicians do it today,' Alex went on, 'when they know what card you're going to pull out next – it might be a trick deck so they've made you take the one they want, but also they could have somehow learned the whole order, just by doing this kind of trick in their memory. Or they Google stuff about people in the audience and memorise a ton of things that people don't even remember they put on Facebook or something, then the magician picks them out at random and "reads their mind" and everyone's amazed.

'I know Mr Norton was English, but he taught me a different but similar thing for numbers, which just sounds really silly actually, but it's one-is-a-bun, two-is-a-shoe, three-is-a-tree and so on. He knew I struggled with remembering sequences of things, for all my subjects. So you can do the same thing – I don't really use that one, because I can't think of any time when I have to remember numbers like that, though I did use it to remember your phone number before I had my mobile. Remember, you made me say it over and over? There was an even longer set of words you could learn, to connect up bigger numbers.'

His generation never had to remember phone numbers, Carrie realised, a task which would have seriously disadvantaged her son. He even didn't have to read the names properly in his phone's address book, either, just know roughly how the word started, at which point it would be promptly paired by the app with a thumbnail image of the friend he wanted to call – easily Alex's preferred point of reference.

Returning to the stove, Carrie tasted the pasta sauce and adjusted the seasoning slightly before turning the power off. She wiped her hands on the kitchen cloth, and sat back down at the kitchen table with Alex. 'So you use this – trick – to learn lists of things, for exams? When else have you used it?'

'Well, I haven't really thought of it so much lately,' he admitted. 'Since I got the laptop – and it's so brilliant to have my own – I can just make my own lists of anything I need to remember, and our exams now aren't so much about things we've remembered so that's better for me. And the dictation app is fantastic, now it's really learning my voice. Even the Stephen Hawking reading app is better than it was on the old computer. Having an app actually made for dyslexic kids to learn from is just awesome. Maybe your friend could get it for her son? You could send her the link about it?

'Also now we're doing GSCE stuff there's less facts and more working things out, thinking about things – it's actually harder work but the way of asking and answering the questions, it's easier for me. In some ways I've got more stuff in my head than some of my friends, as I can't rely on keeping it anywhere else!'

Carrie was once again awestruck by the things her son, who couldn't read at all until he was nine years old, had already accomplished academically. Samar was right, there *were* positive advantages that their boys had in their unusual brains. They were amazing. People who relied on being able to read things easily actually never had to develop the skills to store all this stuff, or of being able to link it together when they needed to in new and revolutionary ways.

'I still use that technique for revising though,' Alex said, 'like for science when we have to just remember things they can ask us about directly. Mrs Novak says that even if you just pick up an extra mark here or there for recalling something, then it's worth it, and that can be the difference of one grade becoming another. So I used it for arm muscles and things like that. Took a bit of imagination when it's like the words themselves don't have any other meaning, though. You can do it if you think of a word which is similar and will remind you of the thing itself, so long as it wouldn't remind you of anything else on the list. Like for the deltoid muscle I used a river delta and actually remembered a diagram from my geography book – to learn stuff for a biology exam! Hope that's not cheating!'

'That's just amazing, Alex,' Carrie said, still blown away by her incredible son. 'Does it help with that history composition though?'

'Not a bit!' he declared, ruefully returning to his laptop. 'This is one of those questions where you have to read this boring long text, then think about it and make up your own opinions about pros and cons and things, then somehow get them organised into an essay.' He groaned and rolled his eyes. 'What really helps there is the reading it aloud app, and now I've heard it through a few times I can more or less remember it, so I can answer the questions. It's much easier to remember some paragraphs and maps and families than it is a list of random words. Well, it is if they're more interesting than this stuff about Corn Laws.'

Carrie returned to the stove and listened as the murmuring laptop re-read key passages from the text he was analysing, while she assembled the lasagna. She marvelled at the combination of technology and creativity that let her son compete on a level playing field with his classmates and gradually increase his grades steadily throughout the past year or so, despite his challenges.

In a quiet, shamed part of her heart, she had occasionally wondered if all the apps conferred some kind of unfair advantage on him, making reading and writing suddenly a means to all his academic studies instead of a terrible barrier to overcome. She would never have said it out loud – though god knows Mark had done so, more than once, and had even used it as an excuse to delay getting the new computer.

But Carrie realised that the kind of work Alex was doing now was more about showing real understanding and the ability to think, and when that was the metric, suddenly her son was streets ahead of many of his peers. Those were the skills which would get him on his feet on the other side of GCSEs, the thinking which would let him make his way successfully in the world – far away from here, she thought bitterly, as she opened the oven door. How sad to wish your only child a safe distance from the tinderbox tension of the family home. She slipped the seasoned lasagna into the oven.

Later, during the family meal, Mark ridiculed and belittled Carrie's carefully prepared dinner and told her off for helping Alex too much with his homework: what could she possibly know about history anyway, she'd probably pull his grades down, that's what she'd do! For heaven sakes don't go listening to your stupid mother! But Carrie just reflected internally that memory was a strange thing, and the mind was strange. Alex had to listen to all of this unpleasantness night after night, but he still came to her for help when his dad was out at work, and she would still do anything to help him achieve what he was capable of.

⋯⋯⋯⋯⋯⋯⋯⋯⋯⋯⋯⋯⋯⋯⋯⋯⋯

MomsBoard private message:

Oh my dear friend,

I cannot begin to share with you the amazing outcome of your advice about Alex's memory technique!

At first Jamal wasn't at all sure, but he had to learn a long list of chiefs and towns and battles for a history test. It sounds like just the kind of thing that your Alex had to do, and just as bad a fit with Jamal's style of learning. Get him to write a story about one of the battles, or paint a picture of it, well he would be amazing. Just don't ask him which one happened before the other one, or in what order the towns were taken! He was getting so stressed and agitated, and I have never been able to help him before.

But, we sat down with the list, and together we built it using the pictures, just like you described. I won't explain to you what they were as they were all Arabic words, but I thought about all that you said about making it vivid, and using all the senses and emotions and even the feelings, about the image. I am sorry but I did laugh inwardly, at what you told me about Alex remembering taking the other boy's confectionary and how it still made him guilty and shy, that he could use that bad feeling to help him remember a name of a book written a century ago!

With Jamal there was one link we made in the list which was about a dessert he adores, that we mainly have only on feast days and religious festivals, and I made him really imagine anticipating the taste of it as it was baking and then cooling, perfuming the whole house as it sat on the side table. I promised to make it for him if he did well in the test, and I am so proud to tell you that this dessert is in the oven right now! Then he had to imagine there was a model car in the middle of it, but that was about connecting with the next word, I won't elaborate. But the point is we did just like you advised, used all the senses and emotions to make it really sharp in his mind. And now he will enjoy his reward!

Because it worked! He got ninety-two percent on his test – this was just amazing, the teacher even thought maybe he was copying or cheating – he got upset when she asked him, and then they called me in and I explained, she wound up saying sorry to him after all! She was amazed by the technique but she had heard of something like it before. She was from a faraway area where they still had visiting Sufis who travelled for miles and were said to learn some things in a similar way: they could recite endless religious verses and they never wrote anything down. She called it a 'memory palace' – though I know the people she speaks of and they do not live in palaces, so far from it, they are very humble in all that they do.

So anyway, my friend, I am so grateful to you because you have not just helped my boy get a good grade in this history test; you have empowered him to master so much in his future learning. It seems that passing through to the studying that he wants to do as an adult all depends on this stultifying and uncreative stage, where they must learn things that other people have created or said and then regurgitate them back out onto the page, with no thought or creativity of their own! This is not evidence of learning! But it seems that it is, for the making of decisions about his future. It has driven me to despair knowing that his future access to study overseas depends on these stupid exams that seemed stacked up against him from the start. And you have unlocked this technique, which he can now use over and over again, to master it all and get to the studying he wants to do!

Which is all on the computer. He loves it, and is spending more and more time on it. He is doing this new programme, which is actually making money – not actual money like pounds and dollars, but he says it is a crypto currency. He's not getting money by earning it, his computer is actually somehow making the money for him somehow, simply computing it – how extraordinary is that? Only the electricity going in, and the power of the computer chips, makes it happen. Although our electricity is sometimes unreliable, it is inexpensive. Jamal says anyone can do it, manufacture these crypto-coins, and it's going to change the world. There are ways to change it for our local currency, but even more important you can change it for real hard money like US dollars. Perhaps even your pounds that you have in England!

It's called Bitcoin, he is going to explain me more about it at the weekend, as he's been reading everything, and they have a discussion forum just like our one here. Well, I imagine it's a bit different to MomsBoard, actually. He is talking to computer and Bitcoin people from America and everywhere. He says it will one day bring down the banks – which I tell him is dangerous talk, even to have online. You might not realise that talk itself can be dangerous, living in a liberated and free country, but we have many secret police here and no end of people who want to ingratiate themselves and inform on others, of things they haven't understood themselves. Jamal just says, Bitcoin will replace money and the banks could just become irrelevant, not be taken down in some revolution, but my neighbours would be too stupid to understand that. I asked him to just keep quiet about what he is doing in the basement, let them think he's playing games all day like their own lazy children. My Jamal is changing the world!

But I must share some sadness now, to answer your question about his sister. I am sorry to change the happy tone of this message, but I want to answer you honestly and fully, and actually I enjoy the chance to talk about this.

My beautiful daughter Aaliyah would have been nearing her twelfth birthday now, but she was taken from us by a short illness, when she was a little child of five. It was a form of meningitis. She just went from being healthy and happy and playing, to a slight cold and fever – and in two days, she was gone forever. Her loss grieves me and Mohit still, and Jamal too, for all that they fought as children. I had indulged her a bit: boys are highly valued in our culture, but had my wonderful son already, and I was secretly so happy when my second baby was a girl! I dreamed of how she would grow into a woman, the world she would enter, how it would differ from my own. I thought about when she would get married, or go to study and travel... There were so many things to be excited about for her – but I never dreamed she would not get the opportunity to grow up.

Losing Aaliyah in that way is my greatest source of sadness in life, but I know you will understand how precious it makes my boy to me. I will never forget his sister, but Jamal makes me so happy and proud. Even after all these years, the pain never goes away. I can look back on the memories, and the precious photos we have of her, with joy now, despite this sadness that will never leave me.

I am glad to share these memories with my friend in distant England, who I know is a loving mother too, and will appreciate the depth of my love and my loss. Nobody outside of our household nowadays mentions Aaliyah's name. I know people believe this is for the best, so as to avoid bringing painful memories to the surface, but she is ever in my heart and just a thought away. To be able to write about the joy she brought me causes me comfort.

Thank you again for being my friend. And also for the amazing gift of the memory chain technique – and for that look on Jamal's teacher's face, when I told her my son was not a cheat, but talented and special and amazing. It was a moment every mother could take pride in!

....

'What an absolute load of nonsense, making money of out nothing on a computer. How utterly typical of you, Carrie, to be taken in my that kind of complete nonsense. If you've downloaded any strange programmes on this thing, I will never let you touch that computer again.' Mark punctuated his furious words with aggression as he stabbed angrily at the keyboard, waiting for the home PC to boot up.

'No, no of course I didn't, I never would!' Carrie protested, eyes wide and hand outstretched nervously. Had she logged out of the browser properly? She had been on the MomsBoard forum, and then did some searching about Bitcoin. But she hadn't downloaded anything, she knew better than that. 'I just thought, you might know something about it, you know, because of your work at the bank?'

'My work? You know nothing whatsoever about my work. Or about money, or about anything at all,' Mark muttered crossly, as he checked over his computer. He opened the browser and immediately looked at the history. All the links about Bitcoin and cryptocurrencies were there, the things she'd been looking at. And the MomsBoard link, a long way down the page – she only ever went there to look at Samar's messages nowadays.

Mark exploded, 'Carrie what the fuck have you been doing? You are so ignorant, but even you can't be so stupid. This cryptocurrency bitcoin stuff isn't money! It's for criminals, drug smugglers, and vice. I don't want any of this shit on my computer! How can you be so dumb?'

'I was just trying to– to understand about it, to learn a little bit…' She started to crumple and shake, cursing herself bitterly for provoking this reaction. How indeed could she be so stupid? Some things she definitely knew better about, and upsetting Mark was one of them.

'People use it for buying drugs or making bombs. Or hiring hitmen, did you know that? You can use bitcoin to buy someone off to murder people for you. I could have you killed and not be cursed with the stupidest wife on the planet. Pay them some bitcoin and no one would be any the wiser.'

Carrie kept silent, it was usually for the best at these times.

'And you asked me why I didn't invite you to Malcolm's leaving party – can you imagine, that I'd take you to meet my new department, when you are so stupid and naïve and ignorant as to think money can be generated on a computer? You deserve to be ripped off and lose all your money. Except, it's not your money is it? And it's not your computer.

'Stay off it, stop talking to people who put such stupid words in your mouth and ideas in your empty head. Bitcoin!' Mark stalked angrily from the room.

Carrie sank onto the settee, her legs giving way. He'd been so furious! She had no real understanding of why. Everything she'd read about Bitcoin made sense, but she didn't think it mattered that much. She'd never dreamed it would provoke such fury. Mind you, anything could provoke Mark, and you'd think she'd have learned that by now. Yes, she'd read about the criminals using bitcoin, but it's not as though she'd bought any or mined it herself, had she? It was strange that he got so angry.

Mark hadn't been so bad lately, and she'd really mastered the trick of not winding him up and making him react like this. All she had to do was keep the peace. How could she have been so stupid as to ask him about this kind of stuff, when he worked with real money in a bank?

She was still shaking, but he hated it if she cried and had stupid red eyes and an ugly snivelling nose, she needed to get a grip and pull herself together. Dinner was nearly ready, and Alex would worry if she looked sad. Carrie had been told over and over again for years that she was stupid, but she knew she was actually very good at some things, including putting the smile back in place like a mask when it was needed. She took a deep breath and blew her nose sharply. She'd got this.

She would never mention Bitcoin again to her husband.

The only thing to worry about now was making sure that dinner was calm and peaceful, and that the chicken breast rested properly before she served it. No one would have any cause for complaint, she knew what to do, and protecting Alex from the way his parents really were with one another was the one cause she was totally committed to. Even so, it was becoming more and more difficult to maintain, as their boy grew up day by day.

*

'I'm sure Mum was just curious,' Alex began, carefully placing his knife and fork together on his empty place before, not for the first time, stumbling awkwardly into the conversational void across the dinner table after his father appeared to be done with his latest diatribe. 'We did something about Bitcoin in maths last year when we had that project on cryptography. The calculations are awfully hard, and even with fast computers it's still slow, but it does mean you can't hack it or anything. It's really weird.'

Mark seemed to be trying less and less hard to control the temper, which always bubbled below the surface. He put his glass down on the table slightly too hard, seething at his son's effrontery in defending his mother.

'It's a trumped-up pyramid scam which blackmailers and terrorists use to rip people off, avoid taxes, and get their computers hacked. It's a lie to prey on the weak, the weak-minded, like your stupid mother! And don't think people aren't watching, scanning for keywords like that, all the government agencies online, not just in the UK!' His voice rose dangerously, preempting his son's interruption.

Carrie was terrified. Mark usually controlled this side of his nature in front of their son, but he'd been simmering throughout the meal. As she and Alex brightly shared remarks about day-to-day happenings at school, Mark's mutterings about bitcoin and crypto con money had escalated to become more and more audible and intrusive, leaving her increasingly paralysed between whether to pretend everything was fine for Alex's sake, or risk upsetting Mark more if he thought she was ignoring and disrespecting him. But eventually her sixteen-year-old son had intervened on his own, and stepped tentatively into the painful silence, trying to mediate.

He hadn't done that before, and Carrie could see that he was scared to. He'd stood up to his father, just a little bit and there was fear in his eyes. Normally he seemed oblivious to his father's emotional distance, unaffected by the lack of attention or interest he received. Carrie worked so hard to be all her son needed, just as he was all of her children. She didn't consciously try to make up for his father's immersion in work and his own life, smoothing the domestic path towards harmony at the cost of her own sanity and integrity, she just loved her boy and would do anything to make him happy and keep him safe. Right now he and his father seemed to be staring each other down as if each had just noticed the other for the first time.

'It's nothing, it was just a passing curiosity, because of something I heard,' she said briskly, getting to her feet. 'Who wants fruit salad?' Carrie started to collect the plates, trying to move things on.

'Sit down. I haven't finished yet'. Mark's hand closed on her wrist, and the plate clattered a few millimetres back to the tabletop

'But you...' Carrie began to flutter her free hand at the empty plates.

'I'm not done. You both need to be quiet and listen. I go to work and I earn the money in this house. Real money. Money that's legal, taxed and earned properly. I pay for the internet, and that damn computer – which you are not to touch again!' His raised voice echoed his hand clamped on her wrist. Carrie discreetly tried to wriggle free, aware that Alex was staring at the tableau of the two of them, frozen over the empty plate. As Mark's volume rose higher, he needed both arms to pound on the table. He lectured her, not about either banking or crypto currency, but her own ignorance and stupidity and the burden it was to him as he struggled to move on in his career. While the cost of everything in their lives kept going up and up, and he was the only one who had any idea what anything cost. Real money, that paid for real things…

He barked at Alex to clear the table, but Alex looked defiant, and turned to his mother – awaiting her permission to depart, scared to leave the room and abandon her.

With a blink she nodded him away, rubbing her right wrist under the table.

After dessert had been eaten and cleared in silence, Alex helped her load the dishwasher. Mark had left the table to return to the television. There wasn't that much to do in the kitchen.

'Mum, I just–'

'No, Alex, don't. There's nothing to worry about!' Carrie jumped in. 'Your dad's working *really* hard at the moment, he's ever so stressed and cross with the new manager and his team at work. He doesn't mean to take it out on us. He's exhausted. Try not to wind him up… I know you don't mean to.'

Alex looked long and hard at his mother. He was growing up so fast. Sixteen years old, but the eyes that stared sadly back at her seemed so wise and weary. He pitied her, she realised, and flushed with shame.

'Mum… Do you still write to that lady, the Arabic one, with the dyslexic son?'

She blinked, at the unexpected remark, the change of subject. 'Samar? Yes, yes I do!' She smiled at him. 'We don't write that often, but she sends the loveliest long interesting letters. Well, they're messages on a website, not actual letters. That tagine we had the other day, with all the cinnamon, that Dad said was a bit too spicy? That was a recipe from Samar. Jamal's doing so much better at school now, since you passed on that, what did you say our teacher called it, the mnemonic trick? Things are hard going for her I think, with her government, there's so much conflict in that part of the world. We're so lucky here…' Her voice tailed off.

'You can use my laptop. When I'm at school. I don't always take it in, only on days when we have English and History, and they have more and more tablets at school now with the reader software on. You can use it to message your friend, to read, or do whatever you like. To do anything. The password – I'll write the password and stick it on a note under the desk. Look for a Post-It.'

'You have a password?'

'Well yeah, duh!' He grinned at his mother, then hugged her sharply. 'Mum, I– I just want to help. If there's anything, I mean, if you're ever–'

She hugged him hard back, trying to shut off the words, just show him she understood and was grateful. That she knew he saw and understood, but that the best way he could help and support her was to keep the peace, not rock the boat, and let things be.

And to share his laptop, with no one knowing. To give her a way to contact the outside world. That was a priceless gift.

CHAPTER THREE

MomsBoard private message:

Warm wishes to you my friend,

Thank you for your lovely words about my daughter Aaliyah. Yes, she will always be with us, once you are a mother, it is always and forever. I can still hear her laughter around our home, her footsteps in the hallway, see her dancing in her favourite dress. Every milestone and birthday, I imagine how she would be now, what her personality would be like, what her passions would be as a teenager... A lot of the time now I can wonder this without a stab of grief, as the time gets further from the moment that we lost her, leaving her frozen in in my heart forever as a little girl. But I still ache for the young woman she would now be turning into, who I will never know.

I pour all of my love into her brother, who continues to make me proud with his heart and mind. Truly his technology expertise and obsession with Bitcoin is amazing me, he is now mining several currencies apparently, and he has set me up with my own wallet to save them. He is trading one coin for another, and making more money each time! Well, nearly each time. He sent me some bitcoin and litecoin and stellar, they are also sorts of cryptocurrencies, and it was so easy. He said he would soon be paying for the food for the house!

I told him he will never need to pay for food for this table, even though he is so proud to be sixteen, and wants to be a man very fast. Disappointingly, I think Jamal judges his father harshly. Mohit is quite a lot older than me, and he's settled for a quiet life in academia. He holds to his principles, but he's not going to change the world at his stage of life. He doesn't like to talk about Bitcoin, it gives him indigestion and gas, he says. He said that people or computers could be reading our email, scanning for words which alert them. Some of the papers people in his institution have authored are viewed as politically controversial, so he is always worried about consequences and backlash. I am sure your husband is much more interested in cryptocurrencies, I think you said he works in finance? You never write me much *about him, while I feel I know Alex quite as well as I know you yourself in many ways.*

So, you asked me about buying cryptocurrencies if you didn't have any special computers for mining them, and I explored this with Jamal's help so that I can answer your questions for you. Actually, it is much easier than the whole mining thing, which I do admit is somewhat mystifying for me.

First thing to answer is, you definitely don't have to buy one whole bitcoin! Jamal did actually laugh at this, which was a bit unkind, but he said just think of it as the amount in dollars or pounds that you want to invest – and then you would just buy however much you want. Right now what one bitcoin is worth is increasing fast in dollar terms. So it might be as much as one thousand US dollars for one bitcoin soon – but each bitcoin is divided into something like one hundred million parts. For this reason, you usually don't buy a whole one. Jamal said there are only ever going to be twenty-one million of them created, so perhaps each bitcoin will be worth one million dollars one day! Then, even owning a small part of one, we will be very rich women, and visit one another on board our private jets, yes?

There are currency exchanges, so you can go on online and just buy them with your credit card, exactly the same as if you need to buy US dollars for a holiday. I think there are ways you can buy them directly from other people too, but the exchanges can be used anywhere, even on a mobile phone. Jamal set this up for me and showed me how easy it was – I am sending his link here and he said if you use this one, he will earn a bit of bitcoin just for sharing it with you, and that you will also get some extra. He never misses a chance to earn something, I don't know whether to be proud or worried about that! But anyway he said you will also gain a little bit of currency to start you off, if you use this link, but that you don't have to.

He also said to follow their instructions to set up two-factor authentication, where you need a code sent to your mobile phone to log in. He doesn't know you, but he knows you are my friend, and he is concerned for your security. He said that if you got a virus on your computer or someone discovers your password, they could easily log in as you and steal all your cryptocurrency, so if you set up the '2FA' it means they couldn't do this unless they also stole your phone as well. He made me do this too, and it just means they send a text to your phone when you are logging in, with a number that you have to enter as though it was another password. He is very smart about things like this, and he says it's an easy to break into most passwords – I don't want to know how he knows this! He asked me, 'Your friend in England, she does know how to make a strong password doesn't she?' So of course I assured him that you did. I think that means that you must make a very long one, and also that you don't use the same one for anything else.

After that you just enter your card details, same as if you were buying something on Amazon, and then it saves it, and next time it's easier. Or you can send money from your bank instead of collecting it in, I think that is a little bit cheaper in fact.

How exciting that we are saving up our bitcoins together! I find it enthralling just watching it go up and down on the exchange. Mostly, in fact, it goes up! But I know it can go either way. Mohit thinks I am daft to watch the jaggedy lines, but I know he is also quietly proud of what Jamal is doing, embracing the future and making it his own, even if he laughs it off when they talk together. I think Mohit is especially proud he involves his old mum in the process! Because of all the instability in this country, even Mohit appreciates the wisdom of saving secretly, and of course it's something we haven't discussed with any of our neighbours and friends.

If you set up your wallet with this link, then we can test it out and learn together. I will send you some bitcoin, and you send me some stellar. Stellar is very new. Oh yes, us mothers can ride the cryptocurrency wave into the future together! And we will make our menfolk proud. Even if Mohit doesn't want me to tell anyone about it.

....

Hmm, Carrie thought, sending money from a bank would never be an option for her, if she ever wanted to buy some bitcoin. It was easy for Samar to say that, but she had no idea. Yes, she knew lots of people had their own bank account, in fact Mark probably did – she'd never given it a thought before. But she only had access to the joint account, into which he put a fixed sum each month for all the shopping and bills – and Carrie knew only too well how much trouble it caused if she didn't budget well and ran short before the end of the month.

The trouble was, Carrie was disorganised, and life was confusing sometimes. Maybe it was because of the medication she still took every day, even after all these years, though it was a lot less powerful than the pills she had taken before. When it came to the bank account, she never thought about it as her money. Her only priority was to feed her family well and make sure Mark had nothing to get cross about.

So, early in the month it was Waitrose and Marks and Spencer all the way, expensive prepared food that took little thought or effort to bring to the table, and only in the final week or so did she have to get more creative and considered. She was a good cook, or she had been. Mark used to love her cooking before he started taking everything for granted in recent years. She was glad that he was spending more and more time out in the evening now, with work things and social events connected to work, which could end every late. TV or kitchen dinners with just her and Alex were much nicer, and they could have whatever they liked. Even vegetarian meals which Mark despised and denigrated.

Her phone rang, jolting her from her recipe reverie. It was the cleaning agency: her regular lady Yolanda had sprained her ankle and could not come tomorrow, possibly not for the rest of the month. Would she like them to send someone else?

Carrie had to think quickly, for the first time in a while. Her mind wasn't used to switching tracks at speed, and she had been deep into musing about getting some money to buy bitcoin with when you hadn't got your own bank account.

She'd known Yolanda for years, but calling 'Matilda's Maids' an agency was pushing the definition a bit – there were only a couple of them, but they were hardworking, reliable and took care of their customers. It wouldn't be easy for them to rustle up someone else overnight either. Carrie always drew out cash from the joint account to drop in to Matilda to pay her girls with – Mark had thought that was strange, and there'd been a brief and predictable rant at the time about encouraging illegal immigrants, but he couldn't argue that the house was spotless, and they were actually great value as well as totally reliable. Above all, he was pragmatic, so the arrangement had continued, and it had been a long time now.

The next monthly payment was due in the next few days.

'Oh no, poor Yolanda!' Carrie replied suddenly. 'Don't worry, we'll be fine for a few weeks. You tell her to rest up and make sure her ankle's fully better before she tries to come back. She should keep her weight off it for now. It's time my son learned what a hoover is for anyway. It'll be good for him! No, honestly, we'll be fine – thank you for thinking of us, but we'll take care of it ourselves for the time being.'

She hung up breathlessly, wondering what she'd done.

All she had done, in fact, was commit to managing without a cleaner this month. But she knew deep down that really she'd taken a much bigger step, and that she was still fully intending to draw out the £300 from the cashpoint as usual on Monday. So long as the house was clean, no one would ask any questions.

Carrie didn't directly examine the thought that she had also committed to deceiving Mark and doing something hidden from him, for the first time in nearly two decades. That thought was best left unscrutinised, scuffling around the edges of her attention, in her peripheral vision but out of focus. There was an uneasiness to the lurking thought which caused a stab of anxiety, a potential threat for overwhelming panic. She wasn't ready to look it in the eye, there was no time for that, after all she was going to have all that housework to do.

She went to the cupboard by the back door and looked almost furtively at the mop, brushes, and buckets, the traditional tools her South American employee preferred to wield along with powerful amounts of elbow grease and good humour. Not today! Yolanda usually came on Fridays. Carrie closed the door, feeling almost like she was being watched. Irritably she shook her head, it was her own utility room in her own home, just a corner of the house to which she never really paid much attention.

The following day, after Alex and Mark had left for work and school as usual, Carrie got busy, cleaning the house from top to bottom. Careful to use gloves and wear her oldest clothes – she didn't have a flowery apron like Yolanda's – she tackled the different rooms methodically. Strangest of all had been cleaning in Mark's study, the very private man-space she never had any reason to enter, where he very rarely worked from these days, but was still completely his domain. Surreptitiously vacuuming and polishing the desk and wood panelling felt deeply subversive and forbidden, similar to how she'd felt touching Yolanda's mop and bucket in the first place.

The challenge was almost fun. It was years since she'd cleaned anything: Mark had started paying for someone else to do it when Carrie was sick and couldn't even look after herself properly.

He'd been generous about that, she reflected. Then she suddenly realised he'd willingly paid for professional care for his carpets and collectables, but not for his young son whose mother had been biochemically incapable and absent. She'd been grateful at the time, and he'd been so vocal about his financial generosity to get her the help she needed, but he'd never called a halt to it all these years later. That's thousands of pounds, Carrie thought. Well, Yolanda and all the others before her had earned every penny of it, she reflected knee-deep in suds as she rocked back on her heels. This was bloody hard work! It was lucky she was used to bearing pain with stoicism.

She had to do the kitchen more or less twice over too, but

she found herself energised despite the exertion and cooked up a storm as evening came. Lamb mince had been on special offer at the supermarket, so she'd made up a triple batch of their favourite curry, hand-prepping to use up all the elderly onions and less identifiable veg from the back of the fridge. She enjoyed filling the house with exotic spicy aromas for her husband and son's return. Mark even remarked absently that it was nice, and she was glad to know that there were two more meals in the freezer for later in the month – all paid for with last month's money, effectively.

*

Over the weekend however she realised there was still a potential problem ahead. On Monday she could go to the cashpoint and draw out £300 like she did every month – but how on earth would she get that transferred to the cryptocurrency exchange, and the empty account waiting there?

She'd set up the account using the link that Samar had sent, but hadn't added a payment source – she'd even added two factor authentication as instructed, because even her ancient phone could receive a text message. It was the next bit she was stuck on – she hadn't thought that far ahead. It had been strange enough setting up an anonymous web-based email account on Alex's laptop to use with the exchange, but it was a necessary precaution: she couldn't be sure that Mark didn't have access to her normal one, that she used for MomsBoard and the school.

She'd become obsessed with the idea of owning some

bitcoin, some secret money of her own. Money which Mark even denied was money – so it wasn't as if he could even object. As she lay in bed Sunday morning, secretly nursing her aching knees and back - how on earth did Yolanda manage, Carrie wondered.

She talked to Alex about her problem, in very abstract terms.

'Well, I guess you'd just use ApplePay or else Paypal or something? But why not just a debit card like mine?' Mark paid Alex's allowance into a current account, for him to use for going out and football and things like that. It was some kind of junior bank account that didn't let him overdraw, but gave him most of the needed everyday things.

'But if someone didn't have any of those things, didn't even have a bank account, just imagine,' Carrie persisted. 'How would they send money electronically, to somebody else's bank account, like to pay a bill or something? What if they had a phone like mine, so forget about ApplePay or basic bananas for that matter!'

'I thought everybody had a bank account?' Alex shrugged. 'Well, I know there's that money transfer place downtown near the bus garage, that Ashok's cousin uses to send money to Bangladesh. He takes in cash from the shop, and they convert it and deliver it to his parents in about a day, but he said it costs a ton. If his parents had a proper bank account, they'd use that instead as it would definitely be cheaper, even with exchanging the currency. But they haven't got any choice.'

She didn't know the place Alex meant, but it didn't sound

like what she was looking for anyway. When Mark went out to play squash, Carrie asked if she could borrow Alex's laptop. 'Of course Mum, but you know you can't mine bitcoin on that, right?' Carrie looked startled, automatically glancing around her at first – but she knew Mark had gone out, and mother and son shared a brief conspiratorial grin. No one had mentioned the word bitcoin since that horrible dinner a few weeks before, and it was like a flash of connection and shared understanding between mother and son.

She started by googling the money transfer place: £5 to send £100 to India! No wonder Ashok's cousin felt ripped off. She recognised the shopfront in the photos now from passing it on the way to the station, a strange and seedy-looking place with lots of posters in different languages, and one boarded-up window, covered in adverts for cheap phone cards and other things she'd never thought about. She couldn't imagine herself ever going in there.

But what had Alex said, 'I thought everyone had a bank account?' Carrie had certainly had one once, because her salary from the temping agency had been paid into it, before she married Mark in her early twenties. She'd been working there after her mother died, having dropped out of her literature degree to look after her and never gone back. Mark had been a client at some place where she'd worked, a bank, but not the one he was at now. After they'd married and moved away with his job, she'd never gone back to work, and less than a year later she'd been pregnant with Alex anyway.

What had happened to that bank account, she wondered? She'd had a little cashpoint card and everything. She had no idea, she only had the joint account card now, which was all in Mark's name and carefully scrutinised. Her money when she worked at the school had gone into there, she supposed, and now Mark put money in each month, and organised all the bills. It certainly wasn't all of Mark's salary, as there was always just enough for the shopping and things, clothes for Alex if she was really careful, and occasionally something from the market for herself, though it wasn't like she needed good clothes for dressing up or going out. Once again she wondered about the black hole in her memories, where the depression and medication swallowed all the details, from the mundane to the vital. She could remember the colour of the bank card she'd had when she was at the college and then the agency, but had no idea about all the years in between then and now.

She googled idly again. Well, she wasn't alone in some respects, apparently nearly two million adults in the UK didn't have a proper bank account! She'd never given it a thought before, any more than she thought about how the money got into an account. She had access to cash advances and instant payments, and if she overdid the Waitrose treats towards the end of the month, the account didn't stop paying for things, it just dipped into an automatic overdraft. She usually didn't even notice until Mark flew into a rage. What happened when people didn't have those normal financial things? She thought about the crowds she now vaguely remembered seeing lining up at that money changing place on certain days of the week, about all Matilda's hardworking cleaning ladies of all ages and nationalities existing mainly on cash. What did they do when the money ran out before the end of the month? She felt ashamed of her 'problem' of having a potential pile of banknotes she couldn't send electronically.

On the search page was an ad for a high street bank. She knew the branch; it wasn't in the shady downtown area like the exchange shop – but it wasn't on the main shopping street either. It was in a quieter side road where no one was likely to see her if she happened to go in there, for any reason. She clicked through – current account, terms and conditions… It sounded pretty easy, actually, to open a new account.

Apparently they needed to 'know their customer', that was the law. Well, so long as nobody else had to know, she supposed that it was OK for the bank to know who she was. It wasn't as though she was a money launderer or anything. *What if they knew it was the cleaning money though?* Nagged that little voice in her head. She ignored the voice. Same as she ignored tense knot of anxiety which seemed to be just under her ribs, and she ignored other physical pains which were nothing to do with the exertions of cleaning, Carrie was good at compartmentalising her attention. Anyway, the cleaning was done. She read more about 'Know Your Customer', and also anti-money-laundering rules. Well, scrubbing the kitchen floor instead of paying someone else to do it instead, that hardly made her a terrorist did it? Death by Dettol – but only to the germs on the kitchen step.

Proof of address was needed, which was more of a problem than the ethics of it. What had her name and address on? Actually, the joint account statements must have. That was hers too, at least in name, because she had her own debit card, but she didn't know where Mark kept the paperwork for those. It could be in the study, but maybe it was at work, as it was the bank he worked for. Her mobile! Yes – her rubbish old 'dumbphone' as Alex called it, at least those bills would have her name on them.

She found them in the drawer in the study – Mark's study. She never came in here, the little room they had converted the garage from years ago. It felt forbidden, just as it had when she'd hoovered the day before and touched the hallowed desk to polish it, while feeling like she'd never really seen it before. Why did he need a study anyway? It wasn't like he worked at home, he hardly seemed to even live there these days. She knew there was a locked safe, a cupboard really, behind the desk – almost hidden, it looked like part of the panelling. She had no idea what was in there and had felt absurdly guilty even running over it with the duster.

The filing cabinet felt less secret than the immaculately tidy desk somehow. The key was in the lock. Mark was still out, and why shouldn't she look at her own phone bills, she wasn't doing anything wrong. It wasn't like she ever even called anybody, she just received the occasional text from Mark telling her things she needed to do, or if Alex was going to be late from school. There they were, the bills, neatly filed away. The organisation of it was oddly pleasing to her and she felt a sense of connection and closeness to Mark looking at the careful filing. It reminded her of her time temping in offices so long ago, a different and long-lost Carrie.

Her heart shouldn't be pounding like this, she thought, just from looking at phone statements, carefully filed in order of receipt. Maybe it was because she was stuffing a recent one, not from the very front but a couple months ago, into the zipped inner compartment of her handbag?

It wasn't as if she was trying to open the locked cupboard behind the desk where she knew he kept a large amount of cash – and how did she know that? She must have seen it at some point. Why did he need that big pile of notes anyway, he worked in a bank? Didn't he trust banks? She knew he didn't trust her, not with more than the month's grocery money. Perhaps he didn't trust anyone. Mark had no other family in his life to speak of, and few friends. Or, at least, he kept his home life completely separate from anything else. Carrie felt like she didn't belong in his study at all. She couldn't remember when she'd last set foot in here: she'd never had a reason to be curious about it before.

She was also going to need identification, but Mark had the passports, of course. They were probably in the safe. But her old driving licence was still folded in her purse, with a photo from a time she couldn't really remember. So actually, there was nothing to stop her, if she wanted to open a bank account of her own.

*

'Mrs Paige, you do realise that it's a motoring offence to have an incorrect address on your driver's licence?' The effeminate and courteous young bank clerk said the following morning, as he took her through the current account application form. 'I think you can get quite a big fine! You really need to send that in to Swansea and get it updated!'

'Oh, I haven't driven for years,' said Carrie. Wow, this lying thing was so easy, the more you practiced it the better you became, and it was dizzily empowering too. 'But it's still me in the picture, though I was a lot younger then, so surely it's still OK as ID?'

They were sitting at one of the little side desks away from the main teller windows, but Carrie had been hoping for more privacy, and tried not to glance self-consciously around the over-lit bank branch. Why hadn't she gone to one in a different town or something? She wasn't used to thinking so dangerously and deviously. She had nothing to feel so anxious about, but oh goodness she was actually rubbish at this lying and deceiving, who on earth was she kidding… It was a stupid idea and she never should have taken the risk. She should just give the money to Mark and explain about Yolanda, or else she could go and see if Matilda had another lady who could come for a few weeks.

'Well, I suppose so, and we can go ahead and open your account today, you said you had some cash to deposit? Ah, excellent, £300, thank you.' He scooped the notes up from the desk, and counted them rapidly but transparently in front of her, as she fought the urge to snatch them back herself. 'Perfect! I'll just give you a receipt for that, and if you can just give me the details from your former bank, we'll arrange to transfer all your debits over here within the next twenty-eight days. You don't have to do anything; it all happens automatically.'

'I don't have a former account,' Carries muttered, feeling her cheeks go hot. There was no air in here, but she was reluctant to take her coat off. 'I'm – a first time customer!' She added, affecting a brittle cheeriness. Surely that must be OK, she wondered… Just one of those millions of people with no bank account, now getting one.

'Oh? Well OK no problem, the balance will be available in your account straightaway, and we'll send the debit card to your home address within the next four working days. Just sign here. Oh, Mrs Paige, that wrist looks very sore, are you sure you're OK to sign? Alright, there you go, that's great… And just here as well.'

Carrie hadn't meant her bruised forearm to slide out of her sleeve and become visible but she hastily hid it again without thinking, instead she asked, 'Do you have to send the card to my home address? Can't I come and pick it up or something? I don't always – we sometimes have some problems with the post, at our house.'

'Ah, I see – right, well I am sure that will be fine to collect the card from us here, but do please talk to the post office, as they have a special department for that kind of thing, to track anything gone missing. I know it's not at all uncommon in this city. I used to be in the Cambridge office, and it was all very different there. When it comes to bank cards, they are so vulnerable to ID theft, so if there's any doubt at all we would actually far rather have you collect it from us here in the branch. Though of course all cards are sent out in an unactivated state.

'We'll call you as soon as it's ready to collect. And yes, understood, you want to operate it entirely online with no paper statements sent to you, ever. Oh, I completely agree, far too many trees dead already, and if you're having delivery problems, then things like bank statements are also very attractive to fraudsters. We'll keep you one hundred percent paperless Mrs Paige – you can set up our app on your phone and do everything from there… Oh, well, maybe not from *that* phone, specifically.' He gave her elderly Nokia a look rather like the one Alex typically reserved for it. 'Perhaps you'll be wanting to upgrade that sometime soon? But, you do have access to a computer at home?'

'Oh yes,' Carrie assured him. 'I do.' She smiled at the friendly young man and gathered up all the bits and pieces. He went through it all with her and identified that she really only needed a single sheet of paper to confirm the account and deposit receipt, really it was admirable that she was so opposed to unnecessary pieces of paper, and yes of course he would see to it that everything else here was confidentially recycled. His name was Ian, by the way, and he'd be her personal banker – if she ever needed anything. She could make an appointment on the app if she wanted to talk to him specifically.

Once she got home, after feeling like she was being watched every step of the way there, she used her new secret email address to set up the banking app on Alex's laptop. Immediately she had a tingle of excitement and adrenaline, because she could see her £300 sitting in her balance. She looked at the currency exchange again, and realised that she could send the money directly from her account to theirs, she didn't even need the debit card she had requested. It would take a little bit longer, but when she compared that with waiting for the card it was probably about the same, and the fees were lower by bank transfer.

Should she send all the money? She'd never had money of her own before. *It's not your money,* the voice started again, but she pushed it away. She had been reading a lot of blogs and education sites about investing in cryptocurrencies, once she found ones which seemed responsible and informative, while also not being totally over her head technically. Samar had sent on links that Jamal had recommended, which helped her understand a lot more. Investing certainly sounded a lot more interesting than it ever had when Mark talked about money and banking and things – not that he really did talk to her about it.

One blogger she liked, who was an American investment advisor, suggested not having more than five percent maximum of your net worth in crypto because it was just too risky and volatile.

What's my net worth, Carrie wondered? She hadn't worked in years and she essentially owned nothing. She had to ask for money to buy clothes for herself and Alex, and she was good at making stuff last. She had no assets, no pension. She supposed that if anything happened to Mark, then she would own the house and things like that. But nothing was going to change for a long time, he was fit and well.

She hadn't got any savings, or other support. Carrie was an only child. Her mother had died of a brief illness before Carrie had met Mark, and her father had since remarried and started a new family. He rarely saw his daughter or grandson, and didn't warm to his son-in-law, so they'd lost touch since they'd moved away from Norwich.

All Carrie had was that £300, but it wasn't safe to keep as it was. No way she could have brought the cash back to the house. She'd been mad to draw it out of the joint account, never mind set up this secret banking website – what had been going through her mind? She couldn't spend it on anything visible, not ever.

So, why not spend it on bitcoin?

She sent the full balance to the cryptocurrency exchange,[1] and could soon see it in her sterling account balance there. Then she clicked to the bitcoin tab and watched as the price kept changing. How on earth would she know the best time to go for it? The advisors she'd read suggested averaging the cost by buying in fixed amounts over different dates, but when she looked at the costs per transaction, she could see that that would only make sense with larger amounts. Some people probably bought loads, but she only had her £300, that was all she owned in the world.

So, she hit the 'buy' button, for the 'spot' rate, which she guessed was some kind of average. She couldn't see any advantage in not selling the full amount of pounds, and within minutes Carrie was the proud owner of a small fraction of the coin she had been becoming obsessed with: She owned some bitcoin.

It was a fraction: a long, long way off being even one whole bitcoin. But the value itself went up and down every few minutes, just like Samar had said it would, and the addiction to watching it was just as she had said as well, a few pence here, and mostly up! After she had finished a nice long message to Samar in another window, she had 'earned' nearly £2 just for holding on to it.

Even though Mark didn't know she used Alex's laptop when they were both out, Carrie was still careful to log out carefully from her email and the exchange site. She was getting quite organised with passwords and things, though she wished she could think more clearly and remember them better.

There had to be a good way of remembering things like that.

....

Momsboard private message:

Dear Carrie,
I received it!
I just wanted you to know that I got it fine in my

wallet, so it worked. The bitcoin you sent me was nearly as quick as an email! Please tell me when my transaction comes to you – I got the request for payment from your app, that came straight away. This is so exciting!

By the way I just gave Jamal a very good excuse to laugh at my expense, in fact he still hasn't stopped. You know I told you that the long string of code was the address to send to? Well, that is what he told me! So, I very, very carefully copied it from your email, one letter at a time, and I checked it and checked it – I knew from everything learned that it could go wrong if I sent to the wrong address or even missed one digit from it, and that the bitcoin would be lost. I thought I did everything right, but I got Jamal to check it before I hit send anyway.

I told him what I did, and he burst out laughing! It was quite disrespectful. When he could speak again he said, you see that QR code there? I didn't know what a QR code was, but it's that thing like a square bar code, in the app just before the long private key I had checked and checked, on the laptop screen. He just grabbed my phone off me and deleted off all my carefully copied code. Then he scanned the screen of the laptop, with the phone camera so it read the QR code. Immediately the long string of letters and numbers completed itself in the field below it, as if by magic. 'Not magic Mum, but it's a lot quicker, and easier not to make mistakes this way.' But he said to still always visually check it.

I had seen those funny codes on all sorts of things, like boxes from the store, and I never knew what they were. They can't all be to do with bitcoin, I am sure of that! But Jamal says they are for machines to read and can contain all sorts of different information that just look like black and white blocks to us.

He said to tell you, look carefully at the app and make sure you understand the difference between your private and public key as well. The public one is the one that you sent me, and you can send it anywhere so anybody can pay you – it's like sending somebody your address, to send the payment to. But the private key, that is the secret one you need to actually send with. He said it's like the keys to your mailbox on the street. Anyone can address a letter to there, but only you can open the mailbox with your secret key, to get the letters out when you want to read them. Do you have mailboxes on the street in Nottingham? I think I have seen pictures of red cylinders in England, but I don't know if those are of historical nature or for community use.

Please let me know when you get the bitcoin. Jamal showed me on the Block Explorer how to watch it, being confirmed and sent to you – now it has four confirmations, so he said it will be visible in your wallet. But, you don't have to worry about it, it's just for checking (I didn't really understand that Block Explorer part of it but he said it's looking right at the blockchain itself, and the blockchain is where the bitcoin that you bought really is.

No I don't understand that part really either, I thought it was in the wallet, but he says no the wallet is really a key chain! All these so very masculine accessories, why can we not have our bitcoin purses, or pocket books I wonder? But Jamal says this is what makes it fair and safe for everybody, that anyone can see it and confirm it, but you alone have the keys. All I know is that it now says my transaction to you is 'confirmed' instead of pending, but that is good!)

It worked!

Samar's payment had hit the wallet in Carrie's app by the time she had finished reading the message.

It gave her a warm glow to think of her friend far away, sending the money straight to her in minutes. It was only the equivalent of $20 which they had agreed to transfer back and forth to each other in order to test it, but it gave her a tingling feeling to think about how it had happened. She imagined the two of them sitting in front of their computers, and sending this secret money, not through a bank or anywhere where someone else could find out about it and check it, but straight from one of them directly to the other.

It was so strange. Carrie didn't do a lot of online shopping because Mark didn't like her to, but she bought things like sports clothes for Alex online by agreement, using the debit card on the joint account. She had never really thought about what happened on the internet, when she hit the 'pay now' button – what had to happen, to make her bank (well Mark's bank) send the money to the clothing retailer.

They seemed to ship the things she bought out really fast, sometimes next day delivery, but surely the money didn't actually move that quickly? She remembered years ago, when she was looking after her mum, writing cheques for things – and they took days to 'clear' from one account to another. Somehow she thought it was similar now, and that even when you paid something in to the bank online, it could take a long time to go from one account to another. So the store had to trust the bank, that they would pay the money to them, otherwise you wouldn't get your package till a week later, and you had to trust the bank to pay the right amount to the store, and– there were so many links in the chain that she'd never considered before!

This way seemed so different.

She clicked on the transaction ID link which Samar had sent her, that Jamal said was the link to the bitcoin Block Explorer.

It was difficult to make sense of, as it just looked like a long list of key addresses, letters and numbers. No nice clear QR codes here. What on earth was she looking at?[2]

It was confusing, but following Jamal's guidance, she found her transaction – or the particular string of letters and numbers which apparently referred to it.

It was all there, for anyone to see it. She thought about

everything she had learned about how the blockchain worked, and that this payment was there on hundreds, no thousands, of computers around the world – right in plain sight, if anyone knew where to look for it. If anyone knew *this* string of letters and numbers meant Samar, and *that* string meant Carrie.

It gave her a stirring of excitement which she couldn't easily put into words. There was something about this which she could imagine changing everything one day.

*

Carrie kept cleaning, and saving, and buying bitcoin. Yolanda's ankle got better, but the agency redeployed her elsewhere, and Mark was none the wiser.

A tiny, victimless rebellion against her helplessness, with no real end goal in mind, just a sense of hugging a secret to herself. She also kept reading and learning about bitcoin and other cryptocurrencies – carefully, safely, and only on Alex's laptop. After all, she was an investor now, in her own right.

She didn't discuss any of this with anybody else, although Alex knew she had a small bit of bitcoin, she was aware, and also that it was a secret from his dad. She knew he had a little bit of interest in it himself though he wasn't an especially techy kid. He was far more interested in what technology could do for him than how it worked, and the cryptocurrency enthusiasm would surely not last long, if the two of them did not discuss it much.

It was surprising then, many months later, for Carrie to be

asked to come early to meet Alex after football. And to find herself sitting in the car with him while they huddled together over a screen in the dark, and he muttered about mining cryptocurrency.

'There's definitely no point trying to mine bitcoin on this, I know that much,' Carrie explained to Alex. 'Jamal says it's hardly worth it at all on any home computer now, though he's doing great guns on some other coins.' They were sitting in the car outside the recreation group where she'd been waiting for him to finish football practice, on a chilly dark February evening. The text about bringing his laptop when she came to pick him up had been quite mysterious, but she was trying to contain her curiosity and indulge his love of being enigmatic.

'Bitcoin is not the only crypto,' said Alex, grinning, muddy, and sweaty, like he hadn't really been listening to her.

'I do know that!' Carrie replied.

'Yes, I know you've been doing your homework Mum! But Dad will be home when we get back, and I wanted to try something out. I'll hotspot on my phone – by the way, when are you going to get a decent smartphone? You can have wallets and all sorts on phones, but not that old thing!' Alex rolled his eyes at Carrie's ancient handset, as he fired up his laptop and connected to 4G via his considerably smarter iPhone.

'Anyway look, this is an app for mining monero.[3] It can use the chips on my laptop, I'm lucky you got me this powerful gaming machine, even though it's a couple years old now. Yeah, I know, it's fine, and there's no chance of Dad paying for another one just now. But I need to update some of the drivers. I've emailed myself all the links from school. We got it running on one of the old PCs there, but it's not very healthy, this is going to be miles better!'

'I've read about monero! It's a coin focused on privacy and anonymity! That's perfect!' Carrie was suddenly glad of the darkened car interior, hiding her sudden flush of colour. What would Alex say if he knew about the cleaning money, she wondered? She feared he would understand only too well, and even applaud her need to secrete some resources for herself, right under the nose of his controlling and short-tempered father. Her mind still shied away from examining whose money it was, and the sense that she had no entitlement to it whatsoever, even though she had now secretly been buying and saving bitcoin for over a year.

What was she saving for?

After all, here Alex was trying to help her mine some more cryptocurrency! She had no idea what the deal was with the code and command line stuff flashing across the screen. Would she have to do that? She knew her way round email and message boards just about, and the bank and exchange websites were clear enough, but this stuff with the white writing on the dark screen was another thing altogether. She didn't interrupt Alex, as he frowned at the notes he'd printed out, juggling between different programmes on the laptop and something else on his phone, in the dark passenger seat. How had he learned all of this? He was copying and pasting long strings of code, and she knew he found this kind of concentration really challenging with his dyslexia. The filtered street lighting wouldn't help either – but he had one earphone in listening to the speech synthesiser reading the instructions to him aloud at the same time.

How many of them were on their separate parallel crypto journeys? She gazed at his profile in its concentrated stare, lit strangely from below by the flickering screen. How grown-up he looked now – well, he was almost eighteen, and taller than she was. She knew he wanted to talk to her about his awareness of the difficulties in his parent's marriage, but the last thing she wanted was his involvement, even though the pretence of his ignorance was long past. Somehow, she felt that if it wasn't ever mentioned, he wouldn't get hurt or have to stand up to his father, but she had had to forestall tentative queries and brightly change the subject with increasing frequency in recent months.

At one point during his tapping away on the laptop he cursed quite colourfully, but she didn't correct him, they were way past that point too now that they were co-conspirators in something secret and grown-up. Eventually, some time after Carrie had started the engine again just to warm the freezing car up, he shouted, 'Yes!' and proudly turned the screen in her direction.

The streaming code didn't make any sense to her at all, but she tried to look suitably impressed.

'We're mining[4], Mum! Mining monero, right here on this laptop! Generating cryptocurrency, secret money!' He grinned at her in the darkness, as data flashed across the screen. 'I'm running the node right here, and I've set you up a wallet on MyMonero. Did you bring the notebook and pen as well, like I said?

'Yes, of course,' Carrie said, rummaging through her bag in the dark to dig out the requested items. It felt surreal and furtive, though this seemed an unusually mundane and low-tech thing to request.

'Write down this list of words on the screen, that's your wallet seed. You never ever copy or save this electronically, you just put the paper somewhere safe, or I can look after it for you if you want,' he said. 'You know what a seed phrase is, right?'

'Yes Alex, I read all about it, and I have one for my bitcoin wallet too, thank you very much. It's a list of short unique words in a specific order, which acts like a password for your password, if you lose it or get locked out. It's the ultimate thing for recovering it, so you mustn't ever put it online or share it anywhere, and you mustn't lose it either.' She hoped that response was good enough for top marks, as she felt quite proud of it.

'Seems ridiculous, doesn't it, for securing cryptocurrency,' Alex replied. 'I thought Miss B was kidding when she told us, or else having a dig at me about my dyslexia and simple words being anything but, for me anyway. But it's for real, I looked it all up. It makes sense that we have original manuscripts and books and things which are thousands of years old, that are just ink and paper and which have survived OK and been handed down without getting lost or spoiled. When the tech we're using probably won't be around in five or ten years. Well, your rubbish old phone might be Mum, as that's obviously going to go on forever!' He grinned toothily in the dark.

'It's from some massive great list apparently,' he continued, 'with like, thousands of words on it. And when the wallet generates it, it's really totally random, in a way that human brains aren't good at. We think we're being random but actually we're not at all, we're too hungry for patterns and meanings and stuff. Well, that's what the thing I read said.

'So anyway, that's why you have to write this down, with a pen, and then keep the bit of paper forever somewhere safe.'

Carrie nodded, and copied down the twelve short words displayed on the screen into her notebook, with the indelible biro she had brought. She was careful to write clearly and neatly, though the words were very distinct and unambiguous. She wondered who had come up with this list of thousands and thousands of words, and how they had even thought of that? Were there word lists in other languages? What about for other cryptocurrencies, or was this only a bitcoin and monero thing?

'Mum have you got somewhere safe? I mean, somewhere you can keep this bit of paper, where it won't get lost or destroyed or– or found by anyone, who shouldn't find it?' Alex looked very serious all of a sudden.

She matched his serious tone. 'Yes, I do. I have a place where I can keep things safe. And I won't label what it is or anything. But look, if I make two copies of it, then you can hide one for me as well – same deal, you just keep the paper safe, knowing you know exactly what it is, but not labelling it or anything ever.'

He nodded, thoughtfully, and looked like he was going to ask something else – then thought better of the idea. 'Now, email – you've a Hotmail haven't you Mum?'

'Er, no. Well yes, but, I've got a new one – a little while ago' Carrie said hastily. 'Thought it was time I updated it a bit.' She told him her completely anonymised, Gmail address.

'Right! OK, well, the miner will pay out to that wallet, I think it's once a day. Though, you know, this is just a laptop, not a commercial rig. It's not going to be like a lottery win, OK? Just a trickle day by day, a few pence worth.

'But, the processors are good for it, and I don't use it at all during the day. I can even upgrade the GPUs when they burn out, according to Miss Brize in Computer Studies. She helped me investigate the miner, though she won't let me run it at school. She reckons it could start a fire in our crappy old IT lab, the PCs there are older than god.

'Then the only cost is the electricity, and that… well, I know it's not free exactly, but, it's just kind of there already in the house isn't it? I mean it's ours, yours, for using. Dad probably won't even notice, it's not as though he ever goes in my room.'

'Alex, it's amazing, wonderful, I– I know you knew I was interested and reading about cryptocurrencies for quite a while now, but I didn't know you were as well, and you were going to do all this.' Carrie glanced at the dashboard clock and realised they'd better get home – lucky there were several very economical meals ready in the freezer to get on the table fast. She didn't really understand anything about mining and how that actually worked, but she could see from her son's proud pointing, that his laptop was actually running the software to generate new money, and sending it to a wallet in her name. That meant a lot.

'It's for you, Mum. I wanted to do it for you. The last time Dad got so cross, and I– I wanted to speak up and do something, say something. I knew you didn't want me to, but I hated myself for letting him talk to you like that, be so rude and horrible. I hate how he talks to you, and you just…

'Anyway, I wanted you to have something. I know you haven't got any income of your own or any choices about anything. One day I might not be here, and he might get worse or angrier or something. They were talking about the Africa volunteer programme in assembly again, and I am really interested in it in one way–'

'Alex, you've got to apply for it, it'd be the experience of a lifetime!' Carrie interrupted. 'You'd be changing lives too, and whatever offers you get from unis – and you will – that kind of experience would be life-changing to have.'

'But Mum! I want to, I just– I'm scared of leaving you behind. With Dad. With nothing of your own and no choices. Can't you, I don't know, get a job again like when I was little, or get back in touch with Grandad and Louisa so they understand more what Dad's like now, or something? I don't even want to go to uni and leave you here with him, with no friends to talk to or anything. I could just study at Nottingham and stay at home with you. I know you were ill for so long, and he still treats you like your stupid or incapable, but it's darker than that, and… I'm afraid for you sometimes Mum.'

That was it, a line crossed, an invitation to talk about all the things he didn't know about, should never know. Part of her, the part which understood the bigger picture, longed to talk to somebody. But not to her baby boy, not even eighteen yet. That was about as unthinkable as talking to her father. Time to stop this conversation, before they got any further into the uncharted quicksand of emotions and revelations they might never survive, not without changing their relationship forever. She parked and put the handbrake on decisively before reaching over to cup his face with one hand like she used to when he was little.

'Alex. Thank you, for the miner, and the love, and the worry. You don't *need* to be scared for me, I'm OK, and I am so lucky to have a wonderful boy like you. I'm fine, I really am, and I can manage your dad's moods, but Alex you've got to promise me you won't let any of this stop you fulfilling your own potential.

'You have got to get that form in for the uni application, and of course for the project – no, listen! You look at me and see someone with no job, financially dependent on someone else, well you're dead right. And if you think that's what I'll let you end up with, you've got another thing coming. The best possible way you can help me and support me, make everything I've ever cared about worthwhile, is to get yourself out of here and off to the rest of your life.

'So when we get indoors, you go and do your homework before dinner, and shower that bloody mud off first, look at you!' She didn't let him get a word in sideways as they stuffed the laptop out of sight in the sports bag, and headed into the house together.

Although Mark wasn't due home for another half an hour, by tacit agreement the conversation ended there as the front door closed behind them, and they went to their separate tasks in separate rooms, before reconvening later on to play Keep Dad Calm Over Dinner.

'Three-nil Dad!'

'That's my boy, well done. Hmm, this is tasty.'

*

Carrie was worried about whether she was becoming obsessed with bitcoin, and everything she was learning about cryptocurrency. It was surely just a harmless diversion? But the risk of getting caught was so high, she didn't want to think about Mark's reaction.

She needed to be organized and alert. She had to make sure everything stayed hidden. Just like the transactions on the blockchain, she had to know exactly where it was if she wanted to look, but be absolutely certain not to point to it or direct unwanted attention to it in any way.

The battered shoebox where she had hidden the list of seed

words for her wallet had to stay where it was. She had read about wallets and understood that that list of words could be used to restore it at any time if she lost her password, or couldn't log in to the application. They had to stay in the box, and there was no way that anyone would recognise them or know what to do with them – would they?

But what if something happened to the box or the piece of paper? She needed a backup plan of some kind. That few hundred pounds-worth of bitcoin she started off with was now well on its way into the thousands – not a lifechanging amount, but it was all she had in the world, and she wanted to keep it safe.

She was using the online wallet that Jamal had recommended to them both, but she knew that an online wallet wasn't as safe as an offline one, which kept the private keys off the internet.

Worse, now she had the Monero miner wallet as well, with its own list of recovery words. What a strange thing to call it, 'a wallet', she mused, as she fired up Alex's laptop to inspect her few pence worth of mining success, Samar was right about that.

A wallet usually kept money in it, if you were a man anyway – so it was pretty obvious who designed and named all this new technology then! Why did you never hear about a cryptocurrency handbag? Or some kind of charm bracelet to collect your keys on? But it wasn't a very helpful term in any case, because if she'd understood it correctly, you didn't keep currency in your Bitcoin or Monero wallet, the money itself lived on the blockchain. You kept private keys to it in your wallet. So, it would be better to have called it a keyring or something then, instead of a wallet or a purse, she thought. Besides, it was software, not a physical thing you could keep in your handbag (although the hardware wallets she'd seen online were more like that).

There was so much to learn. She was glad Alex had showed her how to create a private Google document to hide all her notes in – that was just like the blockchain in a way, it was there on the same internet that Mark used, but he'd never know the long messy URL to her 'bitcoin notes' document, and even if he had it he would actually have to be logged in to her Gmail at the time to use it. She knew that wasn't the kind of security you'd want against hackers or something like that, but it was certainly enough to keep Mark at bay, when he didn't even know she had a Gmail account in the first place.

Her notes now consisted of:

- Her public keys (she knew enough not to put her private keys[5] into a document, they stayed locked tightly in her wallet, backed up on the piece of paper in the shoebox in the wardrobe).

- The addresses for her online wallet, the exchange, and the Block Explorer.

- The bloggers and YouTube channels that Jamal had recommended. She had never properly used YouTube before, and she could see that it was a very confusing place with lots and lots of cryptocurrency information there, but she had been told that most of it was rubbish to be avoided, and she could see why.

- Her own notes and definitions, which were growing every day. Everything she learned from her videos and blogs, from Samar's messages from Jamal – what is a wallet, the different coins – bitcoin, ethereum, monero, litecoin, stellar – there were hundreds of them!

- What an exchange is, like the one she bought her coins on – she knew there were others, including ones where you could change one crypto into another, but for now she just had the one account where she sent money from the bank account to buy bitcoin.

Jamal said it was fairly safe to keep her bitcoin on this one account as they had never been hacked or anything – it was the service he recommended to his own mother – but that it was better to make a wallet account and send the funds there.

Carrie obediently followed his advice, even though it had meant more accounts and passwords and things to keep track of. She didn't understand till a lot later why it was so important to own her private keys and have complete control over them, but she was trying very hard to understand and do everything properly. Being in personal control was a powerful motivation.

Thinking back to her days in the temping agency, a pre-Mark lifetime ago, she remembered always being methodical and organised, writing things down neatly and keeping track of all the important information. It was something she always felt so sorry that Alex could not benefit from due to his dyslexia, the ability to make notes quickly and easily to refer to, although he had worked out good systems of his own using colour and sketches and other things which helped, not to mention his amazing memory tricks.

She wondered idly how Alex would remember the top ten cryptocurrencies by market capitalisation, but she got stuck straight away trying to make a mental image connecting bitcoin and ether, somehow the idea of someone biting into a bottle of medical ether, maybe trying to bite the cork out of a dark medicine bottle – what did ether even look like? She didn't bother, because she didn't need to, she could write it down instead and not use her mind as a hard drive.

Because she did still worry about her memory and its reliability.

She had literally lost years during the time she was on heavy medication. She felt like someone had erased so much of her life when Alex was young, and it was as if she'd been in a kind of daze ever since in some ways. It was so long since she'd tried to learn about something new, it felt like her mind was slowly waking up.

Was it possible? She hoped so. New ideas and new learning, were bringing things to life, within her mind and her imagination.

*

Carrie realised over the next few weeks that Alex had got very good at his game too. She didn't mean football: it was something about his dyslexic perspective maybe, that made him exceptionally attuned to the bigger picture and the long view, particularly when it came to those around him.

For example, he could get his dad almost on the brink of being worked up about something – the refugee problem or the traffic on the ring road, something he could be utterly righteous about – and Alex could flatter his father's ego admiringly, while at the same time stoking Mark's emotional investment in the conversation to a level Carrie found terrifying, with all the barely-contained anger within it. Of *course* Dad was right, if they just fixed the signals on the main access roundabout the whole thing would flow far, far better, especially in the rush hour. It was obvious! If only they'd listen to him! He could masterfully flip Mark's negative energy into pride at being right in a heartbeat, just before it boiled over into the kind of rage where things got broken or thrown.

Then he could either deflect his father from picking on his mother, or he could get what he wanted from him. It was an amazing skill.

Carrie wasn't sure whether to be awed or dismayed when she realised this power her almost-adult son was developing. It was as though Mark wanted Alex's approval just enough that it could be weaponised in the right circumstances. That was the difference between how he was with Alex compared to Carrie: he had no interest whatsoever in Carrie being impressed or approving of his opinions, so he just offloaded them, in a completely one-way process. With his son, though, it was as though he'd suddenly noticed that here was a rather amazing young man who he wanted to impress and show off to. But he didn't realise how much that young man had grown up and could manipulate the conversation for his own ends – l

ike the evening a few weeks after Carrie and Alex set up the mining software, when he managed to convince his father of the wisdom of treating him to the latest iPhone for his upcoming birthday.

Carrie wasn't sure what they cost but she knew it was a lot – hundreds of pounds – and she also knew his present phone was only a couple of years old and still perfectly alright. It was his eighteenth of course, so a big present was in order, but she was still quite surprised when Mark said yes.

Well, good for Alex, if he could wrap his father round his little finger and get him to spend some of his money on his son's birthday, then fantastic! Carrie was well on her way to being a monero millionnaire by that point anyway, having mined nearly £19 worth – though her bitcoin had gone up by quite a lot more, particularly with another month's cleaning money added to it. They each had their secret plans, and she felt like anything Alex could get out of Mark was fair game. It felt like paying him back for so much.

She shifted uneasily in her chair, she had some recent bruising that was uncomfortable, but unconsciously it felt like a price she had to pay for the clandestine wealth she was accumulating. She felt paid back, too, when Mark insisted on ordering Alex the highest spec iPhone model on the market, with a huge hard drive, for all the photos and videos he'd want to take when he went on his gap year. Such beneficence! The provident father figure was very proud of himself.

Regarding the phone, this was the kind of result which really ought to have been credit in the bank for while. Alex was careful to push his father close to the limit and no further, and that had been a big result, so she was surprised to hear Alex flattering and wheedling with Mark at dinner again only a few weeks later, just before his birthday.

The new phone was already ordered and had been delivered, they all knew that, and he certainly wasn't going to be getting any other gifts. So why did he need his father in a good mood? Surely he wasn't finally going to mention The Girl, who even Carrie still pretended not to know about. She was sure he would tell her privately first anyway, and she knew it wouldn't be a moment before he was ready. He was a boy who was learning to keep his counsel and judge his timing and his audience very carefully.

But it wasn't that. It turned out that, instead, Alex had bad news to break:

'I'm really sorry Dad, I always use the lockers, you know that. It was just this one afternoon that I was late for practice, I left my bag in the changing room. I think because the bus was late I wasn't the only one who left my bag out, and I know other people had stuff nicked as well. I feel really bad, even though I know I'm getting a new one, I mean, that handset could have been sold or given to charity or something.'

'Charity!' Mark exploded. 'That phone cost hundreds of

pounds, it was barely more than a year old, far more than any schoolboy needs. You don't deserve the new one, if you're that bloody careless with your possessions. How could you be so stupid!' It was some time since there had been actual yelling across the dinner table, and Carrie flinched, as the plates clattered from Mark's pounding fist.

Oh Alex, why did you let that happen, when things had been so calm and balanced lately? The food in her mouth lost its taste and she couldn't remember how to chew it. The aggression in the air caused a sudden physical reaction she had no control over. She was really surprised, and a little hurt, that Alex hadn't told her privately before dinner about losing his phone, but she supposed there hadn't been a lot of time before they were all sat down together. She willed herself to stay still and invisible as the conversation progressed.

Alex was gesticulating ingenuously, conducting his father's fury directly towards his own sincere expression of regret. 'I know Dad, I am so sorry, I feel really stupid and awful about it. I went right round to the phone shop to stop my SIM before I got the bus home. They're going to send a new one, but I wanted to make sure the thieves didn't get to run up any spending on data or anything. I can't believe I was so dumb. The coach was really upset too because we wanted to call the police, and he said if we did that we'd lose the use of the changing rooms at the rec – they're not supposed to be available for school teams like ours that are over sixteens technically, but you know we've been playing together for so long, and it's really great healthy free exercise that also goes on my UCAS form as a hobby.

'So I couldn't get him into trouble like that, it would have been awful and affected all the team. And when I asked in the phone shop, they said the insurance would laugh at me, for leaving it in my bag. So there was no point doing all the police forms anyway, they told me – definitely no point in reporting it. It's my fault Dad and I'm sorry. I was careless and dumb and I've learned my lesson. I'll clear the table Mum.' Alex deftly swerved out of the room with the dishes, leaving Carrie to sit awkwardly with her husband's simmering rage.

She tried to find her voice, but it cracked into that whispery frail one they both hated in their different ways. 'He's been so good lately, and he's normally very responsible with his things. His laptop, he's had that for a couple years now and it's still working fine – as far as I know, I mean. He's always very careful, I think he's ever so sorry about this,' she volunteered, then bit her tongue. The last thing she'd wanted to do was draw Mark's attention to the laptop, whirring away on Alex' desk, fans straining at all hours of the day and night…

'Well so he damn well should be, that was a bloody decent phone, I'd have done something with it. Traded it in, it was worth a lot.' Mark's voice echoed the volume of the pounding on the table. 'He wants to go off travelling and to uni next year, he's going to have to learn to take better care of his things, I for one won't support him if he's going to be as stupid as this.'

'I'm sure- sure he's learned his lesson,' Carrie continued steadily. Somehow her voice came out more evenly and smoothly than she expected this time. She wasn't used to that: after all these years, was she beginning to learn how to manage Mark's moods from her son ? She knew that when she shook and cried, it just made him angrier. She'd always known that, yet she'd never been unable to control the way he made her react.

Mark stared at her unpleasantly. 'Don't you defend his carelessness and stupidity. You don't understand anything about what he knows, or he's learned, how dare you suggest you know better than I do about my own son! I don't know what's got in to you lately!' His voice rose again.

Carrie dropped her eyes. So, when Alex spoke assertively and reasonably to his father, it calmed him down, but when she did it made things escalate? OK. Alex wasn't the only one learning lessons about how to play things. She could adapt. She could see when her husband felt unsettled even if he'd never admit it.

She smiled weakly back at Alex when he returned to the room with the ice cream dessert, one of Mark's favourites and a good choice. Somehow, the conversation shifted back to safer banalities and a semblance of normal family chitchat, as they finished up their dinner. The theft was never mentioned again, and Carrie knew that the financial impact of a lost phone wasn't a big deal to Mark, it was just something he couldn't do anything about – which was enough to drive him to apoplectic rage.

*

On Alex's birthday morning, after Mark had left for work, Carrie took him breakfast in bed. It was a long tradition of theirs which she wasn't going to break just because her baby boy was somehow now eighteen years old, and officially an adult. But it was a school morning, so it was only toast and tea, and she didn't wake him by singing like when he was little. She enjoyed watching him open his cards while she tucked her feet under the duvet and drank her own coffee. Later he'd go out with his friends for pizza and a first 'legal' drink – already grudgingly paid for by Mark, but with no parents were invited to attend. Which was exactly as it should be, she thought. Her son was a man now.

'Of course you can unwrap your new phone later, even though Dad won't be home he said it's OK, and it's lovely that the boys are coming round here for some cake before you go out. I know it's not always been easy bringing friends round, and I'm really glad you're doing it. I won't embarrass you!' She was looking forward to making the cake and creating something really special for them at home, before he went out to celebrate with friends his own age. How could he be an adult? He looked just the same as yesterday.

He grinned. 'You never embarrass me, Mum! Except when you stare at me like that!' He laughed and then suddenly looked bashful, like he was a lot younger, and really wanted to tell her something but was finding it difficult or awkward. 'Uhm, as well as Ash and Liam, is it alright if– if Katie comes around for some cake too?'

Carrie couldn't remember the last time she'd seen her beautiful, confident boy look so shy, he was actually blushing. She was thrilled, but tried to keep a casual smile in place and not to look too delighted. 'Of course it's alright! I can't wait to meet her, and I'm so glad you're going to bring her home. I promise to be on my best behaviour! And…?'

'…Dad won't be there!' Alex completed the sentence. They both giggled, and suddenly he was her little boy again, ageless and forever her baby. She was so glad he'd finally mentioned this girl directly, after weeks of evasion and hints. That was one lucky young woman, and Carrie was going to meet her at last! She only hoped the poor girl knew what expectations she had to live up to.

She sensed that he still wanted to tell her something; it felt like there was more. Of course, she'd known for a while that this Katie was 'more than a friend', but she hadn't pushed to find out, confident he would share with her when ready and not before. But what wasn't he telling her? She hoped it wasn't something like her having allergies or being vegan, as she'd bought all the things for the cake yesterday, and Carrie had developed an amazing sense of shopping frugality in recent months as she topped up her savings. She paused and sipped her coffee, leaving space for him to tell her more but having no idea what was coming. She didn't have to wait long, and it wasn't what she'd expected.

'Mum, do you remember when I was little, and basically a spoiled brat, and you used to get me a present to unwrap on

Dad's birthday, or even other people's, like back when we used to go to Granddads? You called them "Unbirthday presents?"' Alex said.

'You were never a spoiled brat. Well only a little bit, but I love you anyway. That was years ago since we did that! I can't possibly believe you're eighteen now,' mused Carrie, finding her mind abruptly flooded with a series of still images from birthdays gone by.

'Yeah yeah, I will always be your baby deep down inside, I promise!' Alex's smile shifted subtly from shy to sly, as he reached into a bedside drawer and produced a used padded envelope from the back of it, which he proudly handed to her. 'Anyway… Happy Unbirthday, Mum!'

She looked in the envelope and, mystified, drew out an iPhone. Alex's old phone.

In response to her puzzled glance, Alex spoke in a rush. 'I know, I know, I lied outright to Dad, and that's wrong, I felt a bit bad, but it's not fair that you have to have that crappy old phone. It's just one more way in which he controls you, and everything about you. He probably would have just stuck this in a drawer and forgotten about it anyway.

'You need somewhere private to get your email, and have your crypto wallet, and a way to contact your friends, like that lady in Syria, and anything else you want to do. It's like a human right or something, or else it should be.

'At football that night, Oscar was telling me about getting his phone nicked in town, just pick-pocketed out of his bag, and I knew I had my new one coming. So, I just acted on impulse, telling Dad that mine had been taken. I thought that if he really lost it – like if he went completely mental about it or something – I could "find" it again when a friend had it in the wrong coat or bag or whatever. It seemed worth a try, and fairly low risk.

'So, now it's yours. You can go and get a SIM from any phone shop, or I'll get you one, and you can keep it hidden. When I go to South Sudan, if I go – it was only a first interview! – then I need to be able to message you, and you can't even get proper photos on your crappy old dumphone. I don't want to only be able to send emails to the family computer, and I want you to be able to contact me when you want to. This is the same charger as mine by the way, so you can charge it in here whenever you need to, Dad never even comes in here – there's a spare cable on my desk by the laptop.

'I just wanted you to have it. Everyone needs their own bank account, and their own phone.'

Carrie was stunned into silence, and also waves of shame. She didn't know what to say. Her son was barely hours into adulthood, yet he was caring and providing for her as though she wasn't capable of looking after herself. She couldn't meet his eyes, so she gave him a hug instead.

*

Later on when Alex was at school, Carrie concentrated on getting it set up. She'd have to get a SIM card for it at some point, but it connected to the wifi OK at home for now. She'd never had an Apple ID before, but it was easy enough to create one using her new email address. She wondered what apps to download onto it.

She could have a crypto wallet! She knew it'd be safer in some ways on a phone, especially as the laptop in Alex's room was getting more slow and tired by the minute, running the miner day and night. Alex joked about how it was good at getting his football socks dry in his room, and he'd plugged in other chips and some things he brought home from school that he'd said was some kind of pie? It meant the whole set-up wasn't very portable. She knew it'd be easier to get her email on her own phone, she just had to keep it safely hidden from Mark. She would be able to read her email when she was out, or anywhere she liked! She had her own smartphone! She still couldn't believe it.

The shoebox in the wardrobe where she kept a few letters, photos of her mother and baby Grace, and now also the list of words from her recovery seed and the bank account contract, had room for a small iPhone as well. Mark knew about the box, knew she kept her 'pointless sentimental trophies' in it, and he had zero interest in the contents. It was easier to hide things in plain sight right there in the box, and somehow still felt safer than anything she tried to disguise, which could be found. It was quick to access, and she had time to stash things away in it and put it back in the wardrobe anytime she heard the car in the driveway. When she went out the phone would easily fit in her handbag. She couldn't imagine the potential repercussions if Mark ever found her with it, but that should be completely avoidable so long as she was careful.

She downloaded the cryptocurrency application onto the phone, and carefully logged in. She found that MomsBoard also had an app, so she could message Samar whenever she wanted to! She dug out the last message, in which she'd told her about securing her crypto wallet – something about factors of authentication? She could google on the phone as well, the web browser was good, and although the screen was tiny it was crystal sharp.

Multi factor authentication![6] Was that what Samar's son had been talking about? She supposed it meant the way the bank had made her set up questions, like her mother's maiden name and the place she was born, all of which struck her as a bit unhelpful, as anyone who really knew her – knew her well enough to steal a password – would surely know all that stuff about her as well? *Mark would know all those answers.* Well, he didn't know about the bank account, did he? So that was the most basic level of being secure.

Anyway, apparently that's not what MFA meant, she was reading. Things you know, like a password or security questions, that was only one layer of security essentially. That was what she'd just been thinking! So much for all that. So what were the other layers?

One was a thing you own. So that was the phone itself. She marvelled at the device in her hand, still astonished at what Alex had done, deceiving his father and helping out his mother in this way. His shiny new handset was all set to unwrap in the evening, but this phone, less than two years old, was now hers. That was security alright! Even though it created a vulnerability just by existing, and raised the chance of Mark learning her secrets, she somehow felt one step closer to… to what? Never mind for now. Focus.

She followed the instructions carefully to enable the extra layer of security in her wallet. Now, even if she tried to log into the wallet on her laptop, it'd send a message to her phone as well with a code she had to enter, to prove she had the phone – someone would have to steal her password and her phone, or the phone and the secret list of words she had written on the bit of paper tucked inside her twenty-first birthday card from her mother at the bottom of the shoebox in the wardrobe.

So that was two factor authentication: things you know, combined with a thing you own. That was what Samar had told her about. Apparently, though, from the blog she was reading, there was a third layer – consisting of a thing you *are* as well, something you just couldn't fake.

She knew that her bank in the high street had telephone banking, and they recorded your voice print when you set it up, so that their computers would always know it was you, but she'd never done that. She always took the cleaning money straight round there every first Monday of the month, along with whatever she'd scraped in savings from the food budget through the month before. The nice personal banking manager Ian always looked out for her and asked her how she was, and congratulated her when the amount was higher than usual, and sometimes it was – her cooking was getting more and more creative and frugal.

Mark didn't care if she drew cash out for the butchers and others who preferred it, and if the meat came from the market or a reduced-to-clear bargain he was none the wiser so long as dinner was on the table every night. He went out quite a lot now anyway, and she and Alex were totally happy with something cheap like an omelette or a big bowl of pasta in front of a movie. Oh, how she would miss Alex, if he went off to the Project in South Sudan, but she knew it would be the most amazing opportunity for him.

She carried on reading and then turned to the settings function on the phone. Aha! She could set up fingerprint recognition. So that secured her account a third way. If anyone tried to break into it, from anywhere, they'd need a code sent to her phone, which could now only be unlocked by her own fingerprint! Carrie didn't know much about hackers, and her greatest security worry was always that Mark would find out what she was doing. But she'd now set up her new phone as safely as she knew how, including a PIN code based on one date he would never remember or consider, which was forever inscribed in her own mind – baby Grace's due date. It had three layers of security: things she knew, a thing she had, and a thing she *was*.

Alex's phone, she remembered from the excited discussion in choosing it, could unlock itself based on his face somehow.

He just had to lift it up and look at it. In some ways that sounded less secure than the fingerprint idea. Carrie's mind shifted uncomfortably away from a mental image of an unseen someone holding her own head rigid in front of a screen, or forcing her finger down onto a touch pad involuntarily. No one would know this phone even existed anyway, that was the whole point, and the most secret and secure thing about it.

*

Just a few days later, Carrie found herself buying a pay-as-you-go SIM from the money changing place she'd first thought about months ago, when she was investigating bank accounts. Somehow she felt quite safe going in there now that she was part of this secret and confidential world where people had bitcoin and smartphones and secret lists of words written down on bits of paper hidden in photo albums and birthday cards.

She wondered about the other people in there, curious about how their lives might differ from hers, even though they lived in the same town – people queuing up to remit money to families in distant parts of the world, and buy special cards for phoning them cheaply. She had almost wanted to strike up a conversation with one shy young man who'd nearly caught her eye, a bit older than Alex, but she'd felt intimidated and a bit out of place with her smart handbag and coat. Funny how you can blend in invisibly in one place, and stick out like a sore thumb in another by crossing a street or entering a building. Yet all these worlds coexisted on top of one another in the same town.

'So, it's easy to top it up online here, or just by going to the app, or else texting this number,' explained the stout older woman in a strong Asian accent from behind the grilled teller window. 'You not used pay-as-you-go before ever?'

'No, er, no I haven't. But so long as there's a website, I'll figure it out. I'll ask my son.' Carrie suddenly felt uncomfortable and exposed in the brightly lit shopfront, with the high narrow counter and the long queue of people behind her.

'App is much better than browser, you just get it in app store. Madam, is everything OK? What happened to your arm, that is looking very sore.'

Carrie self-consciously slid down the sleeve of her costly rain mac, trying to shrink back into the coat itself and become invisible.

'How much do I owe you?' she blustered hurriedly, knocking the phone from the countertop as she rummaged quickly in her bag for her purse and tried to pull out the exact number of notes requested for the phonecard. Why had she come in here on the way between the two banks, with her big wad of cash in her purse? She had never felt vulnerable walking around with it before, but here suddenly she felt like everyone was watching her fumbling.

The young man who had almost smiled at her in the queue picked the phone up for her.

'No problem, it's OK, not damaged. But you really wanna get a case for that you know. It's a nice phone.'

'I know it is, thank you very much!' Carrie dropped the

phone into her bag, which she clamped tight across her body with her left arm, also gripping down the sleeve of her coat. She quickly paid the concerned-looking lady, who was exchanging glances with the young man, and gathered up the card and all the bits and bobs. She'd figure it out when she got home. She suddenly felt scared and desperately out of place – what was she doing in this strange scruffy shop? What was she doing even having a secret phone and secret money? A horribly familiar sense of panic welled up in her and she felt like vomiting. There was no way she could allow that panic to rise up and take control.

She couldn't get out of there fast enough, though she did her best to walk not run, in her stupid high heels – Mark didn't like her in flat shoes, but he wasn't here, so why on earth had she put these on today? As she clipped briskly down the high street trying not to look concerned, she jumped when someone caught her arm – someone who then helped and supported her, as she stumbled and swayed on the crowded street.

It was the young man from the money-changing-phone-card place, handing her her purse. He had a floppy shock of hair which stood up at the front and rounded specs. Her first inane thought was that he looked a bit like an Indian Harry Potter. 'You left this on the counter, and Mrs Shah said to make sure you were alright.' He steadied her, still holding her elbow, as she gasped for breath and swayed in the crowd, trying to find the right thing to say.

'Thank you, that's… You're very kind. Yes, I'm fine, thank

you, I'm perfectly… It's really not… Thank you, for coming after me.' She retrieved her arm – it wasn't the painful one, luckily.

'S'OK. You left in a bit of a rush. Your business, but Mrs Shah, she worries. She's like everyone's aunty. Well she actually kind of is my aunty, so she sent me flying after you like that. Though I'd have come anyway.' The young man had a kind smile. He really wasn't much older than Alex.

'And I was thinking, it looked like you'd not had a pay-as-you-go before, actually it looked like you'd never held a phone before, almost!' He laughed, but in a gentle way. 'I know Mrs Shah never got it set up for you before you lit out of there, so, I just wanted to check if you're alright with it? Like, maybe your husband or someone will sort it all out for you. But I work at the big phone repair shop in town, just while I'm at college, and I'm quite good. There's a bit of a knack with the Apple SIM tray and if you're not used it, it's tricky. I could help you? I'm Ritu, by the way.'

Carrie didn't feel like going back into the money shop at that moment, and at Ritu's suggestion they stepped into a café where she bought him a Diet Coke using some of the grocery money. She'd never been in this place before – she never really came to this part of town. Well, at least it meant no one she knew was likely to spot her, drinking tea from a chipped mug at a Formica table, while a strange and polite young man with a deep Brummie accent poked confidently at her phone with what looked like a bent paper clip.

After a few moments of teeth sucking, sounding like

a caricatured impression of an elderly British tradesman, Ritu grinned, and showed her the 4G connection. Then he downloaded and clicked open the new app for the phonecard.

'There you go, you can see the £10 credit on there from the Shah's. That should be good for a load of calls and texts, but it's quite an expensive tariff for what it is, like it's meant for occasional use only. Don't forget you mostly got access to wifi pretty much anywhere nowadays – like here – Stav, what's your wifi key, man?' he yelled at the portly proprietor.

'Fatstav123.' Ritu chuckled as he entered the code in the phone's settings. 'What else? But that's a rubbish password, anyone would guess it. I suppose Stav doesn't mind who uses it, he's got a router like Jodrell Bank, you can surf on here right down to the bus station I reckon. Or half way to wherever you're going on the bus!' He handed Carrie back her phone.

'See you got the Abra wallet on there, good call. Though if you're keeping cryptos on your phone, I'd take the app off the home screen. Stick it on a back page or something, or else in a folder. Not that you got enough apps to have folders, really. I see you got your fingerprint and all that set up which is great, but still, the less people know you're into this stuff, the fewer are going to try and scam you or phish you or rob you.'

'Uh, right.' Carrie didn't explain that the phone itself was a secret, or that she never traded or moved her cryptocurrency. For the billionth time she wondered to herself what she was actually saving it all up for anyway: there was nothing she could spend it on or even cash it out to. It was just there, her secret stash, and no one knew. Well, only Alex. And now this Ritu. But, she'd probably never see him again. He was a kind, helpful young man – a credit to his aunty, who he called by her surname. She didn't want to go back in there again either, but this SIM was really just for emergencies, she didn't intend to use funds much at all. Besides, she should be able to top it up via the app somehow.

'So, you– you like bitcoin and cryptocurrencies then, Ritu?' She asked politely, wishing her tea would cool faster and she could end this conversation somehow, now the mutual good deeds were done.

'Well yeah, a mate at uni got me started! I trade a bit, you know, ICOs and tokens – try to make a bit to help out me Mum, as she's on her own, and I'm trying not to get too many loans while I'm at uni.'

Carrie looked blankly back at him and nodded politely.

'So what you into, just bitcoin, yeah? Well, that's probably good really. I mean bitcoin's the bomb, it's the boss. I don't hodl anything else.'

'Hoddle?' Carrie wasn't sure what to say to that.

'Hold onto, like save up properly for the long haul. It's sort of a joke way of saying that, just about crypto, I think someone once typed it wrong in a rush or something. How d'you get into all this crypto business anyway, as it doesn't sound like you're up on stuff like Reddit and cryptotwitter?'

She had heard of Twitter of course, but could hardly explain that Mark forbade her to have anything to do with social media, or that she was amazed he'd tolerated her using even the MomsBoard forum for so long. She knew about all sorts of things by hearing about them from Alex and other people, like Facebook and so on, but they were like things which happened in another country or to somebody else, and it had never occurred to her till that moment that theoretically now other worlds could open up to her on this new device.

'I'm not really into Twitter and things like that, just some forum websites that I like,' she said. 'But what's Reddit?' She was warming to the polite and enthusiastic young man, who clearly knew about this stuff.

'Oh boy, don't even bother with that. I mean, there is a ton of interesting stuff there, but there's so much crap – I mean rubbish – as well. It's just like a load of people shouting past each other blaring stuff out, and then other people arguing with them and trolling for the sake of it to make things kick off… it's not pretty. Just useful if you want to keep up on something like breaking news about a coin, or an ICO.'

Seeing her blank face again he went on, 'An ICO[7] is when someone makes a coin or a token for a special project, like they have an idea for a business or a new way of doing things, and the token is the way of doing it, of having utility. Usually they build it on the Ethereum protocol, but it's a whole new coin. Most of them are a load of – well let's say rubbish again though that doesn't really cover it. There are hundreds of them now.'

'I have seen there's thousands of coins,' Carrie responded, 'on the Coin Marketcap[8] website. Most of them don't seem to be worth anything. But Ethereum is, I was even thinking of buying some of that. So how are the others built on it, I don't really know what you mean?' She wondered whether she was trying to impress Ritu, dropping remarks about market capitalisations, when she wasn't one hundred percent sure she actually knew what that was. She was on more confident ground with the knowledge that Ethereum was somehow a runner up to Bitcoin, and all the rest came after those two somewhere.

'Well. The currency's actually called ether or eth, and yeah you could get some if you wanted. Might as well stick to bitcoin though. Sure, it's the next biggest one by volume – though that could change – but the thing is it's totally different to bitcoin, just completely another thing. Ethereum itself – that's the protocol – it's like a platform, you can think of it as a computer that's actually distributed over all different nodes globally. So you can build other coins on top of it, and give them specific properties and utilities.'

Carrie sighed. 'Ritu, are you by any chance doing computer science at college? Protocols, nodes… I've got no idea what you're talking about right now.'

'Yeah! Sorry, guess that got a bit technical. I just love geeking out over this stuff! You don't need to know about protocols and nodes, honestly, not if you just want to use cryptocurrencies as money. Same as, I dunno, like you don't have to know how your car engine works - it's enough if you can just drive it safely, and call someone if a warning light comes on. But you were asking about ICOs, and all you really want to know is don't touch them. Unless you're really super careful, because honestly I have actually made some serious money occasionally with them by buying and selling at the right time. I even got enough to go travelling last summer, all from crypto. But you're mostly just going to get burned.

'That's the only reason to go on places like Reddit and Bitcointalk, to learn about token sales and what's coming up – only there's so much hype out there, people scamming each other or just pumping some shitcoin – oh god I'm sorry, I didn't mean to swear Carrie. But I just get really into this stuff! And I hate when people get ripped off, there's been some awful scams and frauds.'

'It's OK, I have a teenage son, a bit younger than you – there's not a lot you can say will shock me,' Carrie reassured him. She wondered about all this stuff he was saying to do with scams and rip-offs; it reminded her of Mark's opinions about bitcoin. But what Ritu was saying suggested it wasn't *all* like that in crypto, you just had to be careful. 'So I'll stick to bitcoin, then, stay away from these ICOs and things, at least until I know what I'm doing?'

'Oh god yeah, definitely. And listen – if you want to ask anything, talk about cryptos or phones or whatever – I'm often at the Shah's shop, or else in here. I do work, and I study too, but I look out for Aunty S when I can since her husband died a few years ago, she still runs that place on her own and she gets all sorts in there. So I make sure everyone knows that me and my cousins drop in a lot too.

I can always stop for a diet coke or something, if you've got any questions. I'll put my number in here. Hey, Carrie, how come you've got no contacts in your phone?'

'Well, it's quite new – new to me at least – and I don't really call anyone,' was all she could think of. 'But I'm often in town for shopping, going to the bank or something. I'm just learning about all this stuff, so it'd be good catch up again.'

'Well no one *calls* anyone anymore,' he laughed. 'I'll WhatsApp you!'

Carrie smiled as she said goodbye. She'd ask Alex about this What's app.

CHAPTER FOUR

....

MomsBoard private message:

My dear friend Carrie,

How wonderful that you and Alex both have new phones, how happy this must make you. I loved reading your account of the birthday tea party, and the beautiful girlfriend. What a privilege to be able to meet this young lady, who is so important to your adult son! In my country it's not so easy. Increasingly, there are restrictions on young people preventing them from spending time together in mixed groups. It seems like every day the mullahs increase their influence, and further dictate how people should behave, deciding what is acceptable and what is cause for shame – not just for the people involved but for their families and communities. My son was freer when he was fifteen, than now when he is approaching adulthood! More and more, it feels like we are living in a different country now.

And it is so much worse for girls. Sometimes I catch myself thinking that I am relieved my Aayliah is not here, to be scorned and threatened for not covering her hair, or for not diverting her beautiful smile from the eyes of her friends. Then I realise the horror of what I am actually thinking, that I am expressing gladness that my daughter did not grow to adulthood in this world, and I feel physically sickened by myself.

My dear friend, I am so sorry for sharing these dark thoughts. Hard times are coming to our city, to our country, it feels like there is little hope for the future. It feels like the West has abandoned us to our own devices, after interfering in our region for so long. Other people are frustrated that the Americans especially are not doing more to intervene, and take responsibility for how we find ourselves living now. I am sorry, these feelings are not directed at you personally in any way at all. But my husband Mohil has been threatened with losing his job and even with being arrested, and I am so afraid. He won't talk to me about what he is involved with, it is all academic and he says it's just politics. He has disagreed with the wrong people, but he won't back down. He says it's too important and that once good people start tolerating bad practice, there is no way for it all to end.

I worry for Jamal too, because I know Mohit is worried for him – and the two of them, they're excluding me from their counsel. Mohit says he is protecting me, Jamal says there is nothing to know about. He just spends more and more time with his friends, but they are not the same friends as before, the crypto computery nerdy ones. Now he is hanging out with different groups and being so secretive, I have come to hope that he is talking to his father because he is not talking to me. These friends… they are also political, he says it's just the same as with the bitcoin, they're people who can see ways to make the world better that others just don't understand because of their limited horizons. To me it doesn't sound so very much the same as making electronic money online. These boys defy the clerics and meet in secret and they don't tell their mothers anything!

I apologise for unburdening like this. Our friendship has endured a long time though we live in such different worlds. It feels as though I can trust you, in a way which is increasingly hard with my friends here. It feels as though everyone is watching everyone else for religious misdemeanours. Some of our neighbours are shunning Mohit for his articles and what people are saying about him – which is all unfair and untrue, anyway. My work at the hospital is busier than ever, although the pay is becoming erratic, even if they cannot pay me how could I not go to work regardless? People are turning up from other parts of the country, where the rebels have completely taken hold. The stories they are sharing are terrible, and the injuries… Mohit says I should not listen to them or talk to them, just help patch them up and send them on their way. But these are human beings here, young men like our sons, with devastation and grief in their hearts as well as damage to their youthful bodies. And where are the families they left behind?

Jamal talks about leaving.

About if things get bad, he should get to Europe – find a place for us. Some of his friends have left, and I know many people have fled from other cities. It seems so drastic, could things really get so bad in this very town? I wish we had more money saved, but the truth is Mohit has not been paid for a long time. And I really, really want Jamal to continue his studies. Some of his friends have dropped out, to join the soldiers, they go away to train and then we never hear anything from them again, or just rumours they are involved in fighting in other cities. Others have made the journey to the north, to Europe – but they must travel through dangerous regions in order to get there and again many we do not hear back from. We have no idea if they make it safely, or whether they are still trying to get there. If even the healthy young men cannot travel and arrive safely, what hope for the rest of us? Because yes, I do think about it, even if the idea of *abandoning my home is not one I relish at all.*

I know we are not welcome in Europe – they call us 'economic migrants' when we are fleeing such devastation, in order to suggest our need is not so great. Yes, there are families in the cities of my country which are destroyed by war, who are migrating in search of better economic prospects – but only because their prospects here are starvation and sickness. Even when the rebels have been routed from a town, no help comes. No one rebuilds the hospitals or schools if they are bombed, there are no shops or crops in the fields. So indeed, people do migrate, in search of better. But it is a long and dangerous road, nobody takes this road unless they have no other way to survive.

I believe in your country when people own property or farms, or they live in a city, they can safely keep their assets and remain there. Perhaps it is even their family land for many generations. In Europe I believe they will not be expelled because the militia want to train there, or the religion wants to rule in a town and change all the rules and expel everyone who is not living in accordance with their views. Jamal said that if we had a land registry on the blockchain, just like cryptocurrency is, then it would be harder for the rebels to just seize it from people who are left with nothing, and wander with only the clothes on their back to our city in desperate need. So the same technology can be used to make a kind of database that nobody can alter or tell lies about. I am sorry, I am digressing now in my stress.

I know in your news media there is much commentary on the arrivals at your borders, but little news of the thousands of displaced people within all the troubled countries in our area. They come to the hospital having walked for thousands of miles, malnourished families and children... Oh Carrie, we live in terrible times.

....

Carrie frowned. She was sad for her friend; it seemed so hard for her, as though everything was changing in her life, which had until recent times seemed middle class and stable. Carrie didn't pay a lot of attention to the news, although Mark liked to have it on the television after dinner sometimes, but she tended to read or busy herself elsewhere when he did. He got very agitated, running a constant commentary on the threat of the wave of refugees heading towards the UK, how they were going to steal his job, dirty his streets, scrounge for benefits and blow themselves up.

Carrie knew far better than to engage him in conversation, even though she hated the way he talked about people like Samar, whose friendship with Carrie he was completely unaware of.

Mark didn't know about Mrs Shah and Ritu at the phone shop, either, who Carrie had stopped by to chat to over coffee a few times lately.

It was dawning slowly on her that these people liked and welcomed her company. They didn't ask anything of her.

They were becoming friends.

It was unfamiliar and overwhelming, another little secret she hugged to herself, that warmed her when she felt cold and afraid at home. It meant more to her than the growing stash of bitcoin, this strange little community of caring individuals who shared their hospitality and kindness with her.

Mrs Shah, the universal aunty, was lovely, and always quick to put the kettle on in her tiny back room when the shop was quiet. Ritu was amazing, he was very knowledgeable about cryptos and they'd had a good chat about token sales – he seemed to take pride in helping and protecting her from getting involved in anything dodgy.

And it was only a few days later that she was catching up over yet another a brew at the back of Mrs Shah's shop. She often saw Ritu there, he seemed to just hang out a lot. When did he do his studies, and his job in the phone shop? He was so busy dispensing cryptocurrency user support to her! The tiny room was cosy and welcoming, even though it smelled powerfully of cigarettes, to the point that Carrie was worried about the smell clinging to her hair and her coat when she got home.

'Just stick to top twenty coins, if you want to diversify, Carrie. For me, I don't see why you need anything more than one, but I believe in bitcoin above anything else. It's the protocol, it's the truth. But – and here's what's most important for money – is that bitcoin has engaged with something called the network effect, which is about getting people using it. There's even a formula for it, called Metcalfe's Law, and it's nothing to do with crypto – OK, OK, just come with me on this, you don't have to know about formulas! Just that there're rules, about how the world works, which are really oddly consistent.'

Carrie was relieved that Alex didn't tend to need help with his maths homework anymore. She had wondered idly about introducing Alex and Ritu, but got caught a moment of sheer panic at the back of her mind about the two separate lives she was developing, and the risks for her son of trying to move between the two of them. If Mark ever– Stop. Kill the thought. Listen to Ritu.

'All it is, is that the more people who use a thing, the more powerful it is. At least, when it's something like this, which is about a network. Like, imagine the first person who ever got a phone – or say it was a new phone app or something, that didn't connect with anything else.'

'Sounds like my old phone!' said Carrie. 'I think I was the only person left who didn't have WhatsApp – so someone must have been the only person who did have it, once!'

'Yeah!' nodded Ritu. 'So imagine this guy, at first he's the only one, and he didn't have anyone to message and talk to. So then he was probably right excited when his first friend got one, 'cause he could use it at last – but soon they'd get bored ringing each other every day. So it's great when one more person gets on it, because now there's like double the number of connections. The new guy can call the first one, and the second one. And then when another one gets in, they've all doubled it again, or almost doubled it, every time – basically the amount of contacts they each have, so the amount of use they get of it, goes up a lot faster than the numbers of users increase.

'And it's the same thing with money. If you have something, it could be really valuable in its own right like a hundred-dollar bill, but you're here in the UK when everyone's got pounds, it's no use to you. It's just paper, the shops don't want it, so you can't buy anything. You got to have a network of people using it, else it's worthless where it is.

'So that's the problem with altcoins, all the new cryptos, not enough of a network, not enough people using it. Because, why would they? You have to have a reason in the first place to have and actually use it, or it's not going to work as money, sometimes projects even just give loads of them away to try and start it off. But none of them have the history and uptake of bitcoin. It's even in what they're called – alternative coins, alternatives to what? Bitcoin! The proper cryptocurrency! All these people buying them, it's like they're actually harming bitcoin in a way, as it just means they're not using bitcoin and helping it grow. I don't care if you mean something like ripple or ether, or else some rubbishy little token from an ICO, they're all shitcoins if you ask me. Ooops sorry.'

Carrie had laughed. 'Ritu, I have told you, I'm unshockable. Except when you call me "Mrs", that's outrageous, and makes me feel as old as Mrs Shah,' she added in a whisper, though the back room was quite secluded from the main counter at the front. 'But truly, all shitcoins? What about monero?'

'Mrs– Carrie. It's just my opinion, 'cause I am passionate about the original Bitcoin protocol itself. Just the maths of it, and the way it balances all the different things that motivate everyone in it, it's kind of beautiful. Any feature, like contracts, or security – even secrecy levels like Monero's got – can be developed on Bitcoin, making the original chain longer and stronger. More decentralised, unstoppable.

'You know my family is from India, right? They're always trying to ban cryptos altogether there, all the exchanges and stuff. But bitcoin still works, because it's so big and spread out: it hasn't got a central point where anyone can turn it off. It's got nodes in every country, including in my flat as you know, validating the whole chain, years and years of it. No way you can ban it, any more than you could, say, ban a popular song. You could ban it from being on Spotify or from being played on the radio, but once it's in people's heads and they know it, they'll sing it and share it, spread it from one person to another, even in private.

'Anyone can get bitcoin - they can buy it off someone, they can even mine it, though that's nearly impossible on most home computers now. But it's all over the world. My friend in Panaji, he can sell bitcoin locally for US dollars, when I send it to him for my family. He's worked out his own network, which lets him buy peer-to-peer from all over the world, and at the same time he's helping families like mine get money through without being ripped off by Western Union.'

'Western Union not a ripoff. They are very good client of mine,' interjected Mrs Shah as she bustled through her back room. 'None of your crypto-nonsense needed here, thank you very much! We never needed in the past, not in India, not here.'

'Ah, Aunty, you pay such high fees to them, how much have you paid all these remitters over the years? You'd break your heart if you knew! If I could just get you using one of these easy peasy wallet apps, god, you'd save a fortune. Look, Carrie learned it all just recently! Closed minds, aged shut, fossilised!' He shook his head with mock horror and genuine affection at the stout, mature woman who cuffed him affectionately on the back of the head as she passed back out towards the front of the shop. She lit another of her evil-smelling Marlboroughs, only to stub it back out again when a customer entered.

'As I was saying. Some little token without a big network, it's only gotta get kicked off one big exchange, get a load of it dumped on the market to tank the price, or else annoy some government – then it's history. Bitcoin though – you couldn't kill bitcoin, even if you were something like the US mint or the Bank of England!'

The two of them laughed into their mugs of tea.

It was still exciting and subversive. Carrie felt like a different world had opened up for her, a hidden one that coexisted alongside the safe suburban life she had inhabited for so long. Bitcoin had unlocked something, because it made her seek out phone cards and apps, but she hadn't expected to find new friends, to find a second community and culture which existed invisibly alongside her own. Just like the cryptocurrency network layered over the traditional money systems like banks and shops, there was this other world in her city – by no means an unprosperous one – where people worked jobs for cash, drove Ubers, traded phone cards, unlocked old phones, and yes, some of them used crypto.

It was a world with its own rules and participants, and a fiercely transparent kind of honesty and reciprocation, where communities helped each other in crisis, and bonded together in times of need. More than a few of Alex and Mark's old clothes had recently made their way to families in her own town who struggled to make ends meet: Mrs Shah knew how to redistribute things where they were needed, and had reacted with enthusiasm to the suggestion that Carrie could bring the next Oxfam bag to her instead. Ritu's mum had shown her how to haggle in the market for cheaper cuts of meat she could slow-cook and create delicious extended frugal dinners from, saving more and more each month from the housekeeping money. She had even enjoyed a couple of lovely curries in their tiny apartment, smiling at her hostess, with whom she shared little language in common, while Ritu translated and proudly showed off the Bitcoin node running on the computer in his bedroom.[9]

The two worlds both called to her in different ways. Whatever was happening with Mark, her home was all she had ever known, and it was Alex's home too. Brilliant if he could get away to Africa for the Project, and then go to university – but he'd need financial support for years to realise his potential. Her little bit of cryptocurrency couldn't fund that. And how could she ever manage on her own? *Ritu's mum manages*, whispered the voice that increasingly refused to be silenced.

It was the voice, in the end, which threatened the uneasy equilibrium of the two worlds, and eventually snapped Carrie's mind, literally fracturing her into panic and paralysis. The pressure of stepping between the two realities took its toll. Hiding her phone and holding the secret knowledge and ideas which Ritu shared in her head until she could add to her notes, as well as doing all the cleaning and scratch cooking meant that in some ways she was fitter and more active than she had ever been, but the mental weight, the conflict and fear of tripping herself up, became more and more impactful.

In some ways it was lucky that she was at home when it happened.

*

'Nothing at all to worry about, Mr Paige, Mrs Paige. Just a panic attack. Now, that injection should be kicking in nicely, and you can relax.' Dr Edwards patted her on her arm. He couldn't see the bruises through the arm of her dressing gown, but Carrie didn't flinch. She had years of practice at not flinching, and the sedative she had just received had made her very, very relaxed, even when the horribly familiar face loomed far too close in towards her own.

'Thanks Simon, I appreciate you coming to the house like

this. I didn't want to take her to the clinic in this state. Have you any idea what brought it on?' Mark hovered behind the doctor, but sounded more irritated than concerned.

'No idea. Mrs Paige!' Dr Edwards raised his voice slightly, and stuck his face down right in towards hers. 'Has anything happened to cause you more stress, more worry, just lately?'

Carrie thought about responding, about the effort of moving her mouth, her lips, to form sentences and find her voice. But she felt like she was far, far away from the room where the two men, squash buddies for years, discussed her for the most part like she wasn't there at all.

Mark gestured dismissively and snorted. 'She has no worries, nothing to be stressed about. All she does is cook, and fuss over our boy. No worries whatsoever. This is the old problem rearing its head again, isn't it? I found her just frozen there, in the kitchen, all trembling like she couldn't even get her breath. I tried to shake her out of it.'

The doctor raised his eyebrows, questioningly.

'You know, get her to snap out of it, concentrate,' Mark continued. 'But she just started gasping like a wet fish, so I called you. I thought she might be having a heart attack of something.'

'Then you really should have called an ambulance straight away, Mark! You know I'll always come and help you out when I can, I owe you that much, for old times' sake – but my surgery's on the other side of town and I could have been anywhere. If it's an emergency you have to get an emergency response.'

'Oh, I knew it wasn't anything too serious really. Maybe she's worried about Alex going off travelling in a few months' time. She says she wants him to go, but what on earth will she do with herself then? I think it's time you put her meds back up, help her cope a bit better. She's not doing so well now, though this is the first time she's been like this in years.'

'What I'd really like to do, Mr Paige – Mark – is admit Carrie, for a few days at least. Get her properly evaluated as an in-patient. You know it's all very discreet, and fully covered by your insurance plan. I feel like we're still trying to treat postnatal depression, decades after the event, and she needs to be properly reevaluated. You can visit any time, and your son – he's over eighteen now isn't he? So he can visit her as well. Maybe a few weeks, enough time for us to check her over thoroughly, make sure she receives any talking therapies she needs, combined with appropriate medication. The way we do things have changed a lot, since that time when she lost the–'

'No! Absolutely out of the question, she's not going in to hospital!' Mark was using the deep and unarguable voice. They both glanced towards Carrie, but though they were only a few feet away from her she showed no reaction in her deeply tranquilised state.

'She doesn't need observing, I'll keep an eye on her here at home like always. Thank you, for coming around so fast Simon. I appreciate it, and your reliable discretion.' Mark was starting to move towards the door, pointedly ushering the doctor from the room.

But Dr Edwards straightened up, as though he was trying hard to resolve an inner conflict, and somehow stand his ground. 'Ten years ago, Mark, I protected you. I covered up what really happened, with the miscarriage. I am not blind, and neither were my colleagues who could see the bruising – keeping things quiet cost me a lot, in more ways than you will ever know. Our loyalties went back a long way, and we agreed at least that she'd recover better at home. I believed you that it'd never happen again, and I knew I could treat her symptoms of depression and withdrawal.

'I can see she's otherwise outwardly physically well, but I am worried Mark. I have a professional duty of care to my patient, to see that she receives proper care and review. I have been remiss and I've let down my–'

'Mum!' Alex burst into the room. 'What happened? Are you OK? Why's the doctor here?'

'Mum is fine!' Mark gripped both of his son's shoulders, in a firm but fatherly manner, and steering him away from the sofa. 'She had a little anxious moment, a little bit of a panic, and she got overwhelmed. She's perfectly alright, she used to do this a lot when you were little. I asked Dr Edwards to come to the house and check her over here, so we wouldn't have to stress Mum out by taking her to the clinic. No, leave her be now, she's had some medicine which will help her to have a good night's sleep, and then afterwards help her stay all calm and relaxed. I will put her to bed in a minute. You can see she's perfectly alright, just rather sleepy.' He was continuing to use the tone which everyone knew to obey without question, and he didn't let go of Alex's upper arms.

'Now, I think Mum was just about to put the dinner on, it looks like that lovely lamb curry we both like. I had thought that was from Marks and Spencer, but it seems like she made it herself, I hope it's as nice as the last one – can you check that's fully defrosted and ready to go in the oven? Go on, we're going to be awfully late with dinner as it is.'

Mark steered Alex out of the living room towards the kitchen, and made sure he'd properly left the room and closed the door, after some long backward glances at his mother. Then he helped Dr Edwards with his coat.

'The thing is Simon, it might have been ten years ago, but your professional ethics and duty of care didn't count for much back then, did they?' Mark remarked quietly as they stood in the doorway of the living room. 'I was able to overlook your self-prescribing problem at the time and let you deal with it yourself, as the professional I knew you to be, for the sake of our long acquaintance. Didn't need outside interference, did you? Neither did I, in the way I looked after my wife. Then or now.

'Speaking of prescriptions, I want her back on the stuff from before, the one which keeps her really calm. Just for a short while. She's been doing too much lately – out and about every day, trying to keep up with all Alex's school work, and I don't think our cleaner's been doing a great job for her. I want my wife to have a proper rest. At home where she belongs. Have you got a pen?'

The doctor gave his old acquaintance a long hard look, then visibly admitted defeat. From Carrie's line of sight on the sofa, had she been capable of taking in the scene at all, she would have seen a perceptible deflation, of surrender, much as she would have seen in Dr Edwards the day Mark discharged her from the hospital after baby Grace had died. But on neither occasion was she capable of observing and remembering, of joining the dots, the links in the chain.

Mark had the situation back under his firm control now. 'Just give me two months' worth then, if that's all you can do. I'll make certain she takes it. I know we understand each other Simon.'

Dr Simon Edwards signed the prescription as directed, and left it on the hall table, unable to bring himself to hand it directly to Mark, ashamed of the piece of paper which bore his signature, and suddenly just as keen to leave as his host was to have him out of the house.

'Will I see you at the squash tournament at the end of the month? The league's really heated up this season, hasn't it? Thanks again for stopping by, I appreciate it!' Mark smiled and waved from the doorway, as his old friend beat a hasty retreat.

Carrie sat passively on the sofa, as Mark came back through the living room, to help her up to bed. On the TV in the living room, the newscaster was talking about bitcoin prices, and market trading cycles, but no one was listening.

*

The next morning, Carrie stared in the bathroom mirror, trying to focus, trying to remember what had happened. She'd lost her grip, panic had overwhelmed her. It was all too much, she hadn't been sleeping, all the secrets and learning and fear had boiled up inside and exploded. And Mark had found her. She'd been terrified: what had he found out, what had he seen, what was going to come crashing down?

The doctor – the doctor from years ago – he had come to the house. She hadn't been sure she remembered him, until he was suddenly back there in their lives.

That was last night. Now she was in the bathroom, and holding two capsules of a familiar medication, though she hadn't seen it for a while. Looking at a stranger with haunted eyes staring back at her, and trying to fill in the pieces in her memory, where the winds of fear and disconnection were howling through the holes like ghosts in a gale.

'…with plenty of water. Have you taken them Carrie, for god's sake, are you even listening? I have to go to work!'

Carrie dropped the capsules into her dressing gown pocket, and slipped sideways out of the bathroom door, to nod absently at her husband without fully meeting his eyes. Mark was busy finishing his tie and checking his hair in the mirror.

'Right, well back to bed with you, you'll probably just want to rest today. Don't worry, we'll order pizza for dinner tonight, you take it easy, read one of your little magazines or something. You need to take the next dose at lunchtime, so I'll call to remind you.'

Another sleep did do Carrie good. It seemed to clear her mind quite amazingly, in fact. She realised that she had had her first panic attack for some years the night before, that's all. And that this had scared Alex, as well as jolting Mark into some kind of concern for what the consequences might be. Dr Edwards – that was his name – he'd been worried enough to come here, to the house, where he and Mark had had the strangest conversation. If only she could remember what had been said. She was sure he had been an obstetrician? But that was so long ago. It was definitely the same doctor though.

Maybe the memories were there somewhere, but she couldn't seem to focus them clearly right now. There was an odd sense of calm hanging over her still. She got her phone from the shoebox and, hugging it to herself, climbed back into bed.

Googling the name on the label of the pills Mark had just given her, Carrie resolved in that instant never to take them again. The description made her feel like a problem to be controlled, to be suppressed and corrected. The most frightening thing was that *she couldn't remember anything properly,* from the moment the doctor came to the house, until she had woken up this morning.

What was in that injection last night? Had it combined badly with the pills as well? If she could remember some parts of the evening, of the conversation, could she somehow connect the pieces in her mind, as though they were a list of Dickens novels or anatomical parts? You had to start with clarity, to encode those kinds of memories. She could remember the twisted strip of paper and Barnaby the bear from that conversation with Alex years ago, but she didn't know what the doctor had said – something else about her pregnancy? The hospital?

She couldn't change what had happened in the past, the voice in her head intoned protectively, she could only decide what she did next.

'Yes Mark,' she replied when he called, making a swallowing sound. 'I am taking them now. Nothing, just resting, like you said, I've been asleep mostly.' She didn't need to exaggerate the tired and disconnected tone of voice much, and at first she'd been trying to answer the wrong phone when Mark called. 'Mmm, yes, I'll just go back to bed now, maybe read for a while.' Was that the first time she could remember telling him a direct lie? Well, she had lied about taking the other dose this morning, too, and he had been right in front of her then.

The medicine didn't flush easily, and she was worried they'd float back up. For the evening dose, she could try disassembling the capsule itself and pouring the powder away, but she'd still have to make sure the shiny outer layer could disappear completely too. What on earth was that stuff, it looked like plastic? How many of these things had she obediently swallowed over the past decade, without even knowing what it was? They must dissolve inside you, so they'd dissolve eventually, surely.

She checked her regular pills on the website she had found too. Well, they were unlikely to be doing her any harm, though according to the site she had been on them far too long. Stopping them suddenly could be harmful. She could decide about that another time. Most important was not to take the tranquilisers that Mark had dashed out to the late-night pharmacist for after dinner.

Carrie spent the next couple of days in bed, not resting in quite the same way as Mark thought, because the powerful medicines were hidden and flushed away each time. Even when Mark stood over her, trying to confirm her compliance, she grew adept at hiding them in her cheek for later disposal. Mark was almost tender towards her care, in a controlling and patronising way, and the more passively she behaved the easier it was to feel far away in her mind.

One sad surprise was how easy she found it to adopt the behaviour, the patterns of speech and concentration, that the medication had induced. There was something horribly comfortable and familiar about it, and in some ways it was a relief to have nothing expected from her on the conversational front. To actually be praised for making dinner. To feel herself making tactical adjustments to her level of alertness over a few days, as she 'got used to the new medicine'. She almost liked being able to function at a level where she fulfilled the expectations of those around her.

On Alex's part, if he noticed a change in his mother's demeanour after the time his father got in from work, in comparison to her reassuringly alert and normal self during the afternoon, he didn't draw attention to it.

Mark in turn continued to be kinder to her than usual, and

that was easier for everyone. Behind the mask of the faked tranquillity, Carrie felt like she was able to start observing him in new ways, perhaps through his sense that she had reduced any potential threat to him by reverting, so far as he knew, to her previous zombie-like state. He'd congratulated her on having a nice walk out to the shops and back – with even less of an idea that behind that vacant smile, sat a woman who had cleaned the entire house that morning, and made the tasty French onion soup from scratch for his dinner.

Carrie enjoyed less talking and more thinking. During her days alone, she did more reading too. Of course, she kept up with her crypto blogs and interests, but with her secret mobile browser she was also researching other things, like a prepaid debit card that she could send her bitcoin to and then spend it. What she would spend it on she wasn't sure yet, but she was piecing together jigsaws in her mind, including the fog of the past decade. She didn't know what the picture was going to look like when it was finished, but she was finding new pieces all the time, turning them over and around in her mind to see where they might fit.

Her future, long-term relationship with Mark was an area her mind was not yet able to examine, but certain practicalities she saw clearly. Firstly, Alex and his Africa relief programme – just a few months away now – meant that he'd be away from her. Far, far away from her, and that thought made her throat catch with sadness.

But he would also be far away from Mark.

Away from the tension hanging in the air, his protectiveness towards his mother, which she was aware her current withdrawn behaviour provoked. Mealtimes were almost silent now. It felt as though Alex hadn't spoken in front of his father since the day he was whisked out the living room, denied the chance to hug his sedated mother… I have to find a better solution, Carrie thought, I have to talk to Alex, talk to someone…

Another vital piece of the jigsaw arrived with Carrie from an unexpected source soon after.

WhatsApp message:

My dear Carrie,

Thank you for your lovely message.

We have been friends for years now, and our correspondence means a great deal to me. Like you, I don't have so many friends in my own neighbourhood, because things are strange here – the war is moving closer, and the difficulties with Mohit's position continue. His institution is aligned to some political group, I suppose you would call it, that used to be in favour but isn't any longer. My Mohit is a man of principle, and while the easiest thing would be for him to distance himself, that does not appeal to him. I am frightened every day that he will be detained by the secret police.

Neither is this easy, what I must write to you. It's

difficult because I feel very close to you in our private messages here, and yet we are thousands of miles distant from each other and we have never met or spoken. All I know of you and your life is what you have chosen to share with me, but from those glimpses, as a friend, I put together a fuller picture in my mind. My imagination completes the gaps and fills in the darker corners. Perhaps I use the wrong colours to paint these missing pieces, and if that is the case, I am only praying that our friendship is enduring enough, for you to forgive my intrusion and judgement – which comes only from a place of love.

Your last letter felt like it filled in a dark piece of the 'Carrie map', the portrait which I had been avoiding looking or asking about, because your private business is just that. But now I must speak – I have meditated and prayed on this at length, and see no choice but to say it, and trust that our relationship will survive these words.

Carrie, I am worried about you, for your safety, and for your emotional wellbeing. What you told me about your breakdown, and the doctor, and everything else I feel you haven't told me over years. I have to speak.

I read about lifestyles in the UK, and the freedom – women can work and travel anywhere, achieve anything they wish. Women are not the property of their husbands, they have so many opportunities denied to many in my culture. But I see you staying with a man who terrifies you. In a marriage with fear and controlling, and no love and affection. I am dreading to learn that he hurts you physically as well, though you have never spoken of this, and I fear too for your lovely Alex, in the centre of all of this.

Carrie, does your husband Mark hit you, injure you? I am so afraid that this is the case.

I am fearful that to put these words to the screen as I do right now, I am overstepping the boundaries of our friendship, treading into areas of privacy behind the closed doors of the family. Of a marriage not my own. I would only dare to risk this, because I care about your wellbeing, and that of your boy, and I am so, so worried for you.

If I am wrong and have misjudged the situation, I hope you will forgive my invasion in this way. I feel so close to you, and that our lives have so much in parallel if not in common… I realise that too can make me project my own thoughts and ideas, run away with the situation in my mind, with not enough truth to build upon. I am only piecing together fragments of things you have related, conversations you've described. All you have said over the years we have been corresponding, as well as things which feel they are being unsaid.

But if I can help you at all, in any way – I don't know how, just to talk to maybe, to be a sounding board, to be a friend? I just want to support you. Your last letter sounded so down and disconnected.

When I read about you losing your baby girl, my heart broke for you. To suffer that grief in isolation, without the love of your family around you and a husband who was emotionally cold: I wept for you Carrie, for you and your baby Grace, just as you told me how you wept for my Aaliyah.

You must never speak of there being this loss greater than that one, there is no hierarchy of this great pain. Yes, I lost a daughter I had held and known for five years, but you never had that opportunity, and I know how the most unforgiveable loss is in all the time you didn't have together. The way you write about it being something people expect you to get over and move on from, I don't know if it reflects your culture or some unusual dynamic in your household, but my belief is that such grief and sadness is completely necessary and normal.

When we lost Aayliah, Mohit wept as well. In the privacy of our home, he sobbed in my arms. He did not cry when his parents passed; he said that was the order of things and a sadness which was natural and expected, compared with the devastating wrongness of losing our child. We were both drowning in our sorrow, but each bit of weeping sheds somehow another tiny crumb of the sadness, spends a little fragment of the hurting. Although it feels infinite, as if it will never leave you, to express each small part of it lets it gradually move through you, so you can accommodate the grief within your new self.

To carry it with you forever, but somehow in its proper place.

Carrie, I fear that you have never had that chance to grieve for your daughter properly, the baby you never got to take home and raise. I am so sad that as well as the emotional distance of your husband, you have no mother and sisters there to share your grief, to wail and rage together at the cruelty of it all.

From here in my country so far away, your sister in spirit weeps with you now, and sends what comfort she may in words.

The image of the smiling little girl in the pink ballet dress which came attached to the message blurred on the screen of Alex's laptop, as Carrie's eyes filled with tears.

There had been tears before, whatever Samar thought, she had wept and grieved. She had been allowed to, for a time, by the lovely nurses, by some kind strangers at the hospital whose names and faces she could not recall. Then the tears had been denied, the time was up – time to stop them tight with pills that blurred the days and nights together in an unforgiving and unspent numbness.

The tears had been her only peace, the only way she had achieved any release of the little crumbs of grief, exactly as Samar had written. But the doctor to which Mark had returned her in frustration, saw the tears as the problem he had to treat, and medicate away. How many weeks, months, years? She felt like she barely remembered the years Alex was in preschool and reception. Her memories were the vaguest snapshots. Why hadn't she noticed that the same doctor prescribed her medication as had attended her when Grace died, until he turned up here the other night? It reflected how her life had been at the time: a series of disjointed fragments, finding herself at the swings with the buggy, or just staring into space at home, her most fundamental emotions pharmaceutically smothered.

How did Samar know? What had she said, or not said? She had been so careful. She wasn't on those tranquilisers now; she didn't have these absences, where she might have written about what life with Mark was truly like. She knew she had never expressed this truth, even in the secret privacy of her own mind, and a complex wave of emotions washed over her. Her friend's kind and insightful probing had ripped away a scab of resistance across her own heart, letting a multitude of feelings and realisations bleed out.

Shame: she *was* the trapped, scared, fearful person that Samar had so painfully identified. She had had so many opportunities, and been born into such privilege and freedom, compared to women in other parts of the world, it was true. How had she let herself become this boxed-in and anxious and terrified individual?

Fear: who else knew, could see, could somehow let Mark know that she was so scared of him that he could do anything? Somehow the realisation of what had been happening made her at first feel more vulnerable, more exposed. With the humiliation now surely written on her face, her subjugation felt absolute.

Anger: how dare someone she barely knew, who didn't even know her, shine this light into her marriage, her weakness, her innermost self? Someone who had never met Mark – never seen the charming, professional, highly-controlled mask he wore in public, and knew him only indirectly, through the words of his wife. Samar couldn't possibly really know what he was like!

But maybe that was exactly why she had seen the truth.

Carrie realised she was gripping the edge of the desk in Alex's bedroom, where she still often went to read messages, out of force of habit now that she could do it all on her phone. She sat, white-knuckled, as the room spun around her. Her whole world spun, wheeling out of control, as she felt herself breaking into tiny bits which whirled and flaked away from her, bits of memory, dreams, patterns and thoughts.

A small, hard part of her mind buried deep below the surface seemed to observe from a distance that the pieces might fall to the ground and reassemble in a very different shape, when they finally came to rest. That in a fundamental and invisible way, nothing would ever be the same again for her. The only point of stillness in her field of vision was the smiling little girl, in the scanned precious photograph that her friend had shared with her to provide some comfort and connection from one bereaved mother to another so far away. Her fingertips reached forward to touch Aaliya's face on the screen, tenderly and carefully.

Carrie closed her eyes, and took a deep breath in, releasing it in slow juddering sobs.

Her nightmare had a name.

She was in an abusive relationship, a violent marriage, where she was bullied and scared and manipulated, and even if Mark had rarely left bruises where anyone else could see them, he had oppressed and beaten and hurt and harmed her for years. She couldn't hide behind a mental illness, a fear of confrontation, or anything else any longer. Where had her thirties gone?

She looked around, blinking in bewilderment, at her teenage son's bedroom – his football posters, band merchandise, and ridiculously large shoes scattered on the floor. She felt as though she'd just woken from a dream, a trance, since he was a little boy going to nursery. There was no way back now. Where had she been?

She ran back to her own room, to her bed, to her cocoon of safety, at least while Mark was at work – and wept and wept. She wasn't sure how long the tears flowed.

Once the initial wave of reaction had subsided, she felt broken, crumpled, spent. But, as the self-pity ebbed away, a new surge of guilt broke over her. What had all this done to Alex? Her beautiful boy. She had believed she was doing the right thing, trying to keep the peace, keep things calm, hide what was going on, and lie to his face every time she said everything was fine or Dad was just a bit tired or stressed and not to worry. But every time she let him think this was a normal relationship between his two parents it must have affected him: what would that do to his ability to be happy in future?

All she had wanted was to be the best mum she could, feeling that she had no choice about anything else in her life. In a few short months he'd be leaving home – leaving forever, she knew – and while that was definitely the best thing for Alex right now, it felt like a bereavement in waiting. The tears flowed freely again. There were so many tears: for herself, for Alex, for Grace. For the Mark she thought she had married, the charming, quick-witted and generous man who had whisked her off her feet. What had happened, to twist him the way he was? Why had he never explained about his complete estrangement from his family? Because it was obvious now that something was very wrong in his past; people like that weren't born that way.

Babies were the most innocent thing on earth.

She had nothing. She was on her own, with few choices, even if she succeeded in getting Alex safely off to another continent, what then? She had no career, her scant few thousand pounds worth of savings, no friends. No family to speak of, with her father completely absorbed in the teenage schemes of his stepchildren. But, she realised, Mark had clearly carefully and systematically isolated her from anyone who could have seen what was happening, stood up for her, in any way held up a mirror to her life and let her see what was going on. She had once had a job, she'd had friends.

But she did have friends.

She had people Mark knew nothing about. She clutched at this thought, like a drowning woman, battered by emotional currents that were rising way over her head. As the waves of panic rose, threatening to obliterate her control and consciousness, she clung tightly to the life-raft of hope, that even though these were people carefully compartmentalised outside her home life, they existed: Ritu and his mother – his mother who spoke hardly any English, but always showed her kindness, and had made Ritu translate for her the friendly statement that she was welcome at their house any time of day or night. Just kindness, or did she perceive something else might be needed?

Mrs Shah, the tea-drinking chain-smoking old lady who had sold her a SIM card then dispatched help to pursue her down the street, who always seemed to be just making a pot of tea whenever Carrie popped in to the shop. The effeminate young bank teller Ian, who congratulated her each time she brought in her money at the beginning of each month – did he know, even before she did, that she was working on an escape fund? Did he know about this debit card that you could add your crypto onto? She realised in that instant how ridiculous it had been, to feel that her money was more safe and secret in bitcoin than it would have been in her own private bank account, but, thanks to the exchange rate her secret stash was worth a lot more than it would have been sitting in Ian's bank.

It was still not enough though. Not enough to… what?

What could she do, where could she go? She had never

thought about a proper plan, never thought beyond the day she got Alex launched on his flight to a new life. Could she begin to see a new life for herself one day too?

And of course the one constant friend of the past few years, the one person who had had the courage to question and name what she saw even from a great distance: Samar. The only person she had written to, after all these years, about Grace's death and her feelings, and the only person to have seen through the carefully-constructed and increasingly brittle outer layer of Carrie's public persona and tried to help directly with what was happening underneath. Despite everything that was going on in her community and in her own family, she offered help and support unconditionally. For one crazy moment Carrie entertained the idea of asking for her address and fleeing to the country which so many were trying to escape from, to be with the only person who had ever truly understood what was happening here.

CHAPTER FIVE

If she had felt like she had an entertaining secret life beforehand, with her visits to the phone shop and her furtive cleaning, the stakes had never been higher than they were now. Carrie knew she had to take care of herself – of her emotions and stability – because another panic attack would be a disaster. She had too much to fight for, too much to lose.

But this gave her energy. She realised there was a connection between her breathless states of panic, and a desperate need to be noticed, to be helped. She had been too fearful to ask for anyone to step up and help her, but needed to somehow be visible, and this was always followed by a retreat inside herself when no help came, when no one looked hard enough behind the veil of middle class respectability. The way people said, 'Why the kind, generous husband, he does everything for the poor woman, she's never been able to work or do anything.' That was easier, for everybody, than to call out what was really going on.

People had tried, she reminded herself. Through her own behaviour she had effectively collaborated in the silence, backing away fast from any affection or connection or attempts to reach out to her. She felt as though years of dust was lifting from her eyes. So many conversations she could now remember could be seen in a different light, if you saw it as someone trying to connect, to tentatively offer her a helping hand or a listening ear, a chance to talk if she had wanted it. It wasn't that she hadn't wanted it, though, she literally hadn't heard what they were really offering to her. It was all so obvious now.

But now she had to help herself. She had to help Alex, and she had to share more with him too. He was eighteen years old, after all. This week, he was going to hear about whether he'd been selected to go on the Africa Project, something he was far more excited and nervous about than the deferred university offer already received, though Carrie knew that Alex was deeply conflicted about leaving his mother too, especially since her recent 'episode'. He deserved better, he wasn't a child anymore, and he deserved to know that actually, his mum was making a plan for her future too.

*

'Well, of course I'm worried, Dad said you weren't going to be driving while you were ill! I could easily have got the bus, I don't know why you had to come and meet me!'

'I wanted to talk to you properly, and it's easier here than at home.' Carrie had got oddly accustomed to the safety and anonymity of discussing profoundly important things in busy cafés full of strangers. Alex had come at once when she texted, leaving football practice early, and surprised to see his mother out of the house.

'Also, I am fine to drive. I had a panic attack Alex, it doesn't affect my functioning a fortnight later. Dad's right though: I am not supposed to drive on the medication I was given. So, it's just as well I haven't been taking it. Not since the first night when the doctor came, actually.' She sipped calmly and returned her cup to the table.

Carrie had read about people's jaws dropping open in disbelief, but wasn't sure she'd ever seen it happen in real life. On her floppy-haired teenage boy, it was endearingly sweet. But she could see him thinking, piecing things together, as his quicksilver mind started joining the dots.

'But in the evenings, at dinner– do you mean– Dad thinks you're still taking them?!' Alex's expression was a strange mixture of awe and infuriation, combined with a growing spark of joy.

'He stands over me at bedtime, and watches me sometimes. Because he's not sure. I have to be really careful. If he thought I wasn't complying with the medication, Dr Edwards would be round again with his syringe, and then I'd have no choice. So I nod slowly, and smile peacefully. Calmly.' Carrie let her features slide momentarily into the vacant, unfocussed manner she adopted when Mark was in the house. 'And I… talk… like… this.'

Then she looked Alex directly in the eye, and said, 'I've also got very good at pretending to swallow – doing a convincing noise – and completely destroying the capsule by dissolving it when I am in the bathroom alone. Alex, I am so sorry!' She reached out and held his hand, grasping it in both of hers across the Formica table. 'I had to deceive you too. I had to, to protect myself, and find space and time to think, to decide. To know what to do.'

'I felt like I'd lost you, like you were slipping away from me! Mum, I was sad, and so scared. And confused. Like, in the afternoons you'd be normal and quite like your old self, even though we didn't talk so much anymore, then by dinner time you were Zombie Mum all over again. I thought it must be about the time of day you took the pill. I had no idea. I didn't know what to do, because Dad seemed to be being nicer and almost kind to you, but it was like you were so vulnerable. I didn't know what do decide about the Project or anything, how to ever leave you.

I still don't, I mean...' He ran out of words, still processing the new information.

Carrie knew her son so well, she could almost see the thoughts whirring in his mind behind his eyes, before he – not for the first time – cut through all the irrelevancies and straight to the point, with a question which got right to the heart of things:

'Why have you told me now, Mum, what's changed? What's going to happen?'

Carrie suddenly found it difficult to meet his gaze. But she had initiated this conversation, and it was time to make the bubbling thoughts and dreams concrete, by saying some of it at least out loud.

'I think, what's going to happen, is that I am somehow going to leave your father. Not straight away, I need to plan, and save. That half a monero which nearly killed your laptop won't get me very far on the bus, though I have some bitcoin as well as you know, it's just not enough. I can't do anything yet, and my number one priority is seeing you on that plane to Africa first. That's all I've been working towards for eighteen years, so, shhh.' She patted his hand to forestall interruption.

'But I can't lie to you any more,' she continued. 'I can't see you confused and hurt about what's happening with me and my health, see you too scared of leaving me behind to focus on your own plans and studies. I had to get it out in the open and tell you. I had to decide to trust you, actually.'

'Oh god, Mum – to the ends of the earth. You can trust me to help you, to protect you, to do anything to help you get away. You're not alone, Mum. I don't want to leave you! And I won't go unless you're really OK, and I mean unless you're away somehow, or you've at least got a plan to be as far away as I'm going!'

'Can I come to South Sudan on the Project?' Carrie smiled. 'I'd be rubbish at teaching English or maths, but I can teach them all how to cook, and how to send bitcoin.' That was pretty much it, she realised, glancing away. Not a lot to show for four decades. She could teach them to do housework in secret. How to take a punch to the ribs, to the upper arms, to areas of old bruising where the pain was worst of all, without giving away the satisfaction of flinching. How to numb it all away with heavy medication. She could teach them how to act like nothing was wrong.

'Well, I told you Katie didn't get through the first interviews. Sounded a bit rough for her, living with no water and no wifi! Apparently they'd be like, really weird about someone refusing meat as well – because meat is a rare privilege there. She just didn't fancy it in the end or at least not enough, and I am not sure you would for the same reasons, Mum. I have to find some other way to keep you safe, I can't take you with me.' He was babbling a bit now, she recognised, letting his mouth run free while his brain buffered in the background.

'No! You absolutely don't have to find me anything, Alex. For the first time in years, far too many years, I am going to take care of myself.

I told you because I love you and I trust you and you deserve to know that I am planning my escape, the same as you are yours. You're not responsible for me, you just need to know that I'm alright, and I am well, as well as I've been in years – whatever it may seem like when I'm around your dad.' Carrie was wondering how well she'd be able to keep that up, now that Alex was in the picture. But she had no choice. It wasn't a game.

'Mum, I'm kind of speechless. And also just mad with myself, because, I've watched you be so unhappy for years. The way he talks to you, patronises you. I've even been scared that perhaps he even… hurts you, physically I mean, sometimes?'

Carrie's glance slid away. She hadn't had any intention of going into details with her son about the form of Mark's abuse, but the level of disclosure they'd been sharing in the last few moments left not a shred of doubt in Alex's mind, about everything his mother's unspoken answer didn't say.

He slammed to his feet, tea cups clinking and spilling. Heads turned in the busy café. 'Right, that's it, I am going straight home, and I'm... No! he'll still be at work, I'm going round his office, I'm– I'm going to–' Alex was shaking from head to foot.

'No, Alex, you're not going anywhere. Sit down. Please!' Carrie took his hand and encouraged him to sit back down. Other customers enjoying their beverages saw the situation as a maternal figure comforting an agitated teenager, and turned back to their own business.

'Alex, I know you want to help me, and even though it's a great deal to ask, a really difficult thing, the very best way you can help me right now is by carrying on in exactly the same way as always. Like nothing has changed. This is a huge weight I have laid on you, coming clean like this, and I knew exactly how you'd react initially. I love you for it, I am more grateful than I can really find words for.' Carrie sniffed resolutely and hurtled on with what she wanted to say before Alex could speak again.

'I've thought and thought about it, because I had to be sure that telling you was the best thing for you truly, rather than just to make things easier for me. I was desperate to confide in you and tell you what was going on, but not at the cost of making life harder for you at this critical time. You're my best friend Alex, but I'm your mum first. In the end I came to the decision that, things going on as they are and my trying to hide it all in plain sight, that must have been so horrible and hard for you, that I considered on balance that it was right to tell you. And trust that you'd be able to join me in keeping the secret. Until we can both get away.

'Dad holds all the power, financially. I have less than £5000 saved – yes, I have been saving. Most of it is in bitcoin, but I do have a prepaid debit card on the way which lets me spend it on anything. It's nowhere near enough. Yes, I know there are places you can go, with no money. There are places where you can disappear completely and never be found, there are charities and organisations, but I need to get clear of him, to a place where I can take him on and be safe from him, making sure he has to play fair financially. I'm forty-five and I've got nothing, no job, no career, no pension – I think I have to divorce him, and get help to make sure I have enough to survive, and that he pays for your uni. Which is why you can't take sides, and why I can't make a move until I have something behind me.'

Alex was nodding slowly, trying to process all the stuff she'd been thinking about for days, and assimilate all the new information and mental models of his parents. His twitching reminded Carrie of when he was little and trying to avoid a completely inevitable reality about something like screen time or baths, she could see him almost physically resisting the situation he now found himself in. 'So, you mean, I have to just act like everything's normal? Like he's not threatening you, hurting you, *drugging you*? I don't know. I just can't imagine how that's going to work, every night at home.' He was really struggling with the whole thing.

'Alex, it's only for a few months, tops. Then you'll be gone. And somehow or other, so will I. Till then, I'll keep going to bed early, but be well enough that Dad feels OK to start going out after work again like before. I won't do anything to provoke him, and if you don't either, we'll be fine.

'We need to sort some things out, like to see if we can get his bank to sponsor your Africa trip – they do have a budget for that kind of thing, and if we can make Dad see it positively and proudly enough, he can really help you there. And we need to confirm where the passports are. I think they're in the locked cabinet in the office at home, at least I can't find them anywhere else. He's going to have to give you yours when you go, so somehow we need to get mine out then too. Not that I'm planning to leave the country, I just want to have it.'

'Oh my god Mum, the cabinet. Do you know what else he's got in there?' Alex interrupted excitedly.

Carrie shook her head. 'I never go in there, I'm not welcome. His domain. Well, actually I go in there every week to clean it, for months now – yes, that's me, and that's how I saved most of the money. It was the first thing I ever deceived him over, and it made me feel ever so powerful, but also scared.'

'Well I'm not welcome in there either, obviously,' continued Alex, clearly ready to park his mild surprise about the cleaning for the time being – like many people of his age he had little awareness of or interest in how housework happened in his environment. 'But I remember when I was little, running in there one day – it was years ago now, I was maybe like eleven or something – but there was money. A big stack of notes, I saw it.

'Dad yelled at me to get out and I did, right away. He scared me then. He doesn't scare me now you know, and I am taller than him! Back then I just got out. I have no idea how much there was, or if it's still there. But I bet it is, and he still keeps it all locked up. Money, Mum! Your money, in a way, if you look at it like that – as you've cooked and cared for me every day of my life, shopped, kept the house for him. Ironed his buttoned-up shirts that all look the same. If we can get that money out, you can go anywhere. Well, depending on how much it is. But it's there in the house, and somehow we can get at it.' Alex had a wild look in his eyes.

'Woah! OK, well, that's good to know and think about. If it's still locked in the cabinet, it's probably with my passport, but we don't know what's there or how much. Also, it'd be stealing – yes, I heard what you said and I know, I know I am owed something for all those years. But, in terms of the police and what would most likely happen, I can't just take that money, it won't work like that.' Carrie was keen to reassert herself as the grown-up in this conversation, take charge of it and set the boundaries and rules for the future.

'For now, we need to go home, so Dad won't notice I've been out with the car. Then I need to make a slightly more complex effort at dinner than I was doing earlier in the week, so he can see I am getting back into my benzodiazepine'd groove – I functioned pretty much on the outside for years on those pills before, for I don't even know how long for. I think he only supported me cutting them out when I needed to drive you to high school.

'I'm sure the reason I had the panic attack was all the lies and fear building up. The money being saved, remembering to do the cleaning each week in secret, the fear of getting found out. So scared that you'd throw away your opportunities because you were worried about me. Scared that I didn't really have any kind of a plan. I have some new friends, they've helped me with some things – maybe you'll meet Ritu sometime, you'd like him, he's a bit older than you. They don't know though, about your dad – they just know that they don't know much about my life and that probably something's wrong at home. Ritu's mum sort of guesses I think, and I am sure there's more of a story there about his father, but her English isn't great and we mostly talk about recipes.

'But I felt like I was leading a double life, split off from my home life, and part of my brain didn't know what was real and what wasn't anymore. It was like when Dad talks about things that have happened and changes things around to make me come off as stupid or forgetful and I know it isn't the truth, it just makes my head spin and I feel so trapped. I think that's why something snapped in me last week, and even then the panic itself didn't seem real. But it mustn't – must not – happen again.

'That was also part of what helped me decide for definite to tell you, because somehow I had to get back on top of things and change the way it was all going. I don't mind hiding from Mark, or lying to him. In some ways I've been doing that in my head for years, even when I didn't know it, just to survive. But it meant I was deceiving you too, and that was breaking me up, that was what was so conflicting. I think it was lying to you that made my head explode, because I'd see you looking at me with that mixture of concern and love, and sometimes even a bit of distaste or contempt – no Alex, you did and you couldn't help it, I was such a victim. For years and years. Now, something has shifted and I'm not anymore. I couldn't bear that I had to pretend to you that I still was.'

'Oh Mum!' Suddenly Alex was sobbing, choking back hot tears. 'I can't believe you– that I didn't realise–' He squeezed his eyes shut, shaking his head, as though he was trying to shake out the rush of troubling thoughts and memories that were flooding through it.

The other occupants of the café, a rather more upmarket one than the one near the phonecard shop, continued sipping their lattes and tapping away on their phones, unconcerned about what was happening over on the corner table at the back now that no one was bumping into tables any more.

'Alex, I am so sorry. This is so much to take in, to take on. And then to act like everything's fine around Dad, you're so honest and sincere and smart, I know it's going to be even harder now in some ways. Every day when I've been scared and I've struggled or worried about what would happen, I've been comforted by how much I love you and how proud I am. Everything you've overcome with the dyslexia and school. How could someone as damaged as me and as cruel as your dad together create someone so amazing? You're like a miracle.' She cupped his cheek in her hand, wiping his tears like he was a little boy again.

'I can do it, Mum. We can do it. I'll smile it him and lie through my teeth it if it'll help you. And if he ever– if he ever–' Alex's voice wavered to a halt, unable to say the word.

He changed track. 'You're not on your own anymore Mum. We'll do it together from today. We'll get you help, make a plan to get away. I'll go to Africa if that's what you really want for me, though I do want to stay and help you more. But you don't have to be scared that I'll do or say anything that'd show you up or make any trouble for you.'

She touched his face again; he wasn't usually much for personal affection these days – her hulking great teenager gave out only rare big bear hugs and shied away from much else – but right now, he was her baby boy as well as her macho defender, all in the same beautiful bundle of contradictions she had fallen in love with the day he was born.

'Let's go home, Alex. I'll get the dinner on, you do your homework, we'll make it through. But we'll do it together now. I am so lucky to have you.'

WhatsApp message:

My dear friend,

I am so proud of you. Your last message brought tears to my eyes. I cannot begin to imagine how you face up to such a situation, and have the dignity and resolve to desire to overcome it.

I think the mind is such a strange and powerful thing. You remember the messages we used to exchange at the beginning of our friendship, about the amazing brains of our special boys? But your brain did a clever thing too, to protect you from the reality of the things in your life that you couldn't address, that you needed to hide away from to survive. Here in my country, people lead double lives often, hiding secrets from the police, from their neighbourhood informers. It is hard. But you hid from yourself, inside your own mind, you built a vault and locked away the truth. Our boys used tricks of the mind to remember things, for their exams, to get through their schooling. I bet Jamal can still remember the list of kings that way, if I asked him now. And your mind built a wall instead of a chain of connections because that is what you needed just then.

You said you had been too scared to examine it, that you felt shame for lack of bravery, but my friend in my eyes you are the most courageous person I know. I am sorry if my words caused you pain, but if they helped you to address your reality and find a path through to a future where things can be different, then every tear has a justification.

It is wonderful that you have Alex in your confidence now, that is so good. I wish it were the same for me with Jamal, but he is becoming increasingly distant from me…

I should be honest with you, despite your personal upheavals I have always tried to share openly – I hope this is not to add to your worries. But things are not so good here. My husband Mohit has been arrested for his 'political activities' – except they are not even activities, just opinions he holds but refuses to renounce, even to keep us all safe. I am only able to see him once a month, and then I have to pay a 'tax' to the guard. Jamal does not want to see his father, but this is for the best for him, I think, to keep that separation, so even though it saddens my heart I do not oppose it.

I am still working at the hospital, but they are conflicted about involvement with my family – although my department head knows that I am not my husband. I do not promote his viewpoints, indeed I never speak of anything political or religious. But it makes them vulnerable. If they had anybody else to do my work, I would be jobless now. As it is, I work when I can for even more erratic pay, because the patients need me, especially the littlest ones, I have become effectively a nurse as well as a radiographic specialist. So many injured are now flooding to our area from nearby cities which have become war zones. My stupider friends continue to talk about how it could never happen here.

Mohit wants Jamal to get away, to leave the country and try to make a new start somewhere. There are people who will take you, help you travel – but they want so much money. I can't bear Jamal to leave me, but I know Mohit is right. He is spending time with the wrong people and he will end up on the other political divide to his father, you would say he is becoming radicalised. My amazingly intelligent and creative son who generated money out of computers, is being alienated from me, and telling me it is not right for me to go out to work, even in the hospital. How does he think we will eat now, with his father incarcerated? He does not listen to my views.

But I know if I presented him with enough money for the traffickers, he would take the opportunity to go. To make a new life in Europe, in the UK if he could get that far. It would break my heart for him to leave, but it's breaking my heart that every day he is moving further from me before my eyes right here. If I knew he was safe in a neutral country, even if it was far from me, I wouldn't be so scared every time he goes out. You said you are scared when Alex comes home; I am scared whenever Jamal is away from home.

We are both trying hard to save money and courage

to send our boys away. This makes me so sad: after all we have been through together raising them to adulthood, through their educational struggles. Now we both want them safely away from their homes, for their own good.

Ah my friend I did not mean to unburden in this way after the momentous news that you just shared with me. Your courageous realisation and planning brought joy to my heart. We are fighting our different battles in our different continents, but our strength as mothers will bring us power. You are one of my only secrets: since you got your number to message directly, I feel really close to you, and that I have a friend who is safe from all the chaos here and not forced to take sides, who I can really talk to. It means the world to me.

Carrie was so worried for her friend. Her husband arrested! An absent part of her mind ran over the idea of walking into a police station and making a statement about Mark, having the fading bruises on her ribs and kidneys photographed and scrutinised, standing in court just like they do on TV and giving evidence. She couldn't imagine – couldn't even contemplate – that ever happening. She would be so afraid.

But she knew that even if she did have the courage to denounce and describe so compellingly that she was believed and taken straight to a secret refuge while they went to arrest Mark, it would be totally different compared to the process in Samar's country. Mark would be taken to a cell maybe, yes, but his rights would be respected, he'd be fed, he wouldn't be tortured or questioned. She tried not to listen when the news was on, but she knew what was going on in Samar's part of the world, and why people were desperate to flee. She couldn't imagine the terror and despair Samar felt for Mohit, the helplessness – never mind the worries about her son.

Over the years, Carrie had entertained idle fantasies of physical vengeance on Mark – but the thought of a state inflicting that kind of punishment, of having that kind of power in the police or some religious militia, that terrified her. How could she help her friend? Could Jamal come here somehow? Could she sponsor him, or adopt him? Her mind ran wild. She would ask Ritu, he might have some ideas, and Mrs Shah would too. She knew if she could just get Jamal over here, then her friends could definitely help him, it was just that the journey was so dangerous and difficult.

It helped her get her own challenges into perspective at least.

A couple of weeks on from her conversation with Alex in the coffee shop, life had settled down somewhat at home. Alex's acceptance on the Africa Project programme had set a hard deadline for his departure, in a couple of months' time, and Carrie was doing her best to accept this positively as a goal to work towards for herself and the very best thing for Alex. If Samar could contemplate sending her beloved son over land and sea in the care of people traffickers, she could bloody well see Alex off to the adventure of a lifetime at Heathrow! And she would.

Mark was in a more mellow mood as well. Something had shifted at work, or maybe outside of work – he was going out two or three evenings a week now, to meetings or socials. Was there someone else? She neither knew nor cared. Their sex life had been non-existent for years, which suited her fine. There was a time she had craved his attention, but now she was quite happy that he kept to his side of bed, when he bothered to come home at all.

When he was out, Carrie and Alex relaxed and chatted, ate pizza on the sofa, talked till late about South Sudan and school and friends – and sometimes even about Katie and the future of their relationship. Alex was so wise for his years, and she loved when they could set the world to rights like this. Carrie was so painfully aware that these evenings were precious in their limited time horizon, and now that she and her son had shifted to a new level of emotional intimacy and disclosure, she wanted to somehow do all the talking and have all the connection to last a lifetime.

It was so different to the times when the three of them were together in the house. Stilted mealtimes, bland small talk, with Carrie carefully showing no overt interest, opinion or initiative, fearful of betrayal by an unguarded glance or smile. The days she went to bed early, despite being afraid to leave Mark and Alex alone together to talk. She retreated into Dickens or Austen on her kindle, or secretly read bitcoin blogs – the curiosity of the combination was not lost on her, but modern literature and dramas held no appeal, in a life already too full of its own dramas.

Alex did have social commitments of his own of course, including with the lovely Katie, although their lives were due to take very different paths in the autumn when she went to study in Bristol while he jetted off to South Sudan. The two of them were still close, but were pragmatic about the prospects for their upcoming separation. They wanted to spend time together when they could, and the consequence of this were the endless nights Carrie dreaded, alone in the house with Mark. She no longer especially feared his anger, so much as she hated the boredom, the absence of any kind of communication or relationship.

One night in late spring she had dinner on the table, and had been bustling around at peace in her own mind's world while Mark worked late – but in his office at home, not the bank, for once. She didn't want the chicken to get cold, so she walked across the hall to get his attention. The office door was half-open, and she carefully adjusted her features back to the tranquilised serenity which now came naturally to wear as a mask, before timidly pushing open the door.

'What are you doing in here!' came the angry response. 'Get out!'

Careful to keep the vacant expression locked, Carrie took in at a glance the open door to the cabinet safe, and the large pile of banknotes on the desk, which Mark seemed to be trying unsuccessfully to obscure with his two hands.

'I just came to let you know that dinner was–'

'Get out of here, you stupid cow!' he yelled, and started to step around the desk – though whether to approach her, or place himself physically between her and the pile of cash was unclear. She didn't look down at the desk, just neutrally and timidly backed away, and returned to the kitchen to wait.

She found she was trembling as she tried to force herself to sit and wait calmly. How much was there in that stack? She was sure the purplish glance she had taken in had been twenties. Alex had mentioned piles of notes in the safe, but she hadn't been able to see into the door of it from where she stood, only what he had been counting on the desk.

Why was he saving cash outside of the bank account? Outside of any bank? He lived and breathed the bank where he had worked for years and years, and doubtless he had savings and all sorts of other accounts, if he had wanted to hide money from her. Who else was he hiding it from? Was it something to do with tax? She had never really had anything to do with tax.

She thought about the money in her bitcoin account, now linked to the prepaid debit card registered at Mrs Shah's address, a card safely hidden in the shoebox and never used. It had taken her over a year to save that little bit of cash. She still felt a mix of guilt and fear about having salted away the cleaning money so assiduously, and scrimped and saved from the groceries budget whenever she could. It had been so hard to get that small amount together, and it was all she had in the world… Yet Mark somehow had this big pile of cash hidden away, from god knows where.

She knew that all she could do was to instantly forget all about it, and fix the smile back in place when he joined her for dinner shortly afterwards, asking him if he needed his warming through at all? No? OK, let's eat. She knew that he knew the medication she was supposed to be taking had a lot of impact on her memory, and it was easiest to simply not mention either the money or his outburst. Mark himself seemed oblivious to any difference in the family dynamic, he was just pleased that Carrie was stabilised on her medication enough to do the cooking and even drive to the supermarket on good days. Neither later that evening nor ever again, did he mention the money or his outburst. Perhaps he really believed Carrie's lack of memory and attentiveness was working in his favour.

Meanwhile, he was curiously proud of his son's selection for the Africa Project, and Carrie was encouraging Alex to exploit this for all it was worth.

Following a little gentle nudging and persuasion, Mark had arranged for Alex to do a presentation at his work to the bank's social action committee, who could realistically provide the bulk of his sponsorship money. Alex was nervous about this, but Carrie knew she could help him do a great job of making slides to create a good case, and his naturally personable and open manner would do the rest. Between them they'd avoid engaging with Mark's outrageous remarks about the 'pygmy children' – she was sure he didn't talk like that at the bank. –

and neither of them would challenge his clearly patronising colonial pride in his boy going over there to sort out everything that was wrong with the poor continent of Africa.

'This is actually jolly good, this presentation. For someone doing science A Levels, you've got a pretty good grasp of the politics and economics of the region, I'd say. This cycle of poverty stuff. Well, that's one view of it I suppose,' Mark added, as he looked over the slides Alex and Carrie had been working on that afternoon.

'It's important not to romanticise these backward tribal lifestyles though. Most of them wouldn't know what to do with proper jobs or civilised infrastructure if was given them on a plate. Which in a way it was – and they threw it back, let it go to ruin. Roads, hospitals, the lot. All these countries have gone back centuries of civilization since we left them to it. It's not politically correct to say so, but all this stuff you've been talking about here, none of it would have happened when we were in charge. Or the French, or whoever had this lot.'

'It was us, Dad. Great Britain I mean. Sudan became independent in the fifties, and then South Sudan became a separate country in 2011, after a long civil war. It's the newest country in Africa, the newest in the world!' Alex said proudly, demonstrating he'd been doing his homework.

'Civil war! Well, that just goes to show, doesn't it?' blustered Mark. 'Leave them to their own devices and it all falls apart. Start fighting amongst themselves and it's back to the bloody jungle already within a few years. Then when they don't like it, they want to come over here and get handouts.

'Oh, I know those views aren't popular, and you're right when it comes to the Committee, this stuff you've done here will play much better with that lot of do-gooders. Give them something nice for the shareholders, the annual report and so on. Haven't you got any photos of the actual school where the money's going?' He prodded one of the slides, which Carrie silently agreed could do with lifting up a bit visually.

'No, I don't, Dad, but I could get some more images of the area, maybe a map to show where the school is in relation to the border and why the area was so vulnerable when the fighting started, and the aid couldn't get through? I agree, that one's too texty overall, it needs something adding. I've got all day tomorrow to finish it up.' Alex looked thoughtful.

'Oh, just get some photo off the internet. Smiling brown kiddies, grateful for the Brits to be back, as aid instead of administration. Doesn't have to be real, just realistic. You know, emotional.' Mark had clearly heard about emotions, then, at least in so far as they related to other people.

'Um, I will ask the Project team if there's any of their photos I can use. Of the actual school and kids that they've got permission to share and use for fundraising. They've had volunteers there for the past two years, so I'm sure there's something suitable.' Carrie could hear a tautness in Alex's tone, that he was fighting to keep out of his voice. He needed his father's help to get in front of this committee, which could unlock the Project financially for him, so Carrie was keen that he didn't rise to the bait about 'brown kiddies' and the benefits of colonial rule, as she pottered in the kitchen on the edge of earshot of the conversation.

Later, over dinner, Alex still seemed edgy, as though there was something he wanted to ask. Carrie knew he was nervous about presenting, even though they had all of the following afternoon for her to practice with him. In the end he blurted it out.

'I'm quite nervous about the bank committee, I hate public speaking. I know, I'll have to do it if I'm teaching a class full of kids, even though they'll be younger–'

'Oh, that'll be no problem. They'll look up to you, be hanging on your every word. The bush kids, that is, not the committee!' Mark chortled appreciatively at his own joke.

Alex flashed his best smile to press home the advantage of his father's self-congratulatory humour. 'It's been so good, all your suggestions and help, and I can get the slides finished at school tomorrow in good time. I was just hoping, because it'd make me feel less anxious about it, that it would be really great if– if you and Mum could both be there!

Oh Alex, thought Carrie. No. Never going to happen. And you can't risk a row now when you're so close to that funding! Don't make him angry!

But unexpectedly Mark burst out laughing instead. 'Your mother? At the bank? Good lord, what on earth would be the point of that! It certainly wouldn't encourage them to sponsor you, that's for sure, more likely run a mile. Mum wouldn't have a clue what was going on, and anyway, she's not well is she? Wouldn't be fair at all.'

He reached across the table and patted her hand, Carrie managing to override a powerful urge to flinch away, and instead pasted the serene smile firmly in place for her husband and son. 'Whatever Dad thinks is best. You've got to make a great impression, this is really important Alex.' She beamed encouragingly round the table, looking for a safe split second to shoot Alex a warning glance because she could see an edge of stubbornness in the set of his jaw that meant he wasn't done. When he was determined on a course of action which other people or circumstances seemed on course to thwart, he occasionally looked alarmingly like his father.

'I'd really like Mum to come too, so they can see me with my family and meet us all together.' Alex persisted, mild-voiced but determined. 'It'd make me present it better, honest Dad!' Alex relaxed his jaw into his winning smile, in a slow and deliberate way. Carrie felt absurdly like he was mimicking her carefully schooled deceptive expressions, and felt a terrifying urge to giggle explosively, while at the same instant wondering if her own forced grins came across as equally non-spontaneous and fake.

'Nonsense. It's nothing to do with Mum, she doesn't know anything about all this stuff, and she'd be totally out of her depth there, anyway. They'll want to have an informal chat after, you know, get your measure as a man – young man. See you're made of the right stuff. Mum would hate it, very stressful, and it's all rather uptight. There'll be wives and so on, but she'd hardly fit in with them, most of them are professionals in their own right.

'And what you've got to understand is,' Mark hurried on, still patting Carrie's hand in a slightly more tense way now, as if to physically forestall any interruption from her. 'Mum's been very ill. Just a few weeks ago she was too sick to get out of bed! Her medicine makes her really tired, so it'd be a real ordeal for her. Sometimes her pills make her say funny things or forget what she's talking about, too. We're used to it, but it'd hardly be a good impression to make would it? She'll enjoy a nice quiet evening in on her own, with one of those Victorian novels she's read over and over.'

Actually, yes I'll enjoy it, Carrie thought.

'You don't get a second chance with this lot you know, they're either going to take to you or they're not,' Mark blustered on. 'I think you've got a good chance, if you practice that talk, polish up those slides a bit, and put your decent shirt on. But don't even think about dragging your mother along. Good god no!'

Carrie could feel his tapping hand picking up in speed and tension as he started to wind himself up into an argument, so she broke in:

'I'll iron your nice shirt Alex, and leave me your good shoes to polish, wear your trainers to school tomorrow.' She made her smile as calm and benign as possible, trying not to slide into a bovine parody of herself which was in danger of making her laugh out loud. She decided to tidy the plates away instead, to break the atmosphere, changing the energy in the room.

'You're going to be fantastic Alex, and you don't need me to worry about. Just concentrate on impressing all those important people, and I'll have your favourite dinner ready for when you both get back. Both of my boys, coming home from the bank together tomorrow night!'

The tension broke with a sudden splutter of laughter from Mark. 'Good god, your mother would probably start asking them about bitcoin Alex, and that'd be the end of that, eh! Remember, that fad from a couple of years back! Can you imagine!' He was so delighted with his own intense amusingness, that he actually carried some things across to the kitchen and started to load the dishwasher.

With Mark's back safely turned to the two of them, Carrie and Alex did risk a sly moment of smiling eye contact.

*

As the year rolled relentlessly into summertime and towards Alex's impending departure, Carrie found it relatively easy to maintain calm on the domestic front. A certain unexpected equilibrium had been reached.

She was now pretty certain that Mark was seeing someone else, probably from work – which was a great relief. He was spending longer and longer at the office, attending 'evening socials' at the bank several nights per week, and they were even more like two strangers sharing a home than ever before. She found the blank look associated with the medication she was supposed to be taking a better shield against everything, from conversation to sex to physical violence, than anything else she had tried in two decades. If only she had remembered this from before.

But that was the problem with actually taking the stuff, it left her unable to remember anything. This way was definitely better, and in addition to the tranquilisers, she was undertaking a steady tapering off from the antidepressant medication she had been on for longer than she could recall. It was going more easily than some of the online advice she'd found had led her to expect, and by the time Alex's flight took off she intended to be totally clear of any prescription drugs. Just her and her own mind to worry about, no biochemical enhancements at all.

Her only worry was that Mark might decide to leave her, before she had worked out a proper plan to leave him. If he was genuinely attached to this other person, then it was a distinct risk – and she had no way of finding out where that was actually going.

In the back of her mind was the pile of notes she had seen in the office. Was he planning to run away too? That was ridiculous, he had everything under his control: the house, the car, all in his name. She remembered with a chill, a cruel remark from years ago, 'I could hire someone, using bitcoin, to have you killed' – a throwaway comment designed to do nothing more, surely, than to make her feel worthless and useless. Mark was the most square and law-abiding man you could imagine – well, if you didn't count the bruises and the lies and gaslighting and the controlling…

It was as though more than one Mark existed, the man who wore a suit and worked at the bank every day, and the man who came home and bullied his family. Just like the charming and charismatic client from twenty years ago, who had become a raging controlling persecutor. For the millionth time she wondered what had happened to change him in this way, but only now was she beginning to see that the potential had been there all along, in the brooding moods and the need to always be in control.

Her only silent revenge right now was that there were also two Carries.

The benzodiazapine'd housewife who shuffled obediently to the shops and made the dinner and laundered his expensive shirts, and the other Carrie, who was – what, exactly? Someone with secret savings, scant though they were, secret knowledge, secret friends. And a secret future, coming somehow.

She had no way of finding out anything, if there was another woman, and Alex hadn't mentioned anything unusual from his presentation and social at the bank. That at least had gone well, and the funding for his Africa Project had been duly offered from their social impact endowment. She was very proud of her son and also relieved that he needn't worry about fundraising events during his upcoming A Levels. A number of his friends were organising all sorts of sports challenges and other things which, although they sounded like a lot of fun, would eat into their study time. It also left more room for Mum and Alex time, which Carrie was starting to measure out in a panic of diminishing weeks.

The two of them had talked recently about the September deadline, and Alex, showing a streak of stubbornness she recognised, had at one point declared he would not get on the plane unless she had a fixed plan in place to leave his father. He was genuinely torn, and she guiltily knew that he was so worried about his mother it was making it harder for him to concentrate on his studies and plans. Although Mark had not raised a hand in months, they both knew that this good mood might not last, that his volatility was such that any small change could make everything different.

Carrie doubled-down on her detoxing and savings, but it didn't feel like a plan. Especially as, with a bitter irony, the sterling cost of her bitcoin stash had been dropping distressingly over the past few weeks. Just a market correction, Ritu assured her.

It came as a bit of a shock, as through the months she'd been saving it had been pretty consistently growing all by itself, in addition to the savings she was continually adding. The sudden decline was a big disappointment, as it seemed to coincide with the crystallisation of her starting to plan to put it to use, and think about what she could potentially spend it on.

Still, there were some months to go, she kept reminding herself. The situation was stable for now. They weren't going away in the summer, and she was looking forward to lots of nice time with Alex, just hoping that nothing would change on the Mark front. That nothing would happen to tip him out of the present mood.

In the end, it wasn't such a small change.

Carrie came home from the shops late one afternoon, enjoying the warmer days of early summer, and with some great bargains from the cheaper supermarket to whip into a luxury pasta dinner with roast pork. She enjoyed walking on days like this, when the lighter evenings transformed the suburban streets into somewhere less mundane and familiar, as the tinge of golden sunlight lent an air of mystery. It was still cool enough to need a light jacket and scarf, but the evening held the promise of proper summer nights to come soon. Out on her own unobserved, the shuffling sickly housewife became a briskly striding purposeful woman focusing on building her strength for unknown challenges ahead, relishing her wellbeing and a productive day enjoyed.

But Carrie knew something was wrong immediately when she saw the front door was ajar, and instantly a world of panic flashed through her mind, crashing her mood to the ground in fear. Was Mark home early? Had she put the box away, where she hid the phone – the phone that she had on her now? What if he shook her, found it on her, found the box with her cryptocurrency keys in and her letter from the bank? She should have taken up Mrs Shah on her offer to keep stuff there. She was terrified as she silently pushed open the door, scarcely noticing at first that Mark's car wasn't even in the drive.

Immediately on stepping inside however, she could see that something different was very, very wrong. The hall floor was cluttered with papers, doors askew in haste, the living room stripped of flat-screen TV, sound dock and the elderly family computer. She moved quietly from room to room, not touching anything, unable to take it in. Chaos and destruction everywhere. There was a crowbar lying on the floor by the dining-room window, the dark silent dining room they never used, for all the dinner parties they never had.

They must have got in through there, she thought, as the window jamb was splintered and it swung loose on its hinges. There was an eerie silence all around, but suddenly Carrie realised they could still be in the house with her for all she knew. Should she climb straight out of the window, go for help? Who would come? She didn't know anyone, in the street on which she had lived for years, and everyone closed their curtains at dusk. It was getting dark outside.

She looked down at the crowbar on the floor. Then, carefully wrapping the end of it in her scarf for reasons she couldn't fully have articulated, she picked it up and tiptoed back to the hall.

Up the stairs, the bedrooms were a mess, drawers torn from her dressing table, the bedside. They would have been disappointed, no treasures to be found there. Carrie had never known what happened to the few bits of jewellery she remembered her mother owning – presumably they now adorned her alien stepmother. Nothing for the burglars to have found, except for packets of antidepressant medication.

She had no feelings, about the underwear and personal items scattered across the bedroom floor, the medicines, the mess. She knew much deeper violation than that, this was a space she already shared with a man who had systematically abused her for years. The burglars didn't know her; it wasn't personal. But the shelf in the wardrobe, where her box of secrets stood in plain sight, was left undisturbed – and that was all that mattered. She left the room without touching anything, realising that that box had been the only thing she cared about in the whole house.

Back down stairs and she went into Mark's office – which had been thoroughly trashed. The filing cabinet, with all the neat bank statements and phone statements, was on its side, the desk drawers upended. The cabinet safe, Mark's secret cupboard was untouched. Well, it wasn't really obvious that it was even there. Not if you didn't know about it.

Carrie knew about it. Her heart was pounding. She couldn't hear anything else. Her brain was rushing to think at record speed, on several different channels at once. Somehow if she thought and moved hard and fast enough, she'd keep any incipient panic at arm's length, unable to overwhelm her.

Clearly nobody had seen anything or called the police, although the burglars could have left moments before she got home – she had no way of knowing. Alex wasn't due back until dinnertime, he had football, followed by drinks with the team later. Their front door was not overlooked from the street, she hadn't seen it was unclosed till she was almost stepping through it, and they had no alarm. She double-locked the door habitually when she left the house, she would have sworn to it, but they had no serious window locks. Mark wasn't due home for over an hour, and she could see the driveway clearly through the study window. The evening sun was fading now, but she hadn't put any lights on, as she had walked quietly through her unrecognisable home.

The safe wasn't actually a safe. It was more of a secret cupboard with a discreet keyhole on it, made of veneered wood. Hiding in plain sight, just like her shoebox of secrets in the wardrobe. Her brain was still racing to join the dots, when she found herself looking down at the crowbar in her right hand, back to the window again, then at the hinges of the forbidden door to the forbidden cupboard.

At that point Carrie seemed to dissociate in her familiar way, and move outside of her body, to a place where she was more of an observer than anything else. From this vantage point she watched somebody who looked just like herself vigorously attacking the cabinet door, jamming in the crowbar in under the beading, working it into the dark slit between the door and the wall and leaning all her body weight against it, the old bruises on her chest ignored as she wrenched it deeper into the gap and pushed with all her might.

She was committed now, as the gap heaved and splintered, she had to see this through, though the door was clearly a lot sturdier than it looked. Finally the veneered wood tore open, ripping around the lock, with a deafening screech in the silent room.

The blood was pounding in her head even harder now, but Carrie felt a million miles from panic, as she gazed on the contents of the secret safe that had been a fixture in her home as long as she could remember. She saw piles of notes – how much? She had no idea, no time to count. Dropping the crowbar on the desk, she realised she still had the supermarket carrier bag at her feet, with the reduced-to-clear pork chops in. Perhaps dinner would end up being a little late tonight.

She dropped the piles of notes, bound carefully in elastic bands, right in on top of the shopping. She didn't dare take the time to look at them. The bag was fairly opaque. Behind them in the safe was a small box, like a jewellery box. Had he bought some extravagant gift for his fancy woman, was that what the secret saving was all about?

But when she opened the lid, her knees nearly gave way, as she recognised a beautiful emerald brooch and earrings which had once belonged to her mother. She hadn't thought about this set for years, never wondered what had happened to the things from the house. So many memories of her mother came flooding back in a tidal wave of emotion that threatened to knock her off her feet. She clutched the little jewellery box to her heart, fighting for balance amidst the sea of memories and thoughts. She remembered when she had married Mark, wishing her mum had been there, but knowing how glad she would be that her only daughter had found someone so strong to love and take care of her.

She wondered what her mother would think of her marriage twenty years later. Or of what her daughter was doing now?

Carrie stuffed the jewellery box into the pocket of her jeans, closing the lid on the flood of recollections and emotions as the little hinge snapped closed, and returned her focus to the safe. Three passports! She pounced on them. She had dreamed about getting hold of her passport somehow, wondering how on earth it would ever be possible, but knowing it was key to getting far, far away. Mark couldn't even come after her if he didn't have his own. Into the bag they went, with the groceries.

What about Alex's? He'd need it in a couple of months, and she didn't want any emphasis on applying for new ones, nor any possible delays – she had no idea how it would take to get a replacement. She wiped it carefully on her shirt, and used the scarf to drop Alex's passport amongst the papers scattered across the office floor. What else was there in the safe? It was getting dark, she knew her phone had a torch, but she was scared of someone seeing in from the darkening street. She didn't have time, she was becoming afraid, panicking about panicking... She forced herself to breathe calmly, to put in place the bovine mask she wore around Mark. Channel the effects of the tranquilizers she dutifully filled the prescriptions for each month, and carefully disposed of daily.

The self-hypnosis worked somehow, and as she settled her face into the familiar aspect, her mind became simultaneously both more calm, and capable of rapidly scanning through options.

No one had seen her come home. Would anyone see her leave the house? Unlikely, their neighbourhood of detached suburbia valued its privacy highly, and the Paige family were far from neighbourly. She abandoned the brief thought of slipping out through the dining-room window, and left by the front door instead, moving through the streets as invisibly as ever – just another housewife carrying shopping in the evening gloom.

She forced herself to walk at a steady, normal speed, not a hundred percent certain at first where she was going. She had her passport, she had a bag of cash, and some pork chops right on their sell-by-date. Not exactly what you'd choose to run away from home with, but she hadn't thought to grab clothes or anything else.

And how could she run away, anyway? Alex would be home soon, she'd never abandon him to his father's rage – and rage it most certainly would be, she realised, and nearly stumbled in the street when she pictured the full impact of Mark's likely reaction to the sight of his home, his office. His money…

She made herself breathe and walk as steadily as possible, realizing that her brisk pace was carrying her downtown towards the station and the bus depot. She put aside lingering thoughts of how quickly she could get to the airport, how far the uncounted bundles of cash in the bag might take her from all her worries and responsibilities. Her plans had been given an unexpected boost but she still had to have a plan, and be systematic.

She found herself at Mrs Shah's shop.

She waited in the smoky back room, as her plump hostess insisted on making her a strong cup of tea. 'You don't look well

Mrs Carrie. You sit down, I look after you. I make tea.'

Carrie was feeling a bit weak at the knees. A quick count of the wads of cash in the tiny shop bathroom she had requested to use urgently had revealed Mark's stash to total nearly £40,000. Most of it was not twenties, but fifties. Enough to get both her and Alex far, far away. She had had absolutely no idea that kind of sum was sitting in the cabinet she dusted every week, or had been slapping against her calves in the carrier bag she had nonchalantly strolled through the darkening streets with, just moments ago.

She couldn't think what to do next, so she gratefully accepted the cup that was offered to her, reflecting that there were few problems in life where a cup of tea did not help at least a tiny bit, if only to delay deciding about anything else. It bought her a few moments to think, behind the chipped but oddly elegant and delicate tea cup, and try to make the beginnings of a plan. A plan which, she accepted, had to include going home again this evening.

'Mrs Shah. You mentioned ages ago, that if I needed to get anything delivered for the phone contract or the bank or whatever, I could have it sent here, to the shop? Like the debit card?'

'Yes of course, my dear. And this is my home too not just business. Lot of people use Mrs S shop to drop off deliveries, or look after their things if they travel. All couriers know me. Not everybody got safe living place to keep their things, or anyone waiting in for them. Not everyone got nice big house.'

Carrie tried not to keep glancing at the bag, aware that she was behaving strangely and showing curious amounts of agitation. She was about to try again, when the older woman leaned forward and patted her hand.

'Mrs Carrie I know on the first day you came in here, you got sadness and you got secrets. Secrets all private, I don't ask, don't tell. But Ritu, he look out for you, keep an eye on you, yes?'

'Ritu is a wonderful young man, Mrs Shah. He's helped me with such a lot, with the phone and everything. And his mother – we barely speak a word of the same language but she's so kind and friendly. This has been a– a strange year so far, but I am glad to have met you all and got to know you a bit.' Carrie really meant that and wanted to convey how much these unexpected friendships had meant to her.

'You sound like you saying goodbye now, or soon maybe?' Mrs Shah arched one of her fearsomely bushy eyebrows to extend this into a definite question. Then, 'I'm not prying. But like I said first time. You need anything, I look after you, OK? I run this place a long time with my husband, now these years I'm alone, but my customers from all over the world, they are like my family now. Some need more family than others, if they far from their own. Or maybe like you, on the face of it have everything, but something inside very, very wrong.

'No, let me say it out. Mrs Carrie, I know things not right for you, something sad, something wrong in your home. You never speak of your husband, but I seen things, many lovely woman with a bad man, and she's afraid. Very lonely situation. But Mrs Carrie you not alone, you have friends. You need a place to stay, place to hide? Mrs Shah look after you. No one know, if you want it. Or I get message to anyone. Not big here, my apartment upstairs, but very safe and secret. You need place to be, I hide you. I know sometimes, some lady need to run. I seen in your eyes, perhaps you need that.

'One time I hid lovely girl up here, from father, brothers, want to send her to Pakistan be married to some guy her father age! She stay in my apartment for three weeks, then we got her away to Scotland. She write me now and again on Facebook, she happy and safe. This was with help of a special group, they got money, houses, collect all clothes and things women need. Some women they run with nothing, just clothes are wearing, it's really hard, but then they are safe and that's better for them. I got the phone numbers, lots of groups and shelters, not just for Asian women, they all work together. Anyone who needs.'

'Oh, Mrs Shah, you're so kind!' Carrie replied, sniffing away tears. 'I… I know there are places like that, and I don't need – well, I don't need that today. I might need a phone number or something, one day. Because, I don't know just know what the future's going to bring.

'Right now, I need to keep some things safe, some… papers. Documents. I just need them not in the house, and where I can get them if I need to. I just have them loose in a bag now and that's not safe,' she explained, reflexively scrunching the top of the carrier bag tightly, as she had been trying to avoid doing since counting the stash.

'That's no problem at all. I help you with gladness. Mr Shah, he was Postmaster, back in day. We had sub-Post Office here, but I had to close it down, cost so much and no profit, now everyone just want remittance and phone cards. But, I got lot of leftover stuff from those days.' Mrs Shah was bustling in and out of the shop and calling back to Carrie, as she rummaged in a store cupboard under the counter, finally revealing a large padded envelope, which she presented proudly.

'You put your letters and whatever is in there, I take it up to the flat and keep safe in my drawer there. No one know. Anytime you need, just come in shop and say to me, Mrs Shah I need my thing – or you send Ritu to get – I know might be big rush when time is come then, so I help you, whatever. But I don't give it over to nobody but you or Ritu.'

Carrie sensed that her kind host was deliberately busying herself in the empty shop, to give her privacy to sort her things out, so she made quick work of stuffing the wads of notes into the envelope, along with the two passports.

Then she thought how obvious it would be, to anyone feeling the envelope, even through the padding, that it contained two stacks of banknotes. So she took them back out, and hastily wrapped the whole bundle in the scarf she had also added to the carrier bag earlier, to make a single fat lump to squeeze back into the envelope.

She trusted Mrs Shah, if she trusted anyone at all. But she

just thought, why make it complicated or difficult? Mrs Shah had assumed they were personal documents. Carrie wished she'd also grabbed the bundle of letters and private keys which were hidden in the shoebox, but they were still in the house. The house with the front door swinging open, and everything ruined… She really needed to get back home.

In the last moment before she closed the envelope by peeling back the adhesive sticky strip, she added the little jewellery box with her mother's earrings and brooch. She felt too emotionally vulnerable to look at them again, but she squeezed the little box hard for a second. Then when the envelope was done she smiled up at Mrs Shah, who had also unearthed a fat permanent marker from her shop cupboard. She wrote 'Carrie' in neat print on the envelope.

'Right, you watch shop, though nobody here right now. I put this safe away upstairs.' Mrs Shah shooed her into the little counter space, so she could open the door to the steps up to her apartment.

Carrie felt both a pang of anxiety and a wave of relief to no longer be carrying the money. It was safer with Mrs Shah than anywhere else she could think of, and while she hadn't really had a plan in mind when she came to the shop, it turned out to be the best one available. Sometimes you had to trust your instincts, or your feet, and they had led her here.

It was all connected, just like the blockchain. Needing a bank account had led to a phone, which led to a SIM card, which led to tea with Ritu and Mrs Shah and a whole new world. Which led to friendship, and hope. And it gave her a place to hide her secret path to freedom.

It was fully dark outside now, but as Carrie got back to the house lights were blazing – and so was Mark. Her heart started pounding before she reached the front door, and she fought hard to control her rising panic. Luckily his anger was being diverted to someone else on the end of the phone at that moment.

'What the fuck do you mean, it may be tomorrow? My house is a crime scene, it's absolutely wrecked! You need to get someone over right now to get fingerprints, to find evidence, and get after the bastards who did this!' He was purple with rage, arms spinning wildly. Carrie stood paralysed in the doorway, terrified by the volume, the energy, even though it wasn't presently directed at her, it was so horrible in its familiarity it froze her to the spot. Far more adrenaline was pumping through her than on her earlier return to the house, and she was in much more danger of being overtaken by panic than she had been previously.

'I don't care how overstretched you are. Yes, I am fucking well angry, and this is how I talk when I'm angry. I pay your salary with my taxes, you don't get to tell me that having my home violated and destroyed isn't important enough. No, I won't mind my language, you just stop telling me my home getting burgled doesn't rate a call. I want to see a police car here right now!' Mark smashed his phone down on the hall dresser, sweeping to the floor a vase which had somehow evaded the earlier carnage.

He had just seen Carrie, cowering in the doorway, fumbling to hide the carrier bag which now contained nothing but dinner, but seemed tainted by association with its former contents.

He ran forward, grabbing her by the shoulder, by the face, forcing her head around to see and shoving her into the living room. 'Look! Look at our home! Where have you been? Look what's happened!' His fingers dug into her jaw as he shook her. 'What the fuck did you do, leave the front door wide open?' he screamed into her face, yanked her by the hair. Carrie felt a yearning to escape into dissociation, to hide within the cocoon she knew her mind could create, and leave her body behind to be battered and abused. But she knew that this time she had to stay present. She could not go wherever her mind took her when it tried to keep her safe, only to wake up bleeding and alone. She had to stay present and face up to this.

She stumbled backwards, trying to put the coffee table between herself and Mark's rage. Part of her mind was wondering whether the police operator had heard the vase smashing before the call was severed. Would someone come? Another part of her mind wasn't thinking clearly enough at all.

'No!' she gasped defensively. 'They didn't even get in that way – I mean, maybe that wasn't how they...' Her words tailed away.

'What the fuck are you talking about Carrie, what do you know?' His tone dropped to a more deadly and threatening level, as he strode across the room and grabbed her by the throat, pinning her back against the fireplace, bruising her shoulders against the mantelpiece. 'What are you saying, Carrie? Talk to me! You'd better fucking talk to me!' His fingers ground into her neck, as her head crashed backwards.

'Dad!' The living room door slammed against the wall, as Alex's kitbag hit the floor. He was across the room in a heartbeat, and grabbing his father by the shoulders, physically dragging him away from Carrie, twisting him clear as they both stumbled and nearly fell across the sofa. Alex was taller than his father by a clear few inches, Carrie noted absently as she rubbed her throat, though Mark was stockier, more heavily built. The squash court built more upper body strength than the football field, though Alex had the reach of him.

And Mark was more used to casual violence to express his emotions and control those around him. One powerful right hook, and his son was flung backwards across the living room, blood spurting from his nose, head bouncing against the wall as he fell backwards over the console which until recently had supported a large smart TV.

In that moment, seeing her son flying backwards across the room, something shifted, unfroze, within Carrie, even though she was still trying to get her breath after being choked.

He hit had hit her son.

Her baby boy.

He had hurt the baby.

Never again would he hurt the baby. Time seemed to run in slow motion as she threw herself in front of Alex, between him and his father, physically interposing her shaking frame between the two of them, an action which was so unexpected, it stopped Mark's advance in confusion.

Then from somewhere deep inside of her where it had been buried and repressed for years, a voice she'd never heard before bellowed: 'STOP! No more!'

Mark had hit her son, and Carrie had found her voice. One punch too late and she would never forgive herself for that, but right now, everything was shifting. Orbiting around a new centre of gravity deep within Carrie, as she stood her ground, facing her husband. Suddenly, she realised that they were all three of them nearly the same height. How had the power got so unbalanced?

She helped Alex to his feet, never taking her eyes off Mark, who was turning from purple to white, staring in disbelief at his wife and son as they stood supporting each other, confronting him. The two of them together, no more deception or lies, as their twin unflinching gazes stripped away all the twisting and dominating and subverting of the truth which had ruled in their home for so long.

'This is over Mark. It ends now. It stops. You've crossed over a line today, and there's going to be some changes now.' Carrie tried to keep her voice steady as the adrenaline pounded in her ears. *He had hit Alex*, and suddenly she desperately wanted to fight him, to tear into his face, for all the hate and the hurt and fear that she had taken on, experienced and allowed, which had led to this point: her beautiful boy getting hurt. But she maintained a ruthless grip on her control.

Mark was still gawping like a fish at the two of them, and Carrie turned to Alex, who had blood streaming from his face, his arm moving protectively around her shoulder. She touched his cheek, then turned back to her husband. She felt like something fragile and emergent was hanging in the air, crystallising into a new future, a new dynamic of latent power, which had never been a possibility until this moment.

'Well? What are you waiting for? Get some ice and teatowels. His nose could be broken!' She yelled in Mark's face, a voice – indeed, a whole Carrie – who he had never seen before. She jerked in rage as if to strike him, and finally Mark ran from the room to do as he was told.

'Mum,' Alex's voice was muffled. 'Did he hurt you? Mum, I'm so sorry, I should have been home earlier, I just–'

'Shh! It's OK. Well, there's so much that is not OK about all of this, but I think we can make it alright now. Let me see…' She tilted his head back, trying to inspect the stemming tides of blood, but it seemed as though the blow had been more to the eye socket and side of the nose, which hopefully wasn't fractured.

'Mum, we leave, like we leave *now!*' Alex clutched at her shoulders urgently. 'He hit me! He was strangling you!'

Mark came back into the room, proffering teatowels, the kitchen roll, and some ice blocks from the freezer. He hovered awkwardly as Carrie staunched the blood on Alex's face, directing him with a gesture when she wanted more tissue and the icepack to wrap in cloth to press to their son's face.

The tableau was a strange one, with all power roles reversed, both Alex and Mark obediently taking their lead from Carrie, knowing that what happened next depended to a considerable extent on her and the path she set for them.

She dabbed at Alex's nose, which had stopped bleeding, and didn't seem to be broken after all, she thought. Aware she was playing for time, she cleaned him up carefully. She wondered if Mark had made it to the study yet and seen the busted cabinet, knew about the money. She knew that Mark's confusion and bewilderment wouldn't last, and it was up to her to secure the upper hand fast somehow, that he was somehow actually afraid of the combination of her and Alex. *Mark was afraid...* She couldn't think what to do or say next.

The curious bubble of reforming relationships was abruptly punctured by the crunch of gravel and headlamps streaming through the open curtains of the living room window. Headlamps and blue flashing lights.

The three of them looked out of the window, then both of the men looked at Carrie, tacitly seeking her guidance, agreeing to follow her lead. Carrie stood up, giving Alex's shoulder a squeeze, and straightened her top, flipping her hair forward around her neck. No more months of planning remained to her – she knew she had seconds to decide how this was going to play out.

'Mum.' Alex was shaking his head. 'You've got to...'

'Shh! Alex trust me!' She patted him quiet, and gave Mark a long look. 'Like I told you, everything changes. Right here, right now. I can tell them everything – you think life is turned upside down already? You just wait!' She hissed angrily.

'Carrie, please! I never meant– I–' Mark seemed inches shorter, completely deflated, and utterly under her control.

'Shut up, Mark.' Carrie stepped past him towards the hall, as a voice rang out.

'Hello! Is anybody home? We received a call about a break in.'

'In here!' Carrie called out, and two uniformed police officers stepped into the room. The female officer in the lead had a torch, but Carrie flipped the lamp on the console table on, to reveal a living room that was even more trashed than it had been a few moments ago.

'Can you believe this mess? We're devastated, I mean, just look at it! I am sorry my husband lost his temper on the phone, but we'd just got back home to this, our lovely home.' She gestured at the chaos. 'And then our son came home early from football with his nose bleeding. It's like a war zone here. We've no idea how it happened, I know I locked the door as usual.

It's wonderful that you came so quickly. Can I get either of you a cup of tea?'

Carrie stepped past the two police officers into the hall, ignoring Alex and Mark staring blankly after her.

'I don't know if we're allowed to touch anything, but it doesn't seem too bad in here, I don't think they really came in the kitchen, I mean, it doesn't look like it.'

'Mrs Paige?' The police officer who had followed her into

the room opened her notebook and shook her head briefly when Carrie indicated the jar of tea bags. 'I'm Sergeant Ellie Chang, and this is my colleague Constable Malcolm Peters. Can you tell us what happened please, who first discovered the break-in?'

The others had followed them through to the kitchen by now, the younger male PC trying to get a look at Alex's nose while Mark fussed at it with the tea towel and Alex angrily waved them both aside. Everyone was continuing to look at Carrie.

She continued brightly before anything else ebbed into the silence. 'My husband must have been home first, because he was on the phone to you when I got in from the shops. I haven't even taken my coat off yet! You were ever so fast! Minutes later Alex came in from football, he was early as he got hit. With the football, obviously. We were just trying to explain to him what had gone on, while dealing with all this... I just can't think how it happened, I am certain I locked the door.'

'How's the rest of the house looking Mrs Paige? Have you looked around?' The Sergeant had one of those voices which sounded like she was in the process of giving evidence, or reading from a script.

'No! I've literally just got in, Mark was just explaining how he found the house, all messed up like this, and then Alex came home and I was more worried about him. We'll have a job getting the blood out of that shirt, but I don't think it's broken.' Carrie squeezed her son's shoulder reassuringly. 'Alex you get that off, and I'll soak it in cold water. Are you sure you don't want a cuppa, either of you? Or would you rather have coffee?'

'No, that's fine Mrs Paige, we'll just take a look around if that's OK. See if we can see anything, work out the point of entry and so on.' The two officers turned to leave the kitchen.

'Fingerprints?' Blurted Mark, abruptly. It was the first time he had spoken since the arrival of the police, and he seemed to have some difficulty getting the word out at all.

'I'm sorry, Mr Paige?' The senior officer's manner was quite formal and brusque, and Carrie couldn't help but wonder if she had indeed been fully briefed on the content of Mark's 999 call. It must have been all of ten minutes ago. Perhaps they had already been going to send someone round?

'Are you going to, you know, dust everything? Examine the scene? In case they left fingerprints, or some sort of clue?' Mark's voice sounded whiny and fretful now.

'Let's have a look around, shall we sir, then we'll decide how best to proceed, once we see what we're dealing with,' she said, ushering him out in front of them both as though awaiting a guided tour.

Alex and Carrie were left alone in the kitchen, and she swept him into a swift hug – meaning they could whisper directly to each other, and she could feel him trembling with shock.

'Mum! What are you doing? This is your chance, to tell them what he–'

'Shh! Alex, you keep telling me to make a plan, take control. Well, right now I am. You have to trust me.' She cupped his face in her hands, turning it slightly from side to side, examining the nose which had now stopped bleeding, then looking him directly in the eyes. 'I know I've not been the most reliable or effective mother you could have chosen, but right now I am changing all of that. You just have to believe me, work with me right now, OK?'

Whatever Alex's response might have been was drowned by a howl of rage from the study, and Carrie flinched despite her curious resolve. Then, taking Alex's hand, they both slipped quietly into the room together, to see Mark furiously and inarticulately waving his arms around at the chaos, the mess. The ripped-open safe door.

'Is this your office Mr Paige, do you work from home? Any computing equipment missing from here?' The notebook was poised.

'Yes- yes it's my- I don't work from home no, but all my papers, my documents, my things-' He spluttered, gesturing at the floor, which was covered in papers from the tipped over filing cabinet and emptied drawers.

'I am sorry, Mr Paige, it must be a shock seeing everything in this state. They've made a real mess in here. But can you tell me if anything seems to have been taken at all?'

Mark was doing the fish impression again, looking from the open security cabinet to the floor, the mess everywhere. He saw the crowbar on the desk and seized it, gibbering at the two officers. 'This is how they did it, they must have broken in, broken the door open, and- I shouldn't have touched it should it? Oh, god!' He dropped the crowbar, narrowly missing his own feet.

'I take it this isn't yours then, Mr Paige?' Sergeant Chang confirmed, signalling to her colleague to step forward and pick it up. Constable Peters looked at Mark, who was gesticulating wordlessly, then appeared to rethink his initial outstretched hand and instead found a clear plastic evidence bag to wrap the crowbar in.

The senior officer indicated her approval with a curt nod. 'We'll have a look at that then. Now, you'll need to tell us exactly what's missing, make a list. What was in here?' She pushed open the splintered door of the safe cabinet with the end of her pen.

'Paperwork… documents, and… things. Passports!' Mark couldn't stop staring at the gaping empty black space in the cupboard, as though he was trying to see things which were no longer there.

'Passport, over here, ma'am!' the other officer said, triumphantly retrieving Alex's little red book from the papers on the floor in front of the desk. 'Maybe the others will show up, somewhere in all this…' He gestured to the paperwork on the floor.

'Gosh, it's such a mess,' agreed Carrie, squeezing Alex's hand then letting go of it, to step cautiously into the small and crowded room. 'I have no idea what Mark really keeps in here, but it's usually ever so tidy. This is dreadful.' She put her hand over her mouth and looked around at the chaos.

The five of them worked their way through the house,

looking at the damage. The dining room window was identified as the point of entry, the back door as undisturbed as the front, and they all trouped up the stairs. Alex's room was surprisingly unscathed, although this was hard to tell given its day-to-day appearance. While the upstairs was messy, very little had been taken, just some watches from Mark's bedside drawers.

'I am very sorry Mr and Mrs Paige, this must be very difficult for you,' concluded the Sergeant Chang, as she snapped closed her notebook at the front door. 'People say it feels like being assaulted, violated. But the thing to remember is that no one got hurt. Your insurance will cover any losses, and we'll send a community safety officer to take a look at those windows. It won't cost much to fit some locks, just for peace of mind.'

Mark hadn't spoken for a while, he'd been very quiet and subdued since they'd left the office. 'You mean, that's it? You're not going to– I mean, what happens next?' he concluded, a little weakly.

'You can call into the station tomorrow or call this number to get your crime reference code, which you'll need for your insurance report. Don't forget to let us have that list of missing items too, and anything you have photographs or model numbers of, so we can keep a lookout for them. I wouldn't get your hopes up, though, and I'd get going with the insurance claim soon as possible, it can take ages.

'Are you alright Mrs Paige? I can put you in touch with Victim Support if you'd like, have them drop round to see you in the next few days?' The officer looked from her, to Alex, to

Mark. Then back again to Carrie, with a question in her eyes.

Carrie emitted a sound somewhere between a snort and a cough, that she couldn't help but feel sounded slightly hysterical. 'Victim Support?'

'If you'd like to talk to anyone. About the burglary, how it's made you feel. Sometimes it helps, Mrs Paige, to talk about how it feels, and process your feelings, when someone's committed a crime against you.'

'It's OK – I'm OK. I feel fine actually. But thank you for offering,' said Carrie.

'Right then, I'll leave you all to the depressing business of clearing everything up. At least they didn't do anything dirty, that's surprisingly common. That's my direct mobile number on the card, Mrs Paige, if you need anything – anything at all – you call me, OK? All the best.'

And they were gone.

Carrie led the way back into the living room, as the police car crunched its way down the gravel path. She knew she had to keep hold of the initiative she had established earlier, and make the most of Mark still being in a certain amount of shock at the way the evening had unfolded. So she whirled round and faced her husband before he could speak.

'Well, Alex and I will start tidying up in here, while you go and get some clothes and things together. Do you need anything from the office before you go?'

'Go?' Mark looked baffled.

'You can't stay here, Mark. You hit Alex. The police were

here, I have that officer's number on this card in my hand. I have the Victim Support helpline!' But Carrie was done with being a victim, and Mark realised it at last.

'I'll– get some things, and go and stay with a friend for a few days. As for the office, I'd prefer if you'd just leave it for now, as there's nothing… nothing left to worry about in there.'

And twenty minutes later, he was gone from the house. Carrie put the chain on the door and listened to his car drive away.

'Close your mouth Alex, you're making a draught!'

'Well, I can't hardly breathe through my nose! But Mum, you did it – you threw him out! I dreamed about *us* leaving, one day, getting you away from him, but I never dreamed he'd just go like that. I thought you were going to tell them everything. I had no idea what you were going to do, what Dad was doing to do.' Alex burst into tears, and flung himself into her arms, as he hadn't done for many years.

She sat holding him on the sofa for a good long while, looking around at the ruined living room, till his sobs started to subside at last. She rubbed his back, letting him cry himself out, and dreamed of picking up and carrying him off to bed to tuck him in. That must be a memory, from when he was little, one of the special snapshots she was sometimes granted from the years that were lost. They'd lost so much.

Instead, she had a hulking great eighteen-year-old in her arms, and she was concerned about him starting his nose off bleeding again. It seemed to be OK, though it was very bruised and swollen on one side, and no one was seriously going to believe it was done by a football. Carrie knew that Mark obediently leaving the house with a few shirts and pants was not the end of her problems, either. There would be a lot to do in the days and weeks ahead. But she had one secret even from Alex which would help with sorting things out, and her assertive response had bought her some time to think about her next move more clearly.

Right now, there was a different kind of sorting out to do.

'Are you OK to help me with this lot now, Alex?' She asked gently, waving at the chaos-strewn room. The police had obviously assumed the smashed ornaments and kicked over coffee table were all related to the break-in.

With a final shuddering sob, Alex pulled himself together with a visible effort. 'I'll get the bin bags Mum, and the hoover. We'll sort this out, yes, get it all sorted.'

Carrie drew the curtains resolutely against the world outside, and together they started tidying up. There was quite a lot to do.

....

WhatsApp message:

My dear friend,

Your message to me was like a light in dark times, to read about how you confronted your oppressive husband, and threw him from the home – like a lioness, defending her cub, you were not triggered to do so until he crossed that line. How many times had he hit you, hurt you, over the years? I cannot imagine. But it was all just building up, until he hurt your boy. Just making you harder and stronger, saving all that power inside, until you were ready to roar in his face when the moment came.

I still don't understand why you didn't speak to the police, because I believe they would surely help you. Here it is different, it is not so long past that women were legally almost possessions of their fathers and husbands, and the mullahs are trying to revert to those times now. Certainly, the police are the last people you would talk to here, but the British police are famous the world over, and they were right there in your house, they could have arrested him!

But also, I do respect that you are working out what to do for yourself in your time, and my brave friend makes me proud and happy.

I too am living as a single woman now, a widow perhaps in truth but certainly in every functional way. I do not know where Mohit is; he has been moved from the jail in our city, and no one will tell me if he is alive or dead. I cannot visit him, and I do not know if my letters arrive. I pay the expected bribes but hear nothing, and I cannot write of anything of significance anyway.

I live for my boy now, and I am trying to negotiate with the people who could help him to get away to

Europe. But their prices are going up and up as the demand and the danger increases. I am selling my last jewellery and silverware, trying to raise the money to get him away, he has agreed he will go when I can provide for the safe transport fee.

Then I will in truth be a widow, with all my family lost to me.

In love and friendship.

Carrie's eyes filled with tears, reading the sadness and despair in her friend's letter. While some things were starting to come together and be better in her own life, Samar's was falling apart. Was there anything she could do to help? She had to do something. She had meant to talk to her friends, but events in her own life had overwhelmed her.

Carrie was reading the email on her phone, in plain sight in her own living room – not furtively on a park bench or in the back of a shop. Her worlds were blending and whirling up together into one comfortable-feeling whole, as she made tea for Ritu and his friend Romen, who was changing the locks on her front door. Ritu was still looking around himself at the spacious and well appointed family kitchen, the elegant extended living room. Carrie felt a bit awkward that the whole of the small apartment Ritu and his mother shared would probably fit inside it. Worlds blending meant some clashing and assimilating of different universes too, but Ritu was polite and worldly enough not to remark if he found her home unexpectedly upmarket and luxurious.

'Soon be all safe and secure, and all to the spec that Community Safety leaflet said, but you can bet Rom's half the price of any of them,' said Rity proudly. 'And you can even pay him in bitcoin if you want.'

'Oh, you mean my StagePay card? That's still hidden upstairs, I've only transferred a small amount onto it, and I haven't used it to pay for anything yet. I guess I could just keep it in my purse now, I hadn't thought about it.' Carrie was still finding things she could connect and simply interact with normally, in her newly congruent world, but old habits of hiding everything were hard to break.

'Very cool that you got that, it's a big help. The fees are high, but it's like a connection between crypto and anything you like. I wish I had it before when I was travelling and could have used my crypto instead of buying different currencies and being ripped off at every border.

But no, I meant you can pay Romen in bitcoin actually, direct from your wallet. He's one of us!' Ritu winked.

'Really?' Carrie was taken aback. 'I've never actually spent any of it before on anything. I sent some to my friend a couple of years ago when we were just starting out, and she sent some back, just so we knew how to do it and that it worked. But I've never used it for anything else, what an interesting idea!'

'Well, Carrie it's none of my business obviously. But, until you get something sorted with your ex or whatever he is now, you don't know how your money's going to go. It's seriously great that he just up and left, but you said he only took a small bag – so you're going to have to have him back in here to get stuff, and then at some point to talk about what's going to happen. Like divorce or whatever. And till then, is he paying the bills, putting money in your account? 'Cause you don't want debits and that to start bouncing. Meantime, I'd hang on to any cash you've got and settle up with Rom on the cryptos if you can.'

It had only been a few days, and Carrie had been revelling in having the house to herself, in small things like being able to invite Ritu round for tea at her place for once, and not dreading the key in the lock around 7:30pm. Knowing Mark's keys wouldn't work now would make her feel safer still, and the police had advised her to get the locks changed anyway. But she knew too that the situation was far from resolved longer term, and she and Mark had had no direct contact at all.

'I suppose I should get some advice, call the helplines in those leaflets or something – thanks for bringing those over. I know Mrs Shah had some ideas what was going on, and she pretty much guessed right about what I'd need. I have no idea what's going to happen next, but I guess it'd be pretty naïve to think he'll just keep his distance and pay for me and Alex to go on living here indefinitely. Alex is off to Africa in just a few weeks now, and I hope there'll be some way to keep things as normal as possible till then.

'He's texted his father, just to check in, and Mark's staying in a hotel near the bank. I guess that's not going to be sustainable for the long term though, either, is it? Alex doesn't want to see him – which is hardly surprising as he still has a black eye from that night.' Despite the warm afternoon, Carrie shuddered as though she was sat in a draught.

'Please Carrie, call someone. If you don't want to talk to the police, then I get it, I know that's going to feel like something kicking off that you haven't got any control over. But you can't just think he's going to stay away quietly, at some point you're going to have to get legal advice, and start some balls rolling. It sounds like you're pretty certain you want to end it.'

'Oh god yes. I mean, it wasn't till that night that I realised that there wasn't actually any choice. I've never been on my own, and when Alex has gone away, then I really will be alone, but I'll be fine in fact, I'm not even worried. It was as though, until the moment I actually told him to get out, I couldn't picture that situation at all, or that it was even a possibility. If I'd thought of anything it was of me leaving, running away. Everything's gone all upside down, but in a good way hopefully.

'I'm assuming we'll have to sell this place, but I'll be perfectly alright in a small flat somewhere. I can clean, I can cook. I could go back to being a teaching assistant, maybe?' Carrie felt excited about the world of possibilities, even though the details of the multiple possibilities were still hazy. It was the dawning realisation that she truly had choices she could make.

'For years I just lived with the assumption – the belief – that things would never change. That I had no choice but to stay with him and put up with– what I put up with. It was all mixed up with the medicine and the miscarriage and the depression, but it was like I was stuck in a bubble in my head for so long. I just need to get out now.'

'You're amazing Carrie,' Ritu grinned over his tea. 'You're going to be fine, you know. We're all so chuffed for you. Mrs S was punching the air when she heard you threw him out!'

'Well, I didn't exactly throw anything, to be fair. Just my voice, which I didn't know I had. I think that intimidated him somehow and was just the last thing he ever expected. Well, me too! He was a bit shocked about the break-in. Rather disappointed, I think, with the mess they made in his office.' Carrie hadn't told Ritu or Alex or anybody else about the money in the safe, or who'd opened it. She had a feeling that was probably for the best for now. Which reminded her.

'Ritu, sorry to change the subject, but you are still my bitcoin mentor, right?'

'Always Carrie, anything I can do to help. You want to know how to pay Rom? It's dead easy, but we need to know how much it's all going to work out as when he's done, he's got the window locks for your back room as well to do after.' Ritu was ever-helpful for sure.

'No, it was something else, I was confused about, when I was reading and thinking about trust, and – well, that's quite tricky for me right now, you know, knowing who I can trust, with all sorts of things.' Carrie wasn't one hundred sure where she was going with this, but she knew Ritu would help her figure it all out.

'I'll bet. Well, you know anything you want to ask me, it's just fine, alright? I won't even tell Mrs S if you don't want me to.'

'No, it's not that, I just keep reading the word "trustless", when it comes to cryptocurrency and blockchain, and then I read that it's all transparent and on the chain forever, and I just can't make sense of it – can it be trusted, or not? Because trust is surely good, right?'

'Ah right, "trustless", it's a weird and confusing word for sure. But it's not, like, a bad thing – it doesn't mean a lack of trust. What it means is, trust isn't necessary, because you don't need it. You're not depending on it.'

Ritu could see that this explanation didn't make sense on its own, so he tried a different tack. 'You know those big coaches that leave from the depot down the road from Mrs S? They go all over the country, in fact I think some go right over to Europe and all over. Takes days. People line up to get on them, and all the luggage goes in the big underneath bit, it's huge. You can't take it inside. I get them busses back to Dudley to see my cousins, and I have to put my rucksack in the underneath luggage bit.'

Carrie nodded.

'But I'd never ever put my laptop in there, no way.' Ritu continued. 'Because that'd be too much trust, right? Every city they stop in, the hatch on the luggage slides up, and actually the door of it blocks any view of it that you might have got anyway, from inside the bus. I guess you could get out and watch if you were really paranoid, and I got to say I've been on it loads of times and no one's ever touched my scruffy rucksack. But if they had, I might not know it for another hundred miles or something, and everyone who gets off just takes whatever they like the look of and walks off, while the bus pulls away.'

Carrie was a bit confused about how this related to blockchain and everything, but she'd been on intercity coaches before – when and where? She couldn't remember. But certainly she'd seen them, and she nodded encouragingly.

'Now, when I was travelling before uni, in Mexico, it was all different,' Ritu continued. 'Same kind of vehicle, could've been exactly the same model, with the big luggage hatch underneath. But loading and unloading was totally different. You checked your bag on and got a numbered ticket, then when you got off – which could've been a day or two later, other side of the country or even over a border – you showed your ticket and pointed out your bag. The driver checked the numbers matched, before you got your stuff back. If anyone lost their ticket, there was a massive fuss of course, so you basically didn't ever lose it.

"Cause that part of the world's got so much poverty, and there's so much more stealing and everything, as there's plenty of people don't even have enough to eat each day. Being able to grab a bag that wasn't yours would be seen as too much temptation, like anyone might want to go for it, maybe if they thought someone else had a lot better life and stuff than they had, they'd even think their clothes might be worth something.

So they don't rely on trust, they design it out.

'They've made it a trustless system.'

Carrie thought about it. 'So, it's like if you have to check out of a hotel but your flight's not till evening, so you ask if you can leave your bag in reception, and sometimes they just say 'yes sure', and stick it round the back, and you spend the afternoon sightseeing and vaguely worrying if they're maybe going to give your suitcase to the wrong person by mistake, as you've no idea how many they've even got back there. Or when you go to collect it, and they say what does it look like, come and point it out – and you feel like you could choose any one of them!'

'Yes, absolutely like that!' Ritu agreed. 'And that's also different in central America, they always give you a receipt for your bag and tag it carefully, then you don't get it back without handing in that ticket. The default is that you don't trust people to do the right thing, you build in the security so that you don't have to.

Just like with these window locks!' He picked up the packages Romen had left on the coffee table, in advance of his next task. 'You don't just trust no one's going to break in the window, and then worry about it, hope for the best. You make sure they can't.'

'OK, I do understand all that, makes sense. But then, what's it got to do with bitcoin?' Carrie asked.

'Well think about it. When you hit pay now online, or even if you swipe your card in the supermarket, there's all this trust going on. Like, the store trusts that it's your card and you haven't nicked it or skimmed it, right? And then they have to trust the bank that you're definitely good for it, because they don't actually get paid right then. Normally they rush the stuff out to you same day, or you just take it straight home from the shop – but they might not get it actually settled for ages, days at least. So, they've got to trust the bank. Then you have to trust them too, because they'll probably debit it right off your account pretty quick but you haven't got your stuff yet that you ordered if it's online and it's being shipped – and if it's broken or doesn't arrive, you got some comeback.

'With a credit card there's even more trust, as they don't collect off you for maybe a month, and also you've got more protection if something happens. Like when that airline went bust, everyone got their money.'

'All that trust is a good thing though, right, surely? It was good those people got the money back for their tickets?' Carrie still wasn't sure whether this was supposed to be a negative or a positive.

'Yes, but who gets to decide, Carrie? Who says the banks are trustable? What about the bank of England, deciding to print a load more money last year?' Ritu was clearly passionate about this, at an almost philosophical level, Carrie realised.

'It's much better to trust to a system, to trust the mathematics, instead of an institution. Like when my brother used to eBay loads of stuff, but he gave it up in the end, because people tried it on. Said stuff hadn't come, "item wasn't as described", and the payment service just reversed it every time, without any question, decided for the seller. He was losing so much money, it just wasn't adding up any more.'

'I see – I think,' Carrie said. 'So, you're saying you think a payment's been made, but actually it's always just promises and trust, instead of a real payment!'

'Yeah exactly! Well, unless you pay cash, from one person to another, like down at the market for a bag of potatoes or something. You can't change your mind, no bank can reverse that transaction, not unless you both agree, anyway. But anything else, any other kind of payment, there's these "trusted" institutions sitting overseeing it all, controlling it.

'That's what's so different with blockchain. Like, if you want to pay Rom with bitcoin for this work, you'll use your private key to transfer those assets to him, and it just goes right to him, straight into his wallet. Gets confirmed on the blockchain, which is what makes it secure, but there isn't anybody, any institution in the world, can get in the way of it, or decide it's not on and needs refunding, or that the money wasn't yours like you stole it or something.'

'Stole it?' Carrie exclaimed, suddenly jumpy.

'But you don't even have to have had to, could be your money but you want to pay it to someone the banks don't agree with. Like WikiLeaks, they got cut off by PayPal, all the credit cards. The banks didn't agree with funding whistleblowing, or they got lent on by the CIA or something, so they just shut it off, to try to stop people sending them donations. It doesn't matter whether you agree with them or not about whether funding whistleblowing's a good idea, the problem is they control it. It's like someone put PayPal and the credit card clearing companies in charge of what's right or wrong, what people can and can't pay for. You can't do that with crypto, it's your money and you can do what you want with it. No one can trace who paid for it or where it came from in the first place.'

'Right, I think I see now,' Carrie went on more calmly. The locks were taking quite a long time, so she thought she'd carry on with her line of questioning.

'But if someone bought the crypto from an exchange, then they'd know where it came from, right? Because of all that "Know Your Customer" stuff and having to send your ID?'

'Well, yeah,' Ritu admitted. 'I guess if you bought it off an exchange, you could probably trace it right back through transaction IDs. I think that's how the FBI caught a load of drug dealers or something. People think crypto's anonymous, but it isn't, specially not bitcoin, it's all there in the blockchain and you can work it back. Lot of people been caught out like that. That's why they made privacy coins. Didn't you say you had a bit of monero Carrie?'

'Yeah, a bit! We mined it! Alex and me, on his laptop – well we pretty much burned it out just mining a little bit of it actually, but the idea was fun.' Carrie still had the monero on her wallet, she'd never got around to converting it to bitcoin or anything else.

'Those are much harder to trace, and I think a lot of criminals use stuff like that now – beam and dash and so on. If people have dodgy money, they don't want the FBI to come looking, so it's much easier to do it in privacy coins. And of course, banks raise all sorts of suspicious flags if large amounts go through them suddenly. If you wanted to make a big donation to a cause that was out of favour, you wouldn't want to do it like that.'

'Do they?' Carrie tried to sound only very casually interested in this vital fact.

'What?'

'Banks! I mean, they're not bothered where money comes from, are they, if it's just your own money, that you pay in?' Carrie asked, doing her best to keep her voice casual.

'Depends how much I guess. Usually banks have kind of a paper trail for anything bigger, like if you have your wages paid in or something regularly there'd be a payslip or something. If you suddenly paid a big load of cash in, they'd ask a load of questions about where it came from – that's the "anti-money laundering" laws, but probably a lot of it's about making sure tax gets paid on it too.

'That's one more reason people use bitcoin, or something like monero or zcash. Because they don't agree with some "trusted" institution deciding what you can support or send your money to. But that means of course that some people use crypto to send to criminals, terrorists, pay for really bad stuff… I'm not saying this is straightforward, Carrie,' Ritu continued.

Carrie thought of the fundamentalists terrorising Samar's country. Were any of them funded by cryptocurrency? But she was worried by what Ritu was saying, about banks wanting to know where money came from.

'But where else would you buy it? I mean – say you had a

load of cash, and you wanted to buy bitcoin – how would you do it then, if you wanted to be really untraceable? Just imagine!' Carrie kept her voice light and curious.

'Well, you'd want to buy it directly off someone I guess: peer-to-peer. Different kind of exchange. They're more like eBay if you like, a marketplace where you match up with someone else and do a deal with them direct. The exchange can do like an escrow, so you upload the money to them, and they hold it till the crypto transfer is confirmed and they can see it's been done, then they release the funds and everyone's happy.'

'Upload it?' said Carrie. 'But that wouldn't work with cash would it? Say, if someone had a certain amount of cash that they wanted to buy some bitcoin with?'

Ritu looked long and hard at her. 'No, you'd need to transact that kind of buy in person then. You can make that kind of deal on a peer-to-peer site Carrie. But you have to watch yourself, yeah. Be really careful who you're dealing with, as they'd know you were fetching up with a load of cash on you, and you'd have to be dead certain who you were meeting and where.

'Some of the sites have kind of a review and rating system so you can choose who you want to deal with, if they've got good feedback from other people. And then you'd have to be safe to hang around wherever it was for like maybe an hour, as you'd want to make certain of the transfer. Normally for any larger sum, you'd want to wait for six confirmations, before you handed over the cash.

If you did need to do a big deal like that, anything like that, the most important thing would be to take someone with you who you trusted, and who really had your back.'

Carrie nodded thoughtfully. She thought about everything Ritu had just said – about the inequalities in central America and how you just didn't deliberately put them to the test unnecessarily, not when you could avoid it with a bit of forethought. She remembered the way that her immaculately-mannered young friend had tried not to whistle as he glanced around her home for the first time – actually, Carrie realised, he was the first friend she had ever invited back for tea. She had no intention of lying to him, but she had learned in her many years living with Mark that there were ways to hide a truth in plain sight with just the right amount of disclosure and no more.

'Thing is you're right, Ritu, I am going to need money. The burglars took most things of value in here, but they missed some things – some antiques, a few bits and pieces. Mark bought them all, over the years – I think, it's possible that some even came from my old family home, I don't really remember. But I do remember when you were talking to me at the café a few weeks ago, about tokenisation. How even unpaid domestic labour might be tokenised and have a value put on them one day, and I have worked hard in this house over the years, cooking and caring, and dusting the bloody things even.' This was safer ground, and she knew Ritu wanted to help her.

'Carrie, I reckon what you've put up with over the years, all you've had done to you – pretty much anything's fair game. I wish my brother was here, the eBayer, as he'd know right off what was worth anything. But I might know someone else who could take a look. Let me ask around. But I'll help you, OK, don't you go fixing up to meet with any strangers in dark alleys to do deals – they'll see you coming a mile off, and – well, it's best to do things trustlessly. If you can.'

'Gotcha. Thanks, Ritu, you're so wise about all this stuff, and you always know what I need. I'm so lucky to have a friend like you. I am actually a really fortunate person, I know it.' Carrie smiled.

*

When Carrie got off the bus some weeks later, she was in a city she'd never been to before.

She watched the luggage hatch go up, and was reminded of her conversation with Ritu before – he was right, the door really did slide right up over the windows, so no one in the middle seats could see out, and a handful of people got off and chose luggage without any checks or supervision before strolling away with it.

It was a system that relied on trust, and also on a certain baseline of equality – that people would have personal belongings on board of approximately equal value, and on balance maintain a preference for their own clothes and things over anybody else's. She'd never thought about all the little social assumptions before, which relied on the same kind of shared understandings. What had Alex called them, when he was doing his sociology essay? Social contracts. If the conditions were right, and the incentives lined up, they pretty much worked OK, for enough of the time, that it wasn't worth doing anything differently. Just like baggage reclaim at the airport: what really was the protection against someone slipping away with your bag in a busy terminal? The whole thing demanded a shared belief that people were mostly honest, roughly equal, and valued their own dirty clothes and holiday souvenirs over other peoples. She'd never thought of things like this as being part of a complicated set of unwritten rules and assumptions, which made the world go around.

The system also assumed that it was mostly dirty knickers in the cases on the carousel or under the bus, and that people kept their valuables within arms' reach in their hand luggage. Blinking in the sunlight, Carrie tried not to reflexively grip the top of her handbag, every time she thought about its contents.

She hadn't wanted to do anything in front of Mrs Shah, the ultimate trusted and trustless custodian, of secrets and secret envelopes. So she had found herself counting money out carefully in yet another toilet, this time at the café by the bus garage down the road from the shop – even though Mrs Shah had accompanied the handover of the entrusted jiffy bag with a stiff smoky hug and tears in her eyes. 'Me and Ritu's mother so, so happy to hear, Mrs Carrie. Ritu told me all about what happened. He give you the helpline, yes? Very important you get the law on your side! Protect yourself!'

Without looking down at the envelope at all, Carrie had

agreed with her and reassured her, then hurried away in order to make time for the necessary cuppa before her bus departed.

£35,000 was the amount agreed for the deal, all in cash. That meant a few thousand left over as well for future spending. Counted out and recounted, on her knees in the smelly cubicle – why on earth hadn't she collected the money the day before, and taken it home to sort it all out? But she still had a mental block about the idea of even leaving her mobile phone lying around openly in the house, so the thought of taking the money back there simply hadn't occurred to her. She still didn't feel safe in her own home, truly, unless she consciously remembered she was supposed to. In the bundle from the jiffy bag, wrapped in the scarf she'd been wearing that day, was a mixture of fifties and twenties, and as she washed her hands she wondered how just long Mark had been saving it, stashing it away secretly in his office. And why?

Having come on this mission forearmed with elastic bands and envelopes, she now had everything sorted and bundled up carefully, ready to do the deal, with the rest of the money and the passports tucked away in an inside zip pocket of her bag. She needed to get some of it into the bank and onto her debit card, she realised, if she wanted to buy anything with it indirectly, and if it was done a few hundred pounds at a time she was sure Ian at the bank wouldn't ask questions about it. Yet, for the rest she felt safest with secret untraceable money: cash and bitcoin. No questions asked, no refunds. For all anyone else knew the money from the safe, which Mark had not to her knowledge even told the police about, was long gone anyway – in the hands of the unidentified burglars. The officers had assured Carrie and Mark that there was barely any possibility of tracking down those responsible and successfully prosecuting them, there was no real prospect of ever getting their stolen things back..

Mark's passport would never be found either, and she hoped the tiny pieces wouldn't damage Stav's plumbing at all. She had brought scissors from home, and spread the pieces around different toilets and the incinerator bins in unrecognisable shreds.

While sitting on the bus, Carrie had dug deep into her conscience and instincts, trying to work out if she felt bad about the money. Mark had clearly been devastated by its loss, and she knew very well that it was the shock of whatever losing this money really meant to him that had thrown him sufficiently off balance to significantly contribute to her ability to stand up to him and tell him to leave. But she still had bruising on her arms and neck from that night, and combined with the persistent mental image of Alex with blood streaming down his face, they blocked any sense of pity she might have had for Mark. Alex had made her carefully photograph the injuries on them both before continuing with the clearing up, regardless of who she might or might not want to report Mark to at any time.

She thought about all the bruises through all the years – and the less visible injuries as well, the put-downs and threats, the controlling and lies, the rules and the intimidation. She realised that try as hard as she might, in amongst the complex blend of feelings she was carrying with her that day as the bus ploughed steadily up the motorway, she could not unearth a single shred of guilt for taking the money. Maybe it was something to do with what Ritu had said, about tokenising work and putting a price on domestic slavery, blockchaining all that she was owed and making it transparent and visible in the world. In a way which did not compromise her identity. Definitely no guilt whatsoever, she decided, and she felt a new wave of calm and an accepting sense of entitlement to the money in the envelopes in her bag.

It was one of many emotions churning within her: excitement, certainly, as well as anxiety – just walking around with that much cash made her feel a bit uncomfortable, unsurprisingly, but the once-seductive lure of panic seemed a long way distant, as though something had switched over in her mind with the opening up of new possibilities. Somehow, she felt safe in the crowd, hiding in plain sight, looking completely 'normal' to the outside world as it went about its many layers of business.

There was anticipation, too. She thought about the money, and having it safely in her Bitcoin wallet, where she could send whatever she needed to her prepaid card at any time. She knew she'd have to leave the family home at some point, and actually face up to dealing with Mark, and she had given in to Alex and Ritu's separate pleading – though she still hadn't crossed what felt like an irrevocable line in her life and introduced the two young men for some reason – and had agreed to an appointment with a volunteer advice service in the week ahead, where she would take the first steps in finding out what her rights were and what she could do to start putting her life back together. The money was her secret fallback position, the knowledge of which she would burden none of her helpers with just now.

When it came to Mark himself, she felt very little.

Contempt, for the way he had walked away when she finally stood up to him, and disgust for the way he had treated her. No regret, no pity. She knew she still feared him and his anger, but it felt distant, like something that had happened to a different person in a different time. She also knew she wasn't free of him yet – but simply not sharing a home and a bedroom with him made her feel lighter, the air clearer and full of potential for better things.

She also felt loss and bereavement for so much: for the marriage everyone thought she had had and the lost years of family life. For baby Grace, too, on some level, which she didn't quite yet dare examine fully, but she knew it was there in the mix, exactly as Samar had said so long ago. The memory stuff was the greatest loss. Alex's childhood, the years on the tranquilisers. It was like looking back through an old photo album full of blurry home snaps, where there were disjointed images with only certain elements in focus.

She had a notebook and pen in her handbag, the same notebook on which she had written out the recovery seed for her Monero wallet so long ago, on the torn-off sheet of paper which was still in the shoebox in the wardrobe. She tried to make a list – to put the facts in order and remember the chain of events. Could she organise it by year?

The Pickwick Papers, Oliver Twist… As the bus droned on up the road, she started to write down facts in order, using each one to remind her of the next, the way Alex had explained to her all that time ago. But it didn't work. She had individual links, but she couldn't make the chain connect, as she turned the shining pieces over and over in her mind and tried to commit them to paper. Happiness at her second pregnancy, then something happened, and she was losing her beautiful baby girl… She'd been on her own in the hospital, but Mark had been there before. And that doctor was there, who had come to the house this year. Had he taken her? What had been happening just before the miscarriage started? There was a still-frame image in her mind from the hospital chapel memorial book, and the tiny photo and foot prints that were still in the shoebox in an envelope from that kind nurse, but she hadn't brought herself to look at them for years. It was enough to know she had these precious things safely preserved.

The next glimpses seemed to be years later. Alex at the play park on the swings – but she couldn't be sure where this image fitted, as he seemed to be both a toddler and a schoolboy at the same time, which made no sense. But of course, they must have been to the park many times! It was no good, she couldn't link the memories together, couldn't make sense of it. She knew it must all be in there somewhere; it was just a case of accessing the right bit of the hard drive.

She remembered the research she had done years ago, when both Alex and Jamal had been struggling to overcome the limitations of their dyslexia to memorise things for tests, she'd read a lot about memory, and from all she'd learned then she was sure the memories of those lost years were somewhere inside her still. Perhaps one day with therapy, or hypnosis, or enough calm and stability in her life and feelings of safety, they'd be able to come out. For now, they were stuck where they were, and she had to focus on new learning and doing. So she closed the notebook and dozed lightly on the long bus journey, hand reflexively holding the clasp of her handbag tight.

So when she reached her destination and got off the bus in an unfamiliar city, she was rested but actively maintaining a vigilant, calm state of mind. Controlling her breathing, aware that nobody in the world knew where she was, except for the stranger she was about to meet – so she was responsible only to and for her own self. In some ways what she was doing seemed insanely risky, but she was committed now, and felt like she'd set things up as safely as she could given the circumstances.

The decentralised peer-to-peer exchange had been straightforward enough to use. She'd set up an account with an anonymous username that did not indicate her gender and looked for someone with bitcoin to sell for cash within a defined geographical area. Nothing had come up closer to home, but obviously finding the right deal for the right amount at the right time meant a bit of flexibility. She wasn't a confident motorway driver – Mark had always said it was too risky with her medication anyway – but she didn't mind getting on the bus and going somewhere new. It felt safer than dealing with anybody she could ever possibly bump into again in her home town, for a start.

The deal had actually only taken moments to set up on the platform, because there was no 'Know Your Customer' process or uploading of ID – the FAQ on the exchange explained that they didn't require them as she would not be sending any money to the exchange itself, the deals were all made directly between users themselves, the 'peers' in peer-to-peer. The site really only acted as a noticeboard to connect the two of them, and as it turned out she didn't even need to place an ad herself, after spotting the perfect counterparty who already had the right amount of bitcoin listed for sale.

The conversion agreed was actually at a slightly lower rate than it would have been at the centralised exchange she couldn't use this time, but as Ritu had pointed out the fees were probably lower – so maybe it all balanced out.

Anyway, a deal was a deal.

She walked to the agreed meeting spot, yet another roadside café, carefully chosen because it was a lively public place just a few minutes from the bus stop. This café had more in common with the nice coffee shop by Alex's school than Fat Stav's where she and Ritu still caught up from time to time (and where they were always happy to let a semi-regular customer dive into the loo to count stolen money). She had chosen it online after an invitation of her purchasing partner to set the location for the exchange. It had excellent reviews, but the street view of the large plate glass window onto the busy high street had been what decided her. She had thought hard about the vulnerability of going to meet someone with a huge amount of cash on her and decided that the five-minute walk down a busy high street was the safest way.

That was the only time she knew she was potentially at risk of being robbed. None of the people milling past her on the pavement could have had any idea what was in her handbag – unless they were connected with her trading partner on the site. She reflected that she had the sharp kitchen scissors in there too, from her careful destruction of Mark's passport… then almost laughed out loud at herself, did she really imagine she would turn into some kind of blade wielding vigilante if attacked? The whole situation felt so unreal. All that mattered was that her trading partner did not know what bus she'd be arriving on or what she'd look like, but she still felt eyes burning into her back.

Carrie purchased a copy of the Daily Mail from a newsagent next door, and sat in the chair by the window where she ordered a latte. Eugh, what a horrible publication, why hadn't she insisted to ArizonaXXseven that they identify each other by copies of the Guardian instead? This rag would have been right up Mark's street, had she ever seen him read anything ever. This realisation occurred to for the first time in nearly two decades – Mark didn't even have any books in his study.

She suddenly wondered if there could possibly be an inherited factor to Alex's specific learning difficulties? In any case, Mark would certainly have enjoyed the latest reports from Samar's country, which made Carrie's stomach lurch in despair as she thought of her friend. She still hadn't thought about a way to help her…

'JubaCiao73?' Said a stranger's voice, startling her. She looked up to see a heavy-set middle-aged man with a European appearance and an unread Daily Mail folded carefully under his arm.

'You must be Arizona double ex…?'

'Joel, if that's easier. Thank you for coming all this way to meet me. Shall I take a seat?' He was polite, well spoken. Carrie had had honestly no idea what to expect, but if anything she was surprised that he wasn't Ritu's age, like everyone else using cryptocurrency appeared to be. Horrible bitten dirty nails, though, she noticed absently as he took out his phone. Well honestly, that really wasn't a problem was it? She felt so far out of whatever was normal in her former life now, a masked gangster would not have surprised her – or put her off getting the money sold. It was like being in a TV thriller or a movie, meeting a secret stranger in an unknown location to make a shady deal, and she hoped she didn't look like an idiot keeping her shades on in the bright sunny café.

'I'm Carr– Karen' she said brightly. 'Good to meet you Joel, would you like some coffee?'

Before Joel's flat white had arrived, the deal was effectively done. Sat in plain sight in the window seat of the busy café, Joel peered into the envelope and checked the bundles of notes discreetly, without withdrawing them. She let him take the lead on who should do what first, as he had used the site before and was clearly experienced and comfortable selling large amounts of bitcoin for cash to complete strangers, or at least he was better than she was at appearing to know what to do.

He scanned the QR receiving address on her wallet app, before they both checked the codes, on both of their phones. After that, he proceeded to transfer the largest single amount of bitcoin that Carrie had ever seen, directly to the wallet on her phone – while Carrie sat trying to look relaxed and wondering what to do with her hands. Why did nobody smoke any more, except Mrs Shah? It had been much easier to look cool when she was a teenager, but she hadn't been watching cryptocurrency transactions going through then.

Leaving his phone on the table with Carrie, Joel went to the bathoom, where in a curious echo of Carrie's performance earlier that day he had suggested confirming the cash amount. He returned a few minutes later with the package secreted somewhere invisibly about him, to thank her politely for her total accuracy.

Together they checked the Block Explorer, and observed the transactions confirming. Carrie realised that they hadn't specifically agreed on a number of block confirmations to wait for – Ritu had said six was ideal, for any large amount. They both shared a little cheer when the first confirmation came in, and the transaction arrived as pending in Carrie's mobile wallet.

After that, by unspoken agreement they made non-disclosing small talk about other things. Joel was from Montenegro, and worked in construction – well, that explained the nails, she thought. What a charming, lovely, hardworking man! He had teenage children too, two girls – and she listened politely to his tales of their hormonal angst and unsuitable boyfriends. He sounded like a caring father, if somewhat traditional in mindset – god help the poor boys his girls were sneaking around with, and she was glad Katie's parents hadn't been at all like that. There was something about those hands, though, in which she sensed the potential for sorting things out with them directly, which made her shuffle uncomfortably, for all his polite words.

She talked to him a little bit about Alex and his upcoming volunteering expedition, wishing she could ask him about the things she was most curious to know: what was his cryptocurrency story? What was his story altogether? This evidently educated and cultured man from the former Yugoslavia, working 'in construction' but not seeming at all like a builder. The big elephant sat right on the coffee table between them was of course what on earth was he doing with thirty-five grand's worth of bitcoin to flog, but she wasn't going to ask him that any more than he was going to ask her questions about the cash.

Actually, she reflected, this controlled sharing was just about right. She knew only what she needed to know – that he'd sent her the bitcoin. All that 'Know Your Customer' stuff was irrelevant. The only address that mattered was the one on her wallet, and she'd never even know his last name. It wasn't relevant, they'd never set eyes on each other again. Who was she to judge where the bitcoin had come from?

They ordered another round of coffees, and nattered politely about YouTube influencers – whatever on earth *they* were – their kids, and the manners and lamentable communications skills of the upcoming generation.

'I said, if Sophia was here, she'd be buried in her mobile phone just now, instead of making conversation!' Joel said, making Carrie giggle as she glanced up from refreshing the Block Explorer in her browser. Five confirmations in, and the wallet app was displaying a green 'confirmed' next to the astonishing balance. She quite liked looking at it, but was keen to play it cool and businesslike, especially as everything had gone so well.

He insisted on paying for all the coffees, after which they shook hands and left the café – abandoning both of their copies of the Daily Mail on the aluminium table – and headed in opposite directions. Carrie's bus home wasn't for over an hour, so she had a stroll around a shopping mall, and ate a sandwich in yet another café, where nobody knew who she was, or what her secrets were.

On the way home, Carrie messaged Samar, to check whether her Bitcoin wallet address was the same one she had been using the year before. At last she was in a position to send a bit of help directly to someone who needed it.

WhatsApp message:

My dear friend,

Your generosity has left me speechless, clinging hopelessly to shreds of joy in terrifying and despairing times. A ray of light in the darkness of my life. Everything else is black.

My husband is dead.

I was forced to use the last of my savings to pay off the guards, so that we could bury him. Jamal and his men from the training camp dug the grave in the hills outside the town. We had no Imam. Mohit faces Mecca as the Koran requires, and this has been my last service to my husband, my partner in life and love. He will be with Aaliyah now, and they are both lost to me in my earthly hell.

I can only whisper the prayers in my heart.

Jamal was angry because the fund that I had saved for his migration was gone. Now we have buried his father it feels as though I am on the point of losing him too, for good, to the revolution – there was no alternative for him, than to get away to Europe.

I have no job, no income, and no family. But your unlooked for generosity, of the bitcoin you sent to me, let me get some cash for my son to leave me as well. This widow has no future to look forward to, but thanks to you I could buy a ticket for my son to leave the hell this country has become. I don't know how far it will get him, but it will start him on his journey away from this life and the scars of the past.

Your friend, in love, and shared memories of happier days.

Carrie slept on her friend's message, going round and round examining the options, but eventually she realised there was only one thing she could do.

Her heart was breaking for her friend's loss and grief but being able to send practical help was oddly comforting, and with regard to her own resources she felt calm and resigned. What would she ever do with all that bitcoin anyway? Samar needed it more. Carrie had no idea how much it cost to pay smugglers to get someone out of Syria, but she knew Samar had been saving for a long time to scrape enough together just for Jamal. It was easier to send it all in one transaction.

She was used to compartmentalising her emotions, and the tearing and visceral grief she felt for her friend so far away was in one place in her heart – an aching sadness, when even though she had done the only thing she possibly could to help in the circumstances, it felt so hopelessly inadequate. So recently, Samar had had a comfortable middle-class existence, worried about her son's grades at school rather than his paramilitary affiliations, concerned about what the neighbours thought rather than what the secret police were doing to torture and kill her husband. The crumbling of her life seemed to mirror in reverse the transformation of Carrie's own situation, making the circumstance yet more obscenely wrong on every level.

As for the money, there would be something surely from the divorce, the house sale. She still had some cash left over from the deal, her passport, and a small amount in her secret bank account. Nobody except the mysterious Joel, who she would never see again, had any idea that she had briefly had tens of thousands of pounds' worth of secret money in her Bitcoin wallet. The adventure on the bus the day before, coffee with Joel and the endless waiting for transaction confirmations, was already fading into the unreality of so many of Carrie's memories, and this one didn't matter as much as many of the others. All that mattered was that Samar had a second chance to buy her son's liberation, after losing her husband and losing her daughter in the way she had.

Essentially, Carrie reflected, she was now in exactly the position which the people closest to her thought she was in any way – left with scarcely a penny to her name, beyond what remained from the money Mark had put in the joint account at the start of the month. She still had a few thousand in cash in her handbag leftover from the money in the safe, but in some ways it felt more authentic, more honest, to be more or less as her friends saw her to be. She had her appointment at the volunteer advice centre to look forward to, and they would surely help her with any benefits or support she was entitled to. She knew lots of people who got by with very little income, within supportive communities where people pooled their resources and looked out for one another. Though of course it wouldn't be easy.

The bottom line was she had no income, few skills to offer the workplace, and the prospects of a messy and unpleasant separation and divorce to look forward to. But, she lived in a country where the rule of law held; she had a loving relationship with her amazing son – even if he was heading to a different continent in a few short weeks' time, that was for positive and exciting reasons and a fixed duration.

She had friends.

She was more fortunate than so many people – and she was determined to be content with that.

Carrie decided to go out for an evening walk, as it was too hot to do anything during the day now. She loved the freedom to come and go, not have to plan around rigid mealtimes and expectations. She might pop in and see Mrs Shah, and thank her again for looking after her things for her. The lightness she felt created a restlessness of spirit, and she was relieved she'd been able to help her friend, it was a weight off her mind.

Alex had been hanging around earlier, and he was still protective of his mum. She had hated lying to him about the trading excursion, but honestly some things had been easier when he was still at school. Now he was out during the day with his friends. At least, he was out with the boys: the whole Katie scene seemed to have cooled considerably, but he didn't seem to want to discuss it, and perhaps with his big adventure coming up that was no bad thing.

When she got back to the house it was nearly nine, and the skies were darkening. She had no inkling that anything was wrong until her key wouldn't turn in the lock of the front door – but the door swung open anyway.

She stepped quietly into the dark hallway, swallowing down a rising wave of panic which pushed its way up through her throat. This was not like last time, there was nothing messed up or destroyed. Why was she tiptoeing? And what on earth had happened to the front door?

She pushed the living room door open, wondering why she was fumbling around in the dark and hadn't put the hall light on. She crossed unerringly to the table lamp by the window, and soon a warm ambient glow flooded the room.

The first thing she noticed was that the curtains were closed – that was wrong too, she had gone out during daylight some hours earlier, so it made no sense. There was a split-second's prescient prickling-feeling, in the hairs on the back of her neck. Then she heard a horribly familiar voice behind her:

'Hello Carrie. You're home late.' Mark was sitting casually on the settee, as though he'd never left his usual spot.

She froze, standing by the window. Measuring the distance to the door, triangulating her escape – could she make it out? Not with her feet rooted to the ground, legs somehow bound tightly as though stuck in resin. Her breath seemed trapped within her. She felt the cloud of medication-like retreat and paralysis coming down over her, while another part of her mind fought desperately for any way out of the situation, eyes darting around the room for possible escape.

'I needed to get some more of my things, and I thought it was time we had a bit of a chat, anyway. As we were interrupted last time, weren't we? Quite a lot to take in that night for sure, and rather a lot going on at once. But there was something you said that stuck with me, something which didn't seem quite right.' Mark got to his feet, speaking calmly but firmly.

Carrie had nowhere to back up to, she was right against the living room window, trapped in the bay.

'You see, I was trying to get everything straight in my head. I was happy to back off for a little while at the time as you were so overwrought. But the more I thought about the events of that night, one thing kept bothering me. I couldn't seem to work it out.

'You'd just come in the door, much as this evening, and I was on the phone to 999. I think I asked you if you'd left the front door open by mistake, and you said something... I don't recall the exact wording, but it seemed to be along the lines of their not having got in that way. Now how could you have possibly known that?' Mark's tone was musing and conversational, as he paced lightly around the living room, all the time staying between Carrie and the door. 'You'd just got home that minute, but it was as though, somehow, you knew more about what had happened with the break-in than I did. Because as I recall, we didn't find the broken window in the back room until the police had arrived.

'I've been staying in this hostel near work and visiting with friends. Very different lifestyle to be sure, to being in the comfortable family home I've worked so hard to pay for. Lots of time on my own, to think. And that's been going round and round in my mind – what could Carrie possibly have meant by that, I found myself wondering.' He stopped pacing, standing directly in front of her now.

'So I thought we'd better have a bit of a chat about that, hadn't we Carrie?'

She felt all the calm and courage draining out of her, seeping away into the floor. The money was gone, she'd sent it far away… Multiple confirmations received. Non-reversible, hard transaction. He had been so upset when he thought it was stolen by anonymous burglars, but if he thought she…

'I just meant, it couldn't be. I know I locked the door, I'm always careful, really careful. Even when I was sick, I never. Of course I couldn't be one hundred percent though.' Carrie's voice choked to a halt, as Mark gripped her neck, his face right up in hers. Her head squeezed back against the window.

'No, you see you were much more certain than that, at the time. Which is why it wasn't adding up for me.' His other hand grabbed her hair, and he dragged her across the room, 'Where the fuck is my money, Carrie?'

She screamed, trying to twist away and protect her face and her neck. Other than that night, he had never once hurt her anywhere publicly visible, but the response now was purely instinctive, to roll in towards the pain in her scalp but protect her vulnerable areas. He hauled her out of the room, pushed her into the study, the rigid fear that had rooted her to the ground now betraying any ability to hold herself in one place, as she allowed him to shove her like a limp puppet.

'All very tidy in here now, I must say. So, you and the Wonder Boy cleaned up I see.' He pounded his fist angrily, sweeping many of the carefully stacked bills and papers from the desk. Alex had dealt with in here: Carrie preferring to avoid the room entirely while she'd restored harmony to the domestic zones, but their son had done a fair job of setting the papers in order as best he could and lifting the filing cabinet back to an upright position. The accusatory void of the safe cabinet, with its smashed lock, yawned towards her as Mark shoved her head towards it – banging her temple hard against the splintered frame. Stars exploded across Carrie's field of vision, as she tried to get her legs under herself and take up her own weight, while Mark continued to haul her around by the hair.

'Too fucking tidy, I realised, once I had time to think. The files were all spilled over, but nowhere else was anything broken or smashed open. And nobody could have known that cupboard was there – no one who hadn't seen it open before.' He was still speaking calmly, implacably, as he forced her down into the office chair – a chair she'd never sat it before that moment. This room was still his domain, she thought abstractly. This was the view he had all the times he had sat here. She remembered the advice of the Community Safety officer who had visited after the break-in and suggested fitting an alarm with a panic button under the desk. But she had been thinking about saving money, she didn't use this room, and there was no alarm installed. Just the new locks – which had clearly proven little obstacle to Mark when he was determined to re-enter the house.

He leaned down over her, dragging her head up close to his. 'I think you've been keeping things from me, Carrie,' he said as flecks of spit rained down into her battered face.

Carrie swallowed hard and tried to breathe steadily. She could feel the fleeting temptation of dissociation at the edge of her mind, a part of her longing to retreat as she had done so often in the past, but the fear and the physical pain of her bruised cheek and burning scalp helped her hold on tight to her presence in the moment. She looked back at him without flinching, although her right eye was swelling closed.

Her silent regard seemed to infuriate Mark further, but with a rough shake he turned away from where she sat on the chair, propped against the desk – his desk – to pace the room angrily. 'Or are you protecting someone else, Carrie, our precious son perhaps? I know he knew about the money too! Neither of you know how hard it was to divert that money from the fund at the bank, how smart I was to have seen the opportunity and taken it when I did, years it took me to save it all up! You think my plans included growing old with you in this place? That was going to be my future, that money! You thought the future was in crypto crap money, mine was in the real world!" Mark jerked back around, as though to catch some betrayal in her expression, but

Carrie remained still where she had been shoved onto the chair, watching him silently.

She knew that he had gone further than ever before, but despite the ringing in her ears and pounding in her head, little warning pains from all over her body, she knew that she wasn't badly hurt physically. Not yet. He had crossed another line, and she didn't know where it was going to end. Her greatest priority was to get away from him, out of the house. The place she had come to think was safe so recently, was now a prison, with Mark between her and the only way out. Why hadn't she listened to Alex, Ritu, and Mrs Shah, and talked to the police, had him arrested? Instead, she had tidied up and played house, kidding herself that he'd just stay away and leave her alone.

Without moving her head, her eyes flicked to the window – the curtains were open to the driveway, and she'd half-expected to see Mark's car there, though he'd obviously hidden it out of sight. It was dark outside, but the only light in the room spilled from the door to the hall. The double-glazed windows would contain any sound her crushed throat could hope to make.

Suddenly the light flicked on and Mark was upending her handbag, which he had spotted dropped in hallway, over the desk.

Various belongings rained down in front of her. The envelope with the remains of the money from the safe was still in there, along with her passport, zipped away in an inside pocket. But he hurled the bag away into a corner of the room with the incriminating contents still hidden within it, and rummaged furiously through the items on the desk. The sight of a small case of tampons made her feel suddenly tearful and vulnerable, but Mark seized on the phone instead, amongst the mundane debris of her life.

'Oh, a new phone, very nice Carrie. Bought with my money? This is stolen property, my property! It's not for you!' He thrust it at her face, then smashed it to the floor, stamping on it, grinding it with the heel of his shoe. Carrie heard the glass screen splintering, feeling her lifeline evaporating as she fleetingly felt relief that he had not at that moment recognised it as Alex's old phone from months before.

'And what's this? Scissors? Want to defend yourself Carrie, going equipped, carrying weapons now?' Again he hauled upwards on her hair while jabbing the point of the scissors threateningly towards her left eye.

Carried tried to stay still and calm, to look small and helpless. The scissors were still in her bag from yesterday, when she had used them to shred Mark's stolen passport, standing in the café toilet. Just small kitchen scissors, but the blades came to a sharp point. Mark looked angry enough to stab her, to blind her, and she wondered if the shiny pointed blade would be the last thing she saw with her remaining good eye. Was this how it ended? Was this her payback for taking the money, money it was clear he had stolen in the first place? Even if he must know he couldn't possibly get away with it and it'd be the end of his freedom and life as he knew it, with no money to run away with. He'd threatened to kill her so many times in the past.

No! She couldn't accept that! She would not die chained to this monster. This wasn't how her story was going to end.

She jerked her body hard and grabbed with both hands to haul on his wrist. She threw herself sideways off the chair, wrenching away from the flashing blades in the same instant. Mark, with his hand tangled in her hair, was flung over her shoulder, crashing against the accusing splintered cupboard door, crying out as he landed, heavily winded. Carrie rolled free, and staggered to her feet as she crawled round the corner of the desk. She could hear her own ears ringing.

She could see his feet lying there, jerking slowly, as he groaned in pain. She walked around the desk to the side where he was lying awkwardly on the floor, his shoulder and left arm looking strangely out of shape, where he had caught it on the corner of the desk with his full weight on the way to the ground.

'You fucking bitch, what have you done! Help me up!' Mark roared, and swiped at her legs with his good arm.

Carrie stepped backwards out of his reach.

Standing over him, she experienced a rush of flashback, a memory, a vision: one of the missing links in the chain. Their positions were reversed, she was lying on her back in pain, groaning and reaching towards him while he towered over her fallen form. Maybe in this very room, that she had not known why she always hated. It was just a fleeting glimpse of a buried recollection, but it flooded her mind vividly. Looking up at Mark, standing by her feet, as he backed away from her.

She had been looking past him, past a stabbing source of

pain in her abdomen – which was swollen with advanced pregnancy.

Like a final digit in a code falling into place and unlocking a secret algorithm, this split-second image unleashed a cascade of knowledge about that night – the bleeding, the wrenching pain, the bundling into the car, the raised men's voices outside a hospital room. A room in which she had woken alone days later, shrouded in the silence of heavy medication and buried trauma.

She looked down on him lying helpless now, trying to cajole her to come nearer and help him, with a blend of threats and pleas. Next to him on the floor was her iPhone, smashed to pieces, bits of glass ground into the parquet – her lifeline, to communicate with Alex and Samar and manage her secret resources for escape. He had walked back in and destroyed it with his angry stamping kick, just as she now knew he had crushingly kicked her belly all those years ago.

Too bad she had on only light summer walking shoes, but her heel came down with the weight of years of accumulated anger and fury and rage. Mark screamed and tried to fold his body around his smashed groin, his right arm striving to protect his battered genitals while still swiping to grab at Carrie's other ankle.

She shook him off hastily, and grabbed her bag, with its secret inner zipped pocket, snatching up her purse from the desk, running as fast as her bruised and shaken legs could carry her.

Which turned out to be quite fast.

Out on the street she realised she couldn't keep running, adrenaline gave way to windedness before long. But she knew that Mark's wind would abate too and he would be on his feet by now. She could not go back to the house, she needed a better plan. She needed to accept help at last – and she could still run, walk-jog-run, putting greater distance between them with every step.

Mrs Shah's shop was closed by the time Carrie made it downtown, shivering despite the warm summer evening – the shock had caught up with her fully, and she was shaking all over. She rang the bell on the apartment door, and Mrs Shah took her by the hand led her up the dark stairs without speaking, seated her on the sofa in the compact living room which mirrored the layout of the shop space below.

'Oh Carrie. I am so sorry. You ready for me to call police now, yes? Then I find Alex?'

Carrie nodded, and sank back into the chair cushions. She was ready to let the law take over.

*

Apart from a few very specific details relating to the break-in and the money, she told the police everything she could remember. She didn't go into the flashback of lying on the floor, pregnant and in pain – that memory seemed both too tenuous and too raw to even examine for herself in that momemnt. She didn't mention her final act before leaving the house, either, when Mark was lying helpless at her feet. But everything else about her relationship with Mark from years before up to the present day that she could bring to mind she shared as she was gently questioned. The polite young DC, Alicia Rawlings, wrote everything down in tidy handwriting, although they also recorded it. Prompting Carrie when she faltered, and probing to clarify detail on occasion, Alicia let her talk it all out. There was something cathartic and therapeutic about letting the words spill forth. It took a long time, but no one rushed her.

They took her bloodied clothes and put them in evidence bags, replaced them with some donated overalls. She was wearing these as she shuffled out of the interview room in the police station, where she was momentarily stunned by the incongruous sight of Alex and Ritu, sitting side-by-side on the waiting room bench, faces looking upwards toward her in unison.

Both of them leapt up when they recognised her, hurrying forward. Alex reached towards her, then froze, in horror at the sight of her damaged appearance and terrified of causing her hurt. He stared at her for a moment and gasped, then burst abruptly into heaving, tearing sobs. Carrie drew her son gently into her arms, holding him close as the waves of shocked and angry crying washed through him.

'It's OK, I'm OK. It probably looks a lot worse than it is, I'll be seeing the doctor shortly,' she said, patting Alex's back while she looked hopelessly around, and caught the eye of her friendly confidant. After a quick word with the custody sergeant, Alicia found a private interview room to usher them in to, Carrie gesturing for Ritu to please join them in there when it looked like he was hanging back.

When Alex had calmed down a little, the boys explained that Mrs Shah had called Ritu after the police had taken Carrie to the station, and he had gone back to their house to wait for Alex – as neither of them had had any other way of contacting him. They'd met the police there, who were examining the study and the rest of the house, and someone had given them a lift to the station where Carrie had been taken to make her statement. Neither of them had seen Mark, and the officers they spoke to would not tell them much at all, except that Carrie was at the station.

Alex remained bewildered and confused, but Carrie briefly filled him in on the evening's events. He was wracked with guilt at not having been there to protect her and not having managed to convince her to talk to the police earlier. He was horrified by her facial injuries, but was subdued and oddly shy with Ritu, who he'd never really known about before. He had been aware that his mum had some friends who she talked about cryptocurrencies and things with, but never asked questions. It was just part of the compartmentalising that Carrie had unconsciously adopted as a defence mechanism, to keep the different areas of her life and thoughts quite separate – and she hoped these two young men, both so important to her in different ways, would become friends in time, even if this wasn't quite how she'd envisaged their introduction. Maybe there would be a future where she didn't feel she had to keep everything in different boxes.

DC Rawlings re-entered the room with a tray of tea.

'I'm sorry to keep you waiting Mrs Paige, the medical officer is on her way in and will be with you shortly.

'Now, I need to ask you not to touch your son or have contact with anybody else, as for the record this will be a forensic examination. Ok well not any more than you have already. We need to ensure the chain of evidence. I am so sorry Alex, I know you're worried sick about your mum, but I've spoken to her for a while tonight and I know she's going to be OK at the end of all this, she's quite amazingly strong. Her injuries look terrible, but apart from that bang on the head which my colleague will check out thoroughly, they're mostly superficial.' She smiled reassuringly at Alex, who still looked befuddled, seeming much younger and more vulnerable than his eighteen years.

'I told you, it's OK,' said Carrie, patting Alex gently on the knee before pushing her chair a short distance away from him. 'But why does it have to be a forensic interview, Alicia, I don't understand? There's no question about who did it.'

'I know, but we still need the evidence secured. My colleagues are out looking for your husband to arrest him for grievous bodily harm, Mrs Paige, along with a range of other possible charges related to the way he has abused you over many years – including psychological abuse.

'We want to ensure we have a rock-solid chain of data ready

to use against him, and that includes any of his DNA which might be present on your clothing or about your body. We can make an immediate assault charge stick fastest, while we go about taking evidence for all the years of mistreatment. The medical officer is an experienced professional, and alongside securing any bit of evidence she can, she'll check you over thoroughly and make sure you're alright. She'll help with making any follow-up referrals which might be necessary, too, then you'll be able to finally get properly cleaned up.

'It won't be that different to the kind of examination you might have at A+E, except I'll be present to witness the cataloguing of anything she recovers, and there will be photographs of all your injuries. Your dignity will be respected at all times. Carrie, Dr Carling is really great – together we've dealt with many sexual assault victims, often young girls, really vulnerable people… Everyone always thanks her for making the process as easy and quick as possible. You'll be fine.'

'But what happens to that evidence?' said Carrie, nodding at the reassurance but still concerned. 'I don't know if I– I mean, I haven't decided, what I want to do yet.'

'You don't have to decide anything right now, Mrs Paige,' Alicia continued. 'Your husband has committed a serious assault against you tonight, and from what you told me in your statement, he has abused and coerced you for years. Our immediate job is to ensure your safety and your wellbeing, and then to consider our force's own mandate under our public protection directorate. There will undoubtedly be charges brought against your husband, who has broken many laws, but your role within this process has a lot of choices, and there will be no pressure. We want to make sure you get the help you need, both right now, and in the longer term, as he has been messing with your head for a long time – help for your son too,' she added, nodding at Alex.

'Living around someone like that has a lot of consequences. Right now you might fear having to see him in court or stand up to him, give evidence – but we'll explain all the options and what's involved as we go along, and the days of you being forced to do anything you don't want to do – that's over. It's ended tonight,' she concluded firmly but softly, squeezing Carrie gently on the shoulder.

'Meanwhile, the crime-scene officers have finished at your house, and secured the property. Once you're done with the doctor, we'll take you home. Unless you'd rather stay somewhere else tonight? I know you lost your phone in the assault, is there anyone you'd like us to get in touch with, or calls you'd like to make?'

'You're both welcome at ours,' Ritu piped up, 'I can call Mum now – you can have my room Carrie, and we've got the sofa bed.'

'Ritu that's so kind of you, thank you – you've done so much for me and I really appreciate it. But ever so late, and it's probably best if we get home once all this is sorted out. What have they done though, in terms of the front door? Because I had all the locks changed last week, to your safety officer's recommendations, and Mark still got back in.'

'Oh, hang on one moment Mrs Paige, I just need to take this call,' said Alicia, stepping out of the room with an apologetic smile.

'The thing is, you were both right,' Carrie explained to Alex and Ritu when the three of them were left alone again. 'I was kidding myself that he had just vanished away. I thought he'd stay gone, at least until I spoke to the advice bureau next week. After so many years in denial you'd honestly think I'd have learned, but with the new locks and him on the other side of them I just started to feel safe in my own home for a little while, and wanted to hold on to that for myself, explore how it felt.

'It was so naïve, because the real Mark wasn't that man who slunk away the night of the break-in. Well, you know that Alex, after all those years, which is why you tried so hard to persuade me to make a statement then. All I wanted to do was make a safe, happy home for us for your last few weeks before you went away, and I thought I could defer dealing with whatever will have to be dealt with, till later on. But now, it's all out in the open, and the law will take its course. I'll accept any help I can get. It's not easy after lying to everyone around me, and lying to myself for so long, but I'll do my best to be open and ask for what I need.

'I'm glad the two of you have met each other finally, though this wasn't quite how I'd planned it. I am going to need whatever help you can give me, to get through this next bit – but I will get through it.' She smiled at them both, in a way that she hoped seemed calm and brave.

'It wasn't how I'd imagined meeting you, Alex, that's for sure!' Ritu said. 'Lurking outside your house while the police were going all over it. I thought you were going to thump me!' He added jokingly, then abruptly he blinked, and he looked mortified at the poor taste in which his remark could be viewed.

'Well, you did startle me, but I'm not my father,' Alex replied, still somewhat subdued, and embarrassed at his earlier emotional outburst. 'But it was great that you and your family thought of it, to come and meet me. I'm sure the police would have explained eventually, but it was a bit of a shock coming back to find blue lights outside the house and them crawling all over it, and no answer from Mum's phone.' He sniffed decisively.

'But all Mum said, about how you helped her, and it was your friend who did the locks – I'm glad I can say thank you, at last. For all that, and for being her friend through all the stuff. I'm here for her, always, but as she's my mum, she still treats me like a kid sometimes – yeah you do, Mum, I know you just don't want to lay the responsibility on me. But the main thing is, I'm supposed to be going away in a few weeks–'

'You most certainly are going away, Alex! There's no way on earth anything your father's done is getting in the way of that. Specially as his employer's pretty much paid for it!' The last part came out in a barking tone with a slightly hysterical edge, Carrie's throat was sore too, with bruising which would soon be photographed and catalogued.

'Yeah, I hear you Mum, we'll talk about all of that tomorrow. But knowing you have Ritu and his aunt, people who've got your back. That helps a lot, in terms of me getting on that plane, you know?'

Alex turned to Ritu and awkwardly extended his hand. Carrie could see the slightly older man really wanted to give him a hug, but he respected Alex's fragile dignity, and solemnly shook hands with him instead.

'Alex, man, I know how much your mum loves you, and how much she wants you go off on your amazing adventure. I promise you, I'll look after her. Keep an eye on things, whatever the future holds. Me and my cousins and Mrs S, and everyone. I'd never even been to your house till last week, but we're there not far away.

'We all wanted to help more. It's so hard, when you know something's wrong, and you wish there were ways to ask outright and call out what's going on. But we're all so polite, right? Too British! We don't want to pry or cross the line – I just can't believe that we all suspected. I tried to help with the Bitcoin stuff, as I've seen that help people in lots of different ways, sometimes to find some independence and freedom financially, but I should have said something, asked directly. I suppose I was scared of having got it wrong and coming off really offensive. So I tried to be around and look out for her and I didn't ask or say anything.'

No one did. No one ever does, thought Carrie. Only Samar, the one person who couldn't see the bruises, but saw into Carrie's heart somehow through her words, and asked the right question. *Where was she?* Why hadn't she replied after Carrie sent the rest of the money? Well, done was done, and right now she didn't even have a phone…

The door opened, and DC Rawlings came back into the room.

'Dr Carling's ready for you now Carrie, this won't take long. Perhaps you two gentlemen wouldn't mind hanging out in the waiting room now? Soon be time to go home.

'And I have some further news for you. We've arrested your husband. No, he's not here, relax, he's not even in this station, and you do not have to see him. But he's in custody where he'll be spending the night, and he'll be charged with serious assault in the morning. Even then, though, you do not have to see him.'

*

Carrie felt safe, waking up in her bed a few days later. In her bed, with no one else around.

That was the first feeling and thought, which washed over her sleep-ridden body. A pleasant sensation, abruptly interrupted as she carefully stretched out by a cascade of aches and pains from her numerous injuries, all of which the doctor had carefully photographed and recorded. There were more than she'd even realised at the time, when she'd only been aware of her head being cracked against the office wall and being dragged around by her hair.

But it turned out that her whole body had suffered: bruises were popping up all over, and as she reached for the painkillers she reflected that it was a shame they couldn't bottle the adrenaline which had flooded her body that night as she ran halfway across town in her battered state.

Right now the pills would have to do, and she had no intention of carefully flushing these ones down the toilet. It was an important day, because Alex had received his equipment grant and the list from the Africa Project, and they were heading into the city to shop. Their time together was now measured in a couple of short weeks, and Carrie was keen that they should spend as much of them as possible together. This was an important errand she could actually help him with, and they could enjoy a day out together.

She hadn't really left the house since the night of the attack, but it was time she did. Mark was still in custody and would not be bailed – Alicia wouldn't discuss very much about his situation with her, but she knew that he had been treated for a dislocated shoulder. No other injuries had been mentioned. Dr Edwards had also been arrested and was being questioned, though Carrie felt that for now she didn't want to know the details, she wasn't ready to deal with all the possible memories and facts that might be uncovered there.

The main thing was the police had promised to keep her informed of any changes regarding Mark's detention, but now that he had been charged under the Domestic Violence Act, she had an occupation order in place. She had had preliminary discussions with the advice centre, who had brought her appointment forward with the police's help, and she knew she had a whole lot of stuff to sort out still But right now Mark would not be able to come anywhere near the house, even if he did somehow get released.

Her main priority presently was to enjoy her precious remaining weeks – days! – with Alex, and also to show him that she was fine and coping well. Make up, carefully applied, wincing over the sore bits – not only to hide the bruises from the world to protect Alex, but also because she didn't want to wear them like a badge outside the house. She felt she deserved a day off, actually. So many conversations in the past few days had required her to embrace the identity and status of a victim, accept help and be honest about the depths of her suffering, about which she had been in denial for years - hiding things so carefully even from herself. It was hard dealing with the huge change. Especially while trying to keep it from impinging on Mum and Alex time, or showing him how difficult she found it all.

Industrial quantities of concealer, a light neck scarf, dark glasses and a long-sleeved shirt helped her face the world though, and brave the city centre traffic. Visiting the specialist travel stores and working through Alex's list of required equipment took several hours. Luckily, one big store had a lot of the travel gear, but the medical items they would have to collect later, and it was good to relax over lunch in a department store restaurant,once they'd finally got just about everything.

Alex was checking back through the list while they waited for their food. He had wisely suggested buying the rucksack first, on the basis that everything else should be able to go inside it – indeed, in a couple of weeks' time it would have to, Carrie pointed out. Hopefully, a lot of the items he was advised to get would not be needed at the Project itself, and were intended to be helpful when travelling around the region where such things would be harder to procure. Thank goodness the fixed cost that Alex had been required to fundraise earlier in the year – largely courtesy of his father's bank's social projects committee – entitled him to an equipment grant, to kit himself out with everything he might need.

'So, do you feel ready now?' She asked him.

'I'm excited, yeah – it's going to be amazing. Ready, I don't know, really. But at least I feel better about leaving you – even though at the same time worse, after what Dad did.'

'Oh, Alex. I wish there was something I could do to turn the clock back, have that time over with you – brought you up as a single mum, even if we'd been on benefits we'd have been alright. I wouldn't feel like I was about to see you off to the rest of your life when I'd hardly got to know you. I can't believe how much he cost us, by making me feel so worthless and useless that I'd never manage on my own. And all that stuff you saw and heard over the years – I could have protected you.'

'You did protect me Mum,' he insisted, 'the minute he raised a hand to me, you were there, like a– like a lioness or something! Yeah, I guess I've got Africa on the brain already. You're my Lion Queen! But seriously, I'll never forget that, how you stood up to him that night, how you roared. If ever I'm scared or homesick or anything when I'm away – and I do know there's going to be moments, probably. That's the memory I'm going to focus on. How brave you were.'

Carrie was touched, and felt the tears welling up behind her tinted glasses. 'I know there's lots of other memories too, and Alicia was right, we should definitely look at some counselling or something for you, when you get back. The fact that I can't even remember most of what happened, stuff he did over the years, that's bad enough. But to know you were exposed to all of it – that's really worrying. We can work through it together, when you're ready, get you whatever help you need. I know you're being super brave right now about your trip and I am cheering you on all the way, but the start of your big adventure isn't the end of anything else. We'll keep talking and messaging all the time – yeah, I know, your wifi might be flakey, but whenever we can then.

'I might not have been able to be the mother you deserved through all those years, but I will be now. And while your father is at the root of all that's happened, I've got to take some responsibility for never snapping out of it, and the fear that kept me there – it wasn't just fear of him, it was fear of managing on my own and having a poorer lifestyle. I didn't believe I could do anything without him. And the things which surrounded us, like the cleaner, and the holidays in the sunshine. They were nice things.'

'Dad was a nightmare on holidays though!' Alex reminded her. 'I think he hated being away from work. And foreign food.'

'And foreign people!'

'Yeah! I wonder why he put us all through it, every year.'

'Oh, it was expected, I suppose. For all that he kept us totally separate from his life at work, there were aspects of that lifestyle which would have looked strange if he hadn't had them, like the new car every couple of years, and the stylish holidays. You said he had family photos on his desk at work when you went to that committee presentation? I guess if he had to keep us physically at arm's length, because of whatever was going on in his mind, he had to keep up appearances at work of this picture-postcard family life. While he was all the time stealing money from the bank, it beggars belief.'

'Mum, it sounds like you're feeling sorry for him now!'

'I'm not, honestly. I just feel like for the first time in my life, I'm trying hard to understand what was in his head, what motivated him and made him like he was. It's hard, because I didn't question anything, all those years. I never even understood why he fell out with his family! What went on there? They do say a lot of this kind of behaviour runs in families, but I believe with all my heart that it's not genetic, it's about what's learned, and expressed, and what someone chooses. Because you are so different to him Alex, your whole character and nature – so, you can't blame genes.

'I am going to see the counsellor again, to try to understand better why I stayed and hid inside myself, instead of facing up to him. I can't just have been scared of losing the nice house in the suburbs – although I have to admit I had no idea, really, how other people lived, alongside us in the same town. Like

Ritu and his mum. I need to talk to her properly, though it's tricky with her English, I think I just need to be more patient. Because she raised him as a single mum for I don't know how long – Ritu never talks about his father – but he clearly had a good loving home and upbringing, and he went off travelling round in South America, and then got to uni, where he's doing all this amazing programming stuff–'

'BSc Bitcoin?' Alex grinned.

'Well, that was one of the first things he helped me with, after you gave me the phone,' she acknowledged. 'When you were into Monero. Even back then, I really wanted the two of you to meet, but it also felt like if you did then the whole world could come crashing down and all the different parts would overlap and flow into each other, in a way where there'd be no bits Mark didn't have control over. That's why it all got too much and led to my breakdown in the Spring. It's so hard to explain. All I know is that despite everything it's all such a relief now, just to be able to lie in bed and look at my phone in the morning. At least it was, back when I had a phone.'

'Like everyone else in the whole world!'

'Well no, Alex, not the whole world – I think you're still in for a massive culture shock when you get off that plane!' Carrie continued. 'But, just to feel normal and safe in my own home – not to be continually hiding things, pretending to take medication, secretly saving – it was all such a strain. I'm not surprised I had that attack, it was doing my head in.'

'I wish you'd talked to me. Or Ritu, or someone, about it all.'

Alex sighed. 'What about your pen friend, the one who used to write to you about her son?'

'Actually,' Carried admitted, 'out of all my friends – and it's not like I've got that many – Samar was pretty much the only one who kind of guessed what was wrong, or both guessed and had the courage to ask directly about it, even though she knew it was risking our friendship.

'But – oh goodness – whatever we've gone through with your dad, it's nothing compared to what's happened in her life. Her husband's been murdered, it sounds like by the government or the police, and ever since her messages have got shorter and shorter. I don't know if she thinks they're being read by someone or something. Her son's being radicalised by a group who want to create a whole religious state of their own, under total control, so she's had to get money together to pay people traffickers to get him to Europe, even though it's a terrifying and dangerous journey. What they've got going on at home is so much worse. She was prepared to sacrifice everything she owned to get him out of there, though she'll be left completely alone.

'I don't know where she is or what's happened, as we just used to WhatsApp, but I haven't got her number even when I get my new phone. I know she has mine, but I've got no way to get in touch with her. I think about her all the time.'

Carrie wished she could tell Alex about the money – but that would lead to too many explanations unravelling, and there were some secrets she still had to live with. He was clearly shocked about what had happened to Samar, and it made her realise how naïve and inexperienced he really was, to be going off to another continent without her.

'We forget how lucky we are, we moan about all that's wrong with this country,' she continued. 'All of us do, not just your dad. But everything that happened since Mrs Shah rang the police that night, is proof that we live in a certain kind of society, a place where the police protect you, and doctors care for you, and justice gets handed out. I know it's not perfect at all, but there are systems, and there are rules. Like the fact your dad got arrested and got medical treatment for his shoulder the same night.' Carrie thought about the final thing she had done before leaving the house. Self defence, to stop him pursuing her? She might yet have to stand up in court and explain, why she had stamped with all her weight and fury of years, on her helpless husband's genitals. But there were some things she didn't want to discuss with his son over lunch.

'I guess when I get to the Project, I'll see a bit of a rougher kind of justice,' Alex said, thoughtfully. 'I know the area was at war recently, but the fact they're doing something, like even getting volunteer teachers from the UK, means they're trying to sort things out and make it better, right? I do feel scared though Mum,' he admitted suddenly. 'That I won't be up to it or won't be any use. I mean, how can I be a teacher? I can barely read and write!'

'You can read, Alex, and write too – my god, the progress you've made in the past few years is just amazing, and it's not all down to the technology. Your memory, your creativity, and your sheer determination to master your studies and win through. It's like the best bits of your dad, the qualities which first attracted me when I met him, when he seemed so powerful and effective.

'Of course it's going to be tough, without all the tech and connectivity you're used to everywhere here, but you can make your way through pretty much all the stuff you need to read now, especially if you've seen it once before – you haven't been using a screen reader with that equipment letter, have you?'

'Well, I think I've more or less memorised this list now anyway, or I can glance at the word shape overall and it reminds me of the next word on it, so I don't have to actually read out the letters individually anyway.'

'But Alex that's all reading is, recognising the words, not sounding them out. Your brain just had to work harder to get there. Besides, you do have your tech. You'll be able to charge your tablet and the spellchecks all work offline.

Just think about the best teachers you had. The ones who helped you find ways to overcome your difficulties and learn despite them – the teachers you wanted to please and be successful for. Think about those people, and what made them stand out for you. Then you'll be just fine.'

After lunch they headed back down to the big chain pharmacy, where Alex's specified medical kit was being prepared. The recommendations were a bit alarming, but he wouldn't necessarily be in a place where he could guarantee access to safe medical care and prescriptions.

The pharmacist was waiting for them, with a basket full of goods that looked like it would fill up the new rucksack completely. She was keen to check they'd not missed anything. 'The list just says one pack of water purification tablets – how long are you going to be away for? As there are eleven months' supply of malaria tabs here, but only water tabs for a few days?'

'Oh, those water tablets are for if we go camping or something', Alex replied confidently and politely. 'They explained in the orientation webinar that we'd have access to safe well-water at the Project. Well, it'd be the same water everyone else was drinking anyway, and we'd just have to get used to it.'

'I see', the pharmacist continued. 'Well, there's a good batch of rehydration salts in case you need them, and some emergency diarrhoea medication – in case you have to travel or something, best avoided if not, always good to let these things run their course if you can, just stay well hydrated. You've had a cholera shot?'

'Oh yes. And about a dozen other ones as well!' he replied. 'I felt like a pincushion, and I could hardly move my arm last week!' Then he flushed and glanced anxiously at his mother.

'He'll have to drink the water, same as everyone else,' Carrie interjected, 'and no doubt get through a bit of Africa Tummy along the way. Hopefully, all the orientation training he's done will help him recognise the difference between that and something more serious. Thanks for packing everything up and labelling it so clearly for him.'

On the way out, Alex asked her, 'Do you think I will get the sh– erm, Africa Tummy, Mum?'

'Well, probably, at some point. Surely they mentioned that in the training, and what to do about it? It won't be that bad, I'm sure, though it will probably be the moment you most wish you were home in your own room – or bathroom! I'll be just a thought away, or a call as soon as you can get to some signal. But honestly it won't be surprising if you have some physical adjusting, as well as emotional adjusting, to do when you first arrive. After all, you've had eighteen years of all the bugs and pollution and god knows what in the UK air and water and food. Probably if you brought one of your students you'll be teaching back over here with you, they'd get sick from those because they'd have no exposure or immunity. Neither of you were raised in a bubble, both of you would have healthy immune systems, but you can only get used to what you're around, I guess.'

'Yeah, that makes sense. Acquired immunity and strength. It's like what Ritu was telling me the other day, about why private blockchains are rubbish,' nodded Alex.

'Er – how did we go from diarrhoea to blockchains?' asked Carrie, as they loaded their haul of shopping into the car. 'I'm glad you're learning from him though, he's very smart!'

'Well, this is just what he was saying, but it sort of makes sense. He was asking about Dad and the bank – just about his work, not asking about anything else,' Alex reassured her. 'He said loads of banks and similar places, they're building with blockchain and experimenting with it, registering patents, because it's such a good way to manage data and see it's not been messed around with. But, they're mostly doing things to use just inside their bank, totally different from a currency that anyone can use.

'Ritu said they're not strong like Bitcoin, those private chains. The institutions think they are, but actually they're quite vulnerable to being broken, and where's their audit trail then? Because Bitcoin's basically been living in the wild, all over the internet, for years. No one's been able to hack it or break it, even though so many people have tried. But all of those attacks, they just make it stronger.'

'What doesn't kill you, eh?' muttered Carrie, as she pulled out of the carpark.

'Yeah, just like you, Mum. You've been attacked, but you're so strong.'

'Hmm. Well, I'm not sure about that saying to be honest. I'm not dead but I'm pretty battered and beat up right now.' She glanced in the mirror – the concealer wasn't doing quite the job it had promised when they left the house, but they'd be home soon. She was weary and aching apart from anything else.

'Yeah, but you're strong emotionally, at least you are now. I think that saying just means that it all makes you stronger in the end, not necessarily right away. I felt pretty crappy last week after the Yellow Fever injection, but I know it's making my immunity better, so I am stronger even if it doesn't seem it at the time. In the same way, if someone attacks a blockchain, like by trying to attack the code all they end up doing is making the proof of work stronger in the end.

That's why you need big public open ledgers, to build that strength. Not private internal blockchains which you need permission to access. Ritu says that in that case, you might as well just have an Excel spreadsheet.'

Carrie smiled inwardly at the 'Ritu says' refrain, which she had heard a lot in the last few days. The boys were well on their way to developing a meaningful friendship, and she hoped it would continue, despite Alex's upcoming travels. They were very much a generation of instant messengers, she reflected, so the distance shouldn't matter too much.

'Well, you know, I don't know anything about that. Yes, I've been really fascinated by all the Bitcoin stuff, and I've enjoyed saving it up and sending it to my debit card, so I could buy things without your dad knowing. But about hash rates and mining and cryptography, I suppose I'm just not interested in that. Maybe I could learn it – I think I spent so many years believing I couldn't learn anything and that I wasn't not smart enough, because that's what I was told. But I was able to learn to use it, what to be careful of, roughly how it works and what I like about it, without having to know the science. I trust that smart people not only know about it, but that the way they're rewarded means they have to do things fairly and for the common good.'

'Well I think you're smarter than you know even now Mum, but you're right. Most people don't know how money works, or really how the internet works, or anything like that – because they don't need to. So long as it doesn't break or do anything weird, it's kind of finished enough and ready enough for everyone to use it easily. I guess bitcoin will get there in the end, if enough people keep working on it and making it easier and easier to access.

'Ritu gave me some links for projects in Africa as well. Not just for people here sending money home from Europe and places like that, but just using bitcoin as local money. He said there're some countries where women aren't allowed bank accounts or to have anything of their own, and so this company's paying them in bitcoin to do graphic design and research – you know, online tasks – for business in America and all over.'

Carrie said nothing. Even in 'free' countries, she reflected, there are women who aren't allowed to control their own lives and resources.

But Alex went on with enthusiasm, 'And because there's no phone lines, in lots of parts of Africa, everyone's got mobiles. Maybe dead basic ones. So there's this payment system people are using for sending bitcoin, direct from one handset to another. Maybe even phones as basic as your old one, Mum!'

'Hey! That is my phone again now until Ritu gets me the new one. Which won't be new – but he said his cousin's got a lead on a working iPhone I can just about afford, so that's good.'

'Yeah, you need a phone Mum, so I can send you all my photos of giraffes and stuff. And then maybe you can get a museum or something to take in your Nokia, so everyone can learn their history in the future?'

The two of them laughing and relaxing like this, even in this odd moment being stuck in traffic, was what she was going to miss.

As least now these moments were forming meaningful memories that she hoped she could hold onto forever. No tricks or mnemonics needed. Once a mum, always a mum.

*

'Is cake! What, you think Indian lady only make curry?' Mrs Shah demanded, as she bustled past Carrie into the kitchen with her contributions to the leaving party spread.

Carrie hugged her. It was so good to see her friend here, in her own home at last, and for Alex to finally meet another person who had been so instrumental in his mother's survival and liberation. Carrie didn't actually have very many friends, and she had never hosted a party before she realised, other than having a couple of Alex's friends round on his birthday. This was to be a joint celebration, for the arrival of a set of perfectly acceptable A-Level results and a deferred university place awaiting his return, and a chance for everyone to wish Alex well before he set off for Africa - and his group of friends dispersed to various university cities around the country. She was so glad Mrs Shah was there, and she and Ritu's mum would be able to talk in whatever language they were most comfortable using, while the younger people chattered and drank lager. She'd been making finger food all morning, and she had a range of soft drinks in too.

Even Katie came, although she and Alex were now officially in the status of 'friends' as opposed to anything else. Carrie hadn't seen her for weeks, and was touched by the warm embrace – though relieved to know that her various bruises were fading from sight, at least on the outside.

Katie searched her face anxiously. 'I love your new hair Carrie!' she exclaimed, then lowered her voice. 'Alex told me what happened, the night your ex-husband came back and broke in, I am so, so sorry. I can't imagine what it must have been like...' The confident young woman's voice tailed off, as she looked curiouslyaround the living room, as though seeking signs of the fight.

Carrie's hand involuntarily touched her new cropped hair, which she was able to style and brush forward over the bruising and scabs around her right temple. She still felt a bit naked around her neck, after years of hiding away behind her mid length anonymous bob. 'Thank you, Katie, and thanks for coming today too. I am so pleased you and Alex are such good friends. Of course he's got the boys he's known for years–' Carrie nodded towards the sofa '–but you two were lovely together, and I'm ever so glad you're staying in touch. Where are you off to? Bristol, is it? What are you doing?'

'Yes, Modern Literature. I can't wait! Such a relief to get the grades confirmed.' For Katie, the matter had been fairly low in uncertainty, as she was very much the diligent straight-A type, but she deserved to look forward to her future with sure expectation.

'Oh, how wonderful. I would have loved to do a degree like that, I never got that far. But I adore books. I'd rather do the classics though,' Carrie said, aware that there was an edge of unexpected wistfulness in her voice.

'Alex told me! How you tried to get him interested in Dickens and Austen, back at GSCE… I can imagine how that worked out!' The two of them giggled together, and Katie rolled her eyes. 'But why not? You, I mean. Why not now? With Alex going away, and presumably you're going to get divorced or something…' Katie hesitated, aware that she might be presuming or overstepping the mark, but clearly really wanting to connect with Carrie and open up ideas for her. 'You could do it, if you wanted – go to uni as a mature student. I mean, you could do anything at all!'

Carrie was brought up short a little by this idea, and paused in the act of removing clingfilm from a tray of sandwiches.

'I guess I really haven't thought through much about what happens next, never mind that I can actually choose for myself. I know that in just over a week I have to drive Alex off to the airport with all his gear, and then there'll be all the separation and divorce stuff to deal with. Honestly, I haven't looked very hard at what I want to do after that.

'My solicitor – how fancy does that sound, saying that, 'my solicitor'? In fact, I call her Ruby, and she's ever so nice. The advice centre recommended her, she's been amazing, actually.

Ruby says the house will undoubtedly end up having to be sold, and that I could push for Mark to have to pay me support for the rest of my life, because he never let me work or build a career of my own, never mind a pension, all that time I was keeping his house and looking after him and Alex. I have no regrets at all about being here at home for Alex, but the rest of it…. Well, never mind.

'But the thing is I definitely don't want that. I really need a clean break from Mark altogether, so she said they'd push for the courts to award a lump sum to me. Financial support for Alex at uni, which will go on till he's twenty-two with the gap year, but nothing ongoing for me. That's why the house has to be sold – but honestly, I don't have any problem with that. It's far too large for me on my own for the next ten months, full of reminders I'd rather forget, and I just need a small flat with a second bedroom so that Alex knows he's always got somewhere to come back to, wherever life takes him.

'I'll need to work, of course. I want to work. My skills are pretty out of date, but I think I'm quite good at learning new things. Maybe I could even study, I hadn't thought of going and being an actual student, but… Well, you've planted an idea in my head now, Katie! No question about that! Thank you.'

'No problem, and– well, I know you're really going to miss him. I'll be away too, term times, but I'm always here, in the same country at least. If you need anything, or just want to talk.'

Carrie was so grateful to the polite, dignified young woman, and felt a little disappointed about Alex cooling things off with her on the relationship front. Well, their lives and locations were going to be very distant soon. It was surely for the best. She had definitely learned that friendship was more important, after all.

Ritu and his mum arrived next, and he followed Carrie into the kitchen after sitting his mum down with Mrs Shah, to get drinks for them all.

'I know it's not your party Carrie, but you get the present today – sorry Alex!' Ritu added, as Alex joined them.

'Ah brilliant, my new phone! It has been hard going back to what Alex fondly calls my "dumbphone", even for a couple of weeks. And this looks great, what a bargain!'

'Well, it's definitely not new, actually it's an older model than the one which got smashed up, but, it's still an iPhone – and I got them to throw in a new battery for you as well, perks of the job!'

'Ritu, you're a star! I really can't thank you enough. It's true what they say about it being addictive, I really do miss it even though I hardly had any apps, and I don't do all the social media stuff or games you kids are into. It's just so much easier being able to find things out, and keep in touch – the other day Alex had to actually phone me, which was quite weird!' Though rather nice too, she had thought at the time.

'Right then, give us your SIM card Carrie, we'll get it all set up for you,' said Ritu.

'Oh. I don't have it. The old phone was smashed to bits, and the police took most of the bits away... If the SIM wasn't damaged it was certainly lost, or hoovered up, he stamped all over it – honestly, Mark's study was a bit of a mess! To be honest, I never really thought about the SIM card. I can get a new one though, right?'

'Yeah sure, and if we can find the paperwork for it, we should be able to port your old number across,' Ritu assured her. 'OK, so, just enter your email and password, and then you should be able to select your latest backup to sync from iCloud. You back up overnight, right?'

'Erm? I am not sure I do, actually. Is that going to be a problem?' Carrie felt sheepish. She knew she was mostly good with passwords and all her crypto stuff going carefully into the little notebook, but she'd not thought about backing up her phone or even whether that was possible. It was another one of those little things which popped up to bite her every now and again, for having been in her shuttered offline bubble for so long. This might be more important than Instagram stories or memes though, and added it to her lengthy mental list of things to find out about.

'It's fine, there is a backup here. Oh, but it's from months ago!' said Ritu. 'Actually, was this the day I put the first SIM in for you, at Stav's? You haven't backed it up since then? Oh no, Carrie, I'm really sorry, I never thought to set that up for you. So any apps, photos, contacts and stuff you added since then won't be on here, I'm so sorry.'

'Honestly, Ritu, don't worry about it. Pretty much everyone I ever want to keep in touch with is right here today, and I should get back in there with them, anyway. Alex, you need to get back to your own party, too! I know it's a camera as well, but never think to take pictures, and I don't download many apps – I probably only have the ones that were on there when I met you. If you can show me what to do to back it up regularly in the future, then I'll be fine from now on.'

'OK, well, just so long as you've got your Bitcoin wallet logins somewhere safe!'

'Absolutely, and my twelve-word recovery seeds, all safe and secure, completely offline. Still hidden in the same place, though I do seem to check it more regularly since the break-in' Carrie promised. 'Shall we all get back to the party now?'

'For real. Even your few apps will take a bit of time to all download and sync up, so stick it on to charge and let's go!'

'I just want to see if I've got any WhatsApp messages... Oh. Oh well. I was hoping there might be one waiting for me, but never mind.'

The party went well and lasted later than she'd expected. Although the boys had been great about tidying everything up, she was exhausted, her body still recovering from its bumps and bruises. The nice new GP that the police station had helped her to register with had assured her this was a completely natural reaction to the terrifying assault, which had caused her delayed shock as well as physical injuries.

Still at least now she could relax in a hot bath, feeling completely safe in her own home in a way she'd rarely known. Alex and one or two friends were still pottering about downstairs, the shiny new locks and alarms were in place, and she could relax and see if all her apps had synced up yet. It wasn't as though she had that many, and she'd never organised them into folders or groups.

She flicked idly through the screens, careful not to drop her precious new handset into the suds: it had been a bargain, thanks to Ritu pulling in favours at the shop where he worked, but it was worth the world to her. Suddenly, her eye was caught by a red counter alert on the MomsBoard app. Goodness, she hadn't used that in months! It had been one she'd installed very early on, but then her and Samar had quickly progressed to WhatsApp once Carrie had her new phone, and she'd hadn't given the forum site and its app a thought since then. Maybe it was just something automated?

She idly clicked it open and found a single direct message. A voice from far, far away:

....

MomsBoard private message:

My friend,

I hope you will see these words. My phone, with your direct number, is long lost to me – along with everything else that I own. But I have been able to borrow this phone for a little while from a kindly aid worker, and somehow I was able to reset the login to this community, where we first met so long ago.

It seems like a lifetime since those days.

But I am alive. I am in Europe – or so I believe. I have lost everything, and everyone, except my Jamal, who I have to hope is somewhere on this continent too. I cannot speak of my loss and grief now, all my memories are buried in a hard tight place deep inside me, but I had to flee from my home the day after my last message to you, the day I buried my husband.

I am now in a place called Moria, I am told this is in Greece, and part of the European Union. It is in many ways a hell on earth. But, when I wait in line for long enough, I have food, and when we women guard each other, we are safe from attack, and in some ways then it is a better life than the journey to arrive here. I am trying to recover from this experience and heal myself in body and mind, The helpers here are kind, but this is hard. My heart is breaking with pain from the losses I have endured, and I also have a deeper understanding of the physical pains you have known for years, at the hands of those who have the souls of animals.

I do not know what the future holds, I have nothing and no way of contacting Jamal, I do not even know if he made it safely here ahead of me. I have no way of leaving here, or of knowing if this message will reach you, ever. If you reply I may never receive it. Phones are precious here, and I have nothing left to bargain with.

But if you read this, maybe one day in the future,

know that your friendship is a precious jewel to me, a shining light in the hell my life has become. I think of you often and your escape from tyranny – perhaps one day there shall be an escape for me too.

CHAPTER SIX

Blinking in the morning sun, Carrie tagged along with a group of volunteer aid workers, as they disembarked from the overnight ferry. They all had transport arranged from the ferry port to the refugee arrival camp, something she had not really thought ahead to, and there seemed to be no objection to her hopping on the bus along with them. A diverse and international group, not very diverse in age though - most of them looked more like Alex's cohort of travellers from Heathrow the previous week. But they had come from all over Europe to help, and some from further afield.

As the bus rumbled up the hill from the small port, Carrie wondered what on earth she was doing here on this remote Greek island, so different from her Ionian holiday memories. It had been such a last-minute decision. The arrival of Samar's message, days before she had to face the emotional labour of seeing Alex off on his travels, had been almost too much to deal with. But it had suddenly dawned on her, why not? Who else and what else did Samar have left to help her? Her friend had sounded utterly defeated and bereft. The only person who'd been there for Carrie right through, despite whatever was going on in her own life, had apparently undertaken a terrifying journey to who knows where, and done so on her own. Carrie's survival had been so shaped by the help of her friends in recent weeks, she couldn't imagine what it was like to be truly without anybody. She had to help Samar, and suddenly realised there was nothing to stop her: she didn't need anyone's permission. So, despite being unable to find a direct flight, here she was just a few days later. There wasn't much left of the money from the safe, but she'd scraped up just about enough. After all, she was accountable to nobody for her movements now.

The bus ride up from the port was bumpy and tough on her various injuries. The excited young volunteers chattered expectantly, and across the dark blue sea in the crisp early morning Carrie could see Turkey, the final waypoint for so many hopeful arrivals on European shores. It looked like no distance at all to cross, but she knew it was an insurmountable and desperately dangerous boundary for so many, an epic distance.

As was this place, a million miles from the Greek island holidays she had once known. They pulled up at something resembling hell, as Samar had said: chaos, dirt, noise, and such human need and loss so starkly visible around her, in the form of desperate faces, waiting patiently in line, their eyes holding no hope. Carrie felt incredibly self-conscious and out of place, then cringed with self-loathing at the sheer self-absorption of this thought, in the face of such suffering. But she didn't belong here, and it showed.

Not for the first time, Carrie wished she had gone back to the department store with the trekking and camping section and picked up a rucksack. Her aching body might not have thanked her, but wheeled luggage was not designed for this landscape, and her shiny gilt-buckled suitcase seemed ridiculous and trivial as she walked past lines of people queuing with bundles of all their worldly goods in their own arms. She tried to remind herself she was there to help her friend, someone lonely and in need, to do good. But she felt as self-conscious as she had going out with bruises on her face back home in town, and like her silly suitcase marked her as somebody way out of their depth.

As they shuffled off the bus and into the camp, she wanted to slip away and immediately start searching for Samar, but realised it would be smart to stick around for the orientation and introduction from variously-designated officials.

This place was so vast. She'd had no idea. She felt bad that everyone else on the bus had come to help generally, so she willingly allowed herself to be assigned to a detail unboxing bottles of drinking water for distribution around the camp. At least it gave her some sense of the place and what it involved, and she was able to park her luggage at a gatehouse with the other volunteers' personal items. Her phone and wallet she stuffed inside the money belt she had bought at the airport, where it was hidden away inside her jeans.

The whole camp was so much bigger than she had expected, and she had no idea where to start when it came to finding one person. Over seven thousand people, she was told, and growing all the time, though many people seemed to move on rapidly to Athens where she'd just come from, or further afield. Was this whole thing a wild goose chase? Samar's message on MomsBoard seemed to imply that she was staying in one place – this place – for some time. Carrie had replied and told Samar she was coming to find her, but she had no way of knowing if that message had even been received, and it was obvious that she had a challenging search ahead of her.

She tried to attach herself to a medical group, because of the references in Samar's last message suggested receiving some kind of treatment. Was there some kind of a hospital zone? She didn't even have a photo of her friend, and she was well aware that along with her phone, Samar might have lost identity documents. She might even have been deliberately travelling under a different name. Carrie could not begin to imagine what had happened in that dreadful time: while Carrie was celebrating her liberation from Mark, Samar had been burying Mohit, and then– what? Had she received the second, much larger amount of bitcoin Carrie had sent her? It would definitely have been more than enough for Jamal to get away, and surely for Samar too? Or had she never received it? Why had her friend suddenly had to flee what was left of her life, while she was in the depths of widowed grief?

Carrie lugged boxes, handed out rations, volunteered to run errands and delivered things around the camp, assuaging her existential guilt at being European and having a home and a life beyond these dreadful barbed-wire boundaries, sublimating some of her emotional pain through physical labour. She felt desperate to help everybody around her, and at the same time urgently wanted to find just one needle in this sprawling and chaotic haystack. When her wounds ached, she felt it as a deserved outlet for her impotence, in the face of the sheer numbers of suffering human beings. She was reminded of the debtors' prisons in her beloved Dickens novels, and their warehoused suffering of people in a place without hope. The boundaries of the camp were ragged and badly maintained, and she asked a veteran aid worker whether people tried to leave, through the damaged fences.

'There's nowhere to go,' she explained wearily. 'They can't get off the island. The people here have no money, no hope. The only ones with money are the traffickers, they come and go easily enough, but these people are just waiting to be processed, to find asylum somewhere. It's hell's waiting room.'

Another queue, another official. Another series of lists riffled through, another temporary-looking building to be directed to, and always Carrie felt awkward and difficult: there were so many people in need here and they all deserved and needed help. It was not her intention to imply that one of them was more important anybody else, but she had come such a long way in every sense, and she had to find Samar. After a long day going from pillar to post, a kindly administrator took pity on Carrie after she burst into tears, and offered her a seat in a tiny back office in a Portakabin, where she was able to rest her aching back and feet for a moment and compose herself. It was a little bubble of peace and isolation, amongst the heaving tide of humanity in the camp that she found so bewildering.

She ended up explaining to her new acquaintance the motivation behind her visit, and even showing the man – a mature bespectacled French UN volunteer – the message on her phone.

'And the two of you have never met each other?' He seemed a little incredulous, but seeing the message in the app clearly helped.

'No. I just got on a plane, and then an overnight ferry, and spent the day humping boxes and taking water cartons from building to building – which I am really glad to do, to try to help out – but I did all that for someone I've never met and don't even have a recent photo of. But I have known her for years, she's been a source of comfort and advice and love in my life, through so much turbulence and disaster. I just want to help her, she's lost so much!' Her voice was in danger of breaking into a wail.

He handed Carrie some tissues, and nodded patiently. 'Well, there's no record that fits under Samar Nazari, according to the latest register – although even that goes out of date several times every day. But, as you speculated, most people lack formal documentation here in any event.

But, if she was brought in from the sea and alone, and if she had any injuries, then she will probably be in this zone here.' He jabbed a finger thoughtfully at a map on the wall. 'Assuming she's not having active, urgent medical treatment. There's a lot of people just stuck in the rehab waiting to be fit enough to be processed, and most of them are undocumented.'

Carrie still had no idea where she was going to sleep for the night, she hadn't been paying close attention in the orienteering sessions, knowing she was only here to find one person. As she trudged up another concrete walkway to another canvas structure, she noticed the light was fading, and wondered for the millionth time what she was doing in this place, when she could be curled up on the sofa at home – an empty home, yes, but safe and quiet, with her whole evening free to relax with her Kindle.

Then suddenly, just as abruptly as any of the other changes which had upended her world in recent weeks, she found her. One more list in one more hospital rehab tent, and one more weary volunteer... Who nodded at her clipboard, and pointed to a body slumped on a corner bed in a gloomy tent.

*

'Carrie? What? How? It's not possible!'

Carrie's legs buckled underneath her, and collapsed her conveniently next to the camp bed, where Samar was struggling to sit up. She realised she was grinning and nodding like a lunatic, and tried to seem reassuring instead. But she was so overjoyed.

'Yes, Samar, it's me. I came. I– I didn't know what else to do, how else to help,' She said wondering why she hadn't prepared something more profound or interesting to kick off with once this moment had arrived. Having spent all day searching, she hadn't really looked beyond locating her friend.

She tried again. 'I got your message – I don't know if you saw my reply – but I was so worried about you. So when Alex finally got away on his trip, I booked a flight, as close as I could get to here. I had no idea how I was going to find you, and I've been searching since early this morning when I arrived on the ferry, god this place is enormous, but – here I am!' She felt as though she was babbling inanely, as she searched the weary and confused face of her friend for the first time, trying to see what had happened to bring her to this lowly place.

'Oh my goodness, Carrie!' Samar emitted something between a giggle and a sob. 'Can it truly be you, here in this place? For so many years I dreamed of us meeting up one day, in real life. This wasn't what I pictured…' She looked around the gloomy rehab tent, where lights were going on as the evening advanced, and most people were slumbering, with little to be awake for even during the daylight. 'Is this happening? You came here, for me? What on earth happened to your face?'

'I came Samar, I didn't know what else to do. I didn't tell anybody, in case they thought I was crazy, but, when I heard you were here… Oh Samar, what happened to you? Where is

Jamal? What on earth has happened to you both?' Carrie took both of her friend's outstretched hands in hers, watching in horror as Samar's face crumbled into pain.

'I have no idea where Jamal is! He had nearly all the money, and a start of more than a day, I pray that he is safely here in Europe somewhere, and we can be reunited somehow. But I have no way to contact or find him. Less than an hour after my last email to you, I was driven from my home. I had no chance to grab anything, I just had to run.'

Samar's voice fell to a whisper, as Carrie held her friend, weeping helplessly against her shoulder. 'My home had become hell, so I ran to survive. I was warned that they were coming for me, someone had told the authorities about me burying Mohit and I was to be punished. My neighbours helped me, warned me, lied for me. I had only what was left of the cash from the bitcoin you sent me to pay the men, to get me here. It wasn't enough, so they took my phone, my clothes, they took everything. I begged, I walked, I lied… I sold all that I had.

'They lied to me too. For a long time, I was in some kind of cell with many other women, the younger ones were taken… One by one. I don't believe they told the truth, that they were going to jobs in Europe. Two of us escaped from there and walked for miles in the desert, trying to find someone else to help us keep moving further from our captors.

'When I finally reached the port, after trucks and walking and hiding and having to surrender utterly to those I could not bear, I had nothing left. Nothing left that could be taken from me.

'Then finally I was at the border, and then I was on a boat, setting off into the night, with so many people, some of them families with babies. Far, far too many people, it was obvious, and not surprising that it overturned – I spent hours in the sea, in the dark. There were children and babies screaming, and I couldn't reach them, in the black water, the screaming faded as they drifted away from me. I tried so hard to find the babies...' Her voice choked off, as she pressed gnarled and chapped hands to her face.

'Then after I don't know how long, there came searchlights, and the rescue boat, which brought us here. We were so close to the shore then, I had not known I so near, to the land, to Europe. We came so close. I nearly did not live. But I thought of Jamal, somewhere here, where I could find him, and I lived. I walked off that boat onto the beach myself, in the sodden rags of my only clothes.

'Then they brought me here.

'I think I've been here a couple of weeks now, I don't even know. Time stopped for me in some ways, when I buried my husband and then I lost my son, I only kept moving out of fear. They are treating me for the exposure, I am told, but they do not know to what I have been exposed, as I cannot speak of it... But they are salving my hands and feet from being on the road and in the water.

'I have no passport, no money. I was able to borrow a phone from a kind nurse from Spain, she let me log in the MomsBoard and send a message to you. I did not know if you even looked there anymore, but I had nobody else to contact. I didn't even know you had seen it, nobody here has a phone, if they do, they are robbed straight away.'

Carrie was speechless, numb in the face of her friend's grief. 'Oh Samar! So, you didn't get my reply – or anything else – the day of your last message from home? Or my reply last week to say I was coming to find you? I can't imagine how you've survived.'

'Carrie, I don't know what I survived for, just this one camp is so big and crowded, and I know it is a tiny stone on the mountain of Europe. How will I ever find Jamal? I don't know if he is alive or dead. I should have died. They should have let me die. I told them to leave me in the water, keep searching for the babies. I haven't found the babies from the boat, here in the camp.' Samar's voice kept faltering to a crackle, but it seemed that she was done with tears: they were all spent after so long.

'Samar, you do have hope, you still have one friend. You were my friend when I had no one – I had pushed everyone away, and everyone around me was afraid to question what Mark was doing to me. I've travelled across Europe and searched all day to find you. I can't begin to contemplate how much you have lost, every one of your family – the hurt you must be feeling! But I'm here, and I want to help you. I'm going to get you out of here, somehow. Together we will find Jamal. I don't have much money, but I've got a little, if we can get out of this camp, off the island... I don't know. But you're not on your own, I am here to help you.'

'Carrie. Oh my dear friend, I still can't believe you are sitting here next to me. What happened to you, to your face?' Samar gently pushed back the hair from Carrie's temple dusty and sweaty, and shook her head at the fading scabs and bruises on her temple. 'Oh Carrie!'

The two women just stared at each other for a little while, all out of words, each silently bearing witness the scars of the journey the other bore, seeing the pain and the cost of this final face-to-face meeting.

'Do you have a phone? A smartphone?' Samar whispered suddenly.

'Yes, of course!' Carrie responded, digging out her phone, then being more discreet as her friend shushed her anxiously. Together they crouched over the glowing screen to try and hide it from sight of the rest of tent's slumbering occupants.

'You have a Bitcoin wallet? No, not yours, we need a new one!' Samar declared. 'You have some bars of signal, yes? Quick, download something – BRD, Edge, anything. I didn't have time to sell every bit of the bitcoin you sent to me the day we buried Mohit. The traffickers took my phone as soon as they saw it, and they did not listen when I said that I could use it to get them more than the handset was even worth.'

Carrie started downloading the first wallet the app store offered her, mystified… But then Samar said, 'Select the option to restore from seed phrase.'

*

'This is all I have left to me, Carrie. The one place they could not touch me, break me, inside my heart and my mind. Every step of the journey, as I lost more and more of my strength, my possessions, my self worth, I learned this list. I clung to it as I fell to sleep, when I felt safe enough to sleep, or when I believed I was dying. Or when I needed to distance my mind from what was happening to my body.

'When the boat went down, I lost my last small bundle of possessions, trying to survive. This list is all I have left, and no one could find it or take it from me.

You are the only person left alive who knows it exists, even Jamal does not know I have this in my head.'

Samar's swollen and frostbitten fingers closed around Carrie's hand on the smartphone, and for a few moments the two women clung to each other by the fingertips, both shaking with emotion as they realised the price they'd each paid for their liberation. Carrie got up from the floor, and sat on the bunk next to her friend, so that they could both see the screen, where a flashing cursor prompted the entry of the first word in the recovery seed phrase.

'The first word of the seed phrase is "dance", and the second is "rose". My daughter Aaliyah, she loved to dance! And she had a rose-pink ballet dress – so my recitation starts with the most beautiful picture to hold in my mind, my daughter in her dancing dress. She looked like a flower herself. She would always be the one not quite in line with the other girls, because the music in her head was too exciting, she'd be putting in an extra wiggle or flourish, making that dress swish madly. She was a unique individual, with her own amazing strength of character!'

Carrie blinked back her tears and smiled, as she entered the first two words into the recovery page. 'I wonder who she got that from? I am sure she would have been just like her mother.'

Samar continued, 'The next word is "tattoo". So that was easy to make a mind picture for as well, though not so attractive, I don't like marking the body in that way. So many in my country now have marks on their body from shrapnel and bullets, why would someone think to be damaging their skin voluntarily? I pictured a white fat man, I am sorry but I think of it as such a Western thing! And I imagined a pretty red rose tattooed on a hairy white belly!' She gasped. Carrie glimpsed a twinkle in her eye, and a faint hint of the generous wit and humour of her old friend, who had lost so much.

'The next word is "whale", and I first thought that a whale could make a design for a tattoo, but then I realised that could be confusing me about the word order, so early in the sequence – I couldn't afford to mix up which came first. So I had to imagine something a bit curious instead, which was a tattoo on a whale. And for some reason it was a tattoo of the outline of a whale, on the whale, in a brightly glowing silver ink somehow. The whale's in the sea with water spurting out of its hole. Like in pictures. I have never in my life seen a whale.'

Carrie nodded, and tapped the words into the phone.

'So far it was easy because of nice words that were

straightforward to visualize,' Samar went on, their voices in the quiet tent barely higher than a whisper. 'But then the next word was "opinion". That was so difficult! But I couldn't alter it of course. How could I think about that word, and connect it in the chain?

'I had such negative feelings about the opinions of politicians and the mullahs and what they had done to my country and my family, all the evil news agencies that told lies about my husband – but still the word is just so abstract to remember. So I tried to have an opinion about whales. I decided they were mammals too, and just wanted to live and swim in the sea, and carry out their business. Maybe some of them were mothers as well.' She shrugged. 'I had to concentrate on the feelings and really caring about whales and what was best for them. About how other people didn't necessarily agree, they didn't have to agree, it was just my opinion.

'Then when I was in the sea for so long that dark night, I rehearsed my list, and I thought about my whales, but I did not see any. One day, I would love to see whales, and remember, that I had my opinions about them.

'Following that I had the word "farm", and that was very hard to make a connection with as well. Well, farm was not so hard, but to link to this difficult word, opinions. I thought finally about the newsrooms and the universities, with all their opinions that had damaged my husband. At least it was a strong feeling, and I made a picture in my head of a big farm where all the bits of newspaper headlines were growing. Their lies were blossoming, like they were little buds of cotton, white in green leaves, waiting for someone to pick them and print them and believe them, to destroy people's lives with their harvest of evil words.'

Samar's expression darkened, and Carrie realised how much the anger at the what her family had suffered had sustained her friend and been a source of strength to her somehow. What an amazing woman!

'Then next I had a silly word, that was "circle", but actually it's a nice one for just a visual picture. In my mind I zoomed out into the sky in my helicopter, over my farm, and saw that the field of crops made a perfect circle, green against the brown earth. And with the farmhouses and buildings right in the centre of it. There was some kind of harvester or tractor going round the edge… in a circle'. Her eyes drifted up and sideways as the depth of focus in her mind's eye visibly altered. It was as though she was in some kind of trance, that Carrie didn't dare to fracture, even by breathing too loudly.

'After that I got "coffee", and I thought how strange to have the words of the same letter like that. So I tried to join them quickly, without changing too much, and just flipped the brown earth around my farm into the centre of the circle in my mind, so was looking directly down into a cup of freshly brewed black coffee. I made myself smell the roasted beans, because I was just above it, inhaling deeply, ready for a big strong gulp. Proper Arabic coffee, not the stuff you told me about in the UK that you stir in the water to dissolve it.'

Carrie could almost smell the coffee herself, right there in the muddy tent, as she silently typed the words her friend was recalling, directly into the wallet app.

'Then the next word was "accident". After so long working in the hospital that was easy, and creating a strong shocking thought of coffee being spilled and scalding a face was vivid to remember. I feel bad that it was a child's face – not one of my children or anyone I knew, maybe a composite of faces from the emergency room where I saw so many sit patiently with their pain. I made this picture before what they did to Mohit. I knew what a bad scald looks like already.' Samar's voice trailed off slightly. Carrie let her sit with the silence for as long as it took.

'Coming after that was "mobile", well, back when I made this phrase I had a mobile phone. I was careful with it as you know, after Mohit was arrested I knew I could never buy another one. It was during that time that I created this chain of words, it helped to distract me from my thoughts when I was scared and alone. For my memory collection I had to make something bad happen to my mobile phone, just not deliberately, so I imagined it falling from the balcony of my bedroom. It was a tiny terrace, just wide enough to drink a coffee and read a book, and I would never have put my phone on the rail like that in real life. So that made it a compelling movie in my mind, when it fell to the ground, as though the movie reel was slowed down in time.'

Carrie was awestruck at her friend's trance-like recall of this list of abstract words, and she nodded encouragingly, scared to make a sound which could break the spell of memory. Samar seemed so far away right now.

'Next on the list was the word "edit", so I made a picture of an icon for editing, on my magically restored mobile phone. You know, just the pencil symbol, I put it on something like a document or note, but in the eye of my mind the icon filled the screen, so I would know that was what I had to remember.' She stopped abruptly.

Carrie looked down at the screen and counted the words, only eleven! How had Samar missed one, she had made such powerful associations, so strong and unique. Were they going to fail at this stage? She waited, listening to the silence of the tent, a bubble of tranquility against the more distant noise of the camp outside.

'Then finally the last word was "earth", Samar eventually continued, in a strange whisper. 'How could I edit the earth? It had to be a strong picture, to lock the whole sequence together, but the words were so random to be connected to "edit". I struggled with this for a long time, and tried different feeble images, but it wouldn't stick, and the whole thing was becoming wobbly. I didn't think it mattered, it was a thought exercise, yes? I would not need to know these words because they were safely hidden in my jewel case in our apartment. So if the last word was less strongly remembered, it did not matter so much.'

Her voice was barely audible now. 'Then I had to bury my husband by moonlight. Jamal's friends dug the earth in the night. I couldn't help them. I sat frozen by the shrouded body of my Mohit, trying to absorb and process what had happened. The last time I had seen him he was tired and thin but so vitally himself, and holding to his views. Then he was returned to me dead.

'We put him in the earth. The boys covered him respectfully, but we dared not use any marker. Only the scars in the soil where it had been turned betrayed that his body was there. When we turned to leave my strength left me, and I collapsed on the earth, willing it to turn back to the undisturbed corner of ground on the edge of the desert where no one had ever buried my husband. Jamal helped me to my feet. It was the last time I felt his strong arms around me, for the next day he was gone.

'Then, twenty-four hours later, I was gone too, and my phone was taken from me, I knew I had to remember these words. But I knew also that I could never edit the earth, and restore my husband to his life.'

Carrie entered the final word after a heartbeat's respectful pause. The screen flashed a different colour and popped up a question – 'Yes, click yes to the BIP39 word list' Samar urged her.

Both women watched as the screen dissolved, and the wallet flashed a zero balance. Then, before their eyes, it refreshed itself:

Balance: 46.0317844 BTC

The two women's mouths fell open, as their eyes flicked from the screen to each other's astonished faces. For a few heartbeats there was silence, and some blinking. Then in the same instant, they both started to gasp and laugh uncontrollably, seizing hold of each other, shaking with amazement and grief and hope, as they blinked from the screen to one another.

'You did it!' Carrie realised there were tears streaming down her face, though she was still laughing.

'But, I don't understand!' Samar whispered hoarsely. 'That's far too much, I had nothing like that amount!'

'I sent you more!' Carrie said. 'The next day! You never knew, you were running by then, but I came across some more bitcoin – and I sent it all to you. All the time you were running and selling your things, you had all this money and you didn't know. But you did it, you got away anyway!'

'No, you did it! You found me, you came to me.' Samar seemed caught between hysteria and disbelief, completely different to how she had been during the intense recall session. She was now a hundred percent present in the moment, yet barely able to breathe and think.

'You got out. You made it, you're free!'

'We're both free!'

They realised people were turning to look at them, in their dark corner of the hospital tent. Suddenly, Carrie felt vulnerable as she realised that even her phone could attract unwanted attention. Thank goodness she'd been able to leave her silly wheeled luggage at the reception centre,.

The two women headed outside into the warm autumn air, whispering furtively. There was a lot to sort out, plans to be made... First up, secure that wallet with a password as well. Then they sent some of the bitcoin to Carrie's payment card app. Within a few minutes, it seemed, the funds were there available to spend: fifteen thousand Euros. They kept passing the phone back and forth to each other to look again at the balances.

They sat on a wall, looking across the valley towards the hills and the dark sea beyond, giggling like a pair of teenagers. The timid, gaslit housewife was gone for good, and the bereaved and abused victim was also out of sight for now.

'Right, now we need to get you out of here,' Carrie said. 'Hire a car. Then maybe we can hire a boat – I can cash out Euros from the card in Mytilene, and we'll talk to some of the fishermen about the best way to get off the island, get back to the mainland somehow. Talk to the traffickers if I have to. I have friends in the UK who can help us, once I can reach them. We can't start searching for Jamal until we're clear, and I might have to come back on my own if he's here. It might take a few days, weeks even, but money will make it happen.'

'Money can make anything happen!' Samar replied, still gasping with shock. 'I know that from my journey. Money can get transport, passports, knowledge. I can't believe that it's already there, available to spend on the card. I can't believe I can get out of here, and start searching for Jamal!'

Carrie was pacing as she talked, starting to organise and make plans.

Her friend was still battered and exhausted physically from her hours in the water and the abuse she'd faced along the journey – things they still hadn't talked about yet. Carrie herself had forgotten her own aches and bruises, but she still carried her scars with her. They both had things to deal with.

But all of that could come later, they would look after each other and get back on their feet. First thing was transport – could she get Samar out of the camp tonight? Where was that broken bit of fence? Then a hotel, somewhere where they could get rid of all this *mud*. For a moment she thought fondly of Alex's mountains of dirty football kit.

Until that point, she hadn't really thought beyond finding Samar, and hadn't realised the extent to which she was going to find herself too in this filthy collection of makeshift shelters. But she knew that she'd rather stay there forever, than go back to her former life of fear and submission.

They'd manage, between them, because they had control of their money. No one could take it away from them – the control was lodged in Samar's brain and Carrie's phone. Neither had a home to go back to or a family, Samar had no physical copies of her ID. But they had choices. They could buy time to plan, travel, decide…

They had no boundaries, and no trust problems. The future was theirs

THE END

GETTING HELP

All of the characters and events in this work are wholly fictional, but the reality of Carrie's abusive marriage is sadly too genuine for many people, men and women. There is always help to be found. If you suspect someone needs help, can you be courageous like Samar and offer it?

If you or someone you know or suspect is in immediate danger, call your local emergency number, 999 or 911 or 112. Things could have ended very differently for Carrie, and the most important thing is to get away to a place of safety, before deciding what to do next:

The phone numbers Mrs Shah gave to Carrie might have included:

- English National Domestic Violence Helpline
  0808 2000 247
  www.nationaldomesticviolencehelpline.org.uk

- Women's Aid Freephone 24hr National Domestic Violence Helpline 0808 2000 247

There are international networks and organisations all over the world to help survivors of abuse, and many are listed here **http://www.hotpeachpages.net/a/countries.html**

AFTERWORD AND ACKNOWLEDGEMENT

This book would not have come into being without the support of a whole network of people, whose assistance ranged from emotional to practical. A story like this is the product of a long path of learning and thinking and conversations and reflections and ideas, which eventually coalesce into a beginning, a middle and an end… but by a very circuitous route.

It is, as indicated, a work of complete fiction, with no characters or events corresponding to real people. But real people generously shared their experiences with me in conversations about everything from their abusive relationships to experiences at Greek refugee camps, and I am so grateful for that input, to allow me to weave their truths into this story, with artistic licence. While being careful to avoid references to specific dates or events, and indeed to cryptocurrency prices, this tale unfolds in early part of the second decade of the millennium, against the backdrop of political upheavals which are still unfolding. Any lack of accuracy about history or geography or indeed technology is completely my own responsibility, but I have striven to make the context as real as possible within that.

The memory chain technique used by different characters within this story I first encountered years ago, in a wonderful book by British illusionist Derren Brown. It's many years since I read it, but I can still remember some of the images I formed in order to remember his example list (including a strong mental picture of a glass cabbage). As soon as I encountered the idea of a seed phrase to recover a cryptocurrency wallet this idea returned to me, and indeed the concept of a 'brain wallet' is far from unique. At the time of this story's inception there were media reports of a crackdown at US borders, with some travellers being forced to unlock their smartphones, prompting advice to reset and wipe your phone prior to travel, simply cross the border with the password inside your head where no-one could touch it. With Europe in the grip of the refugee crisis of recent years and seeing footage of desperate arrivals clambering to our shores with not a possession left in the world, this created the seeds of a powerful redemption story for me, even though it took some time to work out the characters and plot to bring about this conclusion.

Given that this was my first foray into the world of fiction,I have to thank in particular my beta readers, the people who made their way through a very early version of the manuscript – complete with typos and chronology errors – to give me unbelievably valuable feedback on everything from the structure to the level of blockchain explanation in the text. Pilar, Anna, Mo, Jane, Cassie, Richard and Russ, your input was so important in helping me turn the story idea into the book you hold in your hands. And each of you gave me those early spine-tingling moments when you commented on and related to the characters personally. You had opinions and cared about what happened to these people, who had lived completely inside my own head for so long, and helped me to believe that others would relate to them too.

My wonderful editor, Jasmin Kirkbride, I found on the independent author's marketplace Reedsy, and I am so glad I chose her for this work. Jasmin went above and beyond with her editing, suggestions, and ideas, making me tighten up the chronology, keep the point of view, and increase the impact at critical points. Thanks to her I know I have a better book than the one I would have otherwise. In the same way Mark Thomas' cover artwork brought new creative input to my own to make something more than the sum of its parts, and I am very grateful.

But so many others inspired the writing of this story. My colleagues at BlockSparks, Diana, Helen and Babs, as well as the fascinating projects we work with in the blockchain space. The diverse and endlessly interesting guests we meet on the Crypto Confidence podcast, and the many amazing people doing groundbreaking work with this new kind of technology, across so many different industries. Personal networks, from WABAS to the Blockchain Sisterhood to the Ideas Team to my Thursday Stompers who helped me walk out the knottier bits of plot, we are all the products of those with whom we spend the most time, and makes me one of the luckiest people alive.

Most of all I am grateful to Richard and my girls, for putting up with my personal journey to creating this book.

ABOUT THE AUTHOR

Maya Middlemiss grew up in London, and her earliest writing experiences were gained hanging out at rock festivals on behalf of the Amnesty International 'yoof' mag. Following travel around southern Africa and higher education in psychology and management studies she worked in community development and diversity training projects in inner London locations, before founding a research fieldwork agency and discovering the benefits of remote and home-based working.

In 2009 she took her location independence one step further and moved with her young family to the Spanish Costa Blanca, where she continued to lead her distributed research team, and wrote *The Participant Principle (2016)*. She ended up writing a column about tech and social media for the local English language press for many years, and first read about bitcoin back around 2012 (but didn't buy any...). In 2017 she turned to the freedom of full-time freelance writing and consulting, specialising in speculating about the future: the future of work, technology, society, data, and increasingly, the future of money.

Indeed, her journey down the 'blockchain rabbit-hole' happened later that year via an unexpected ghost-writing gig, which was followed by another and then another... And as she learned more and more, she found herself increasingly fascinated by the potential global impact of cryptocurrencies and blockchain technology: the unique intersection of mathematics, motivation, economics and innovation, with the power to revolutionise the global economy. Seeing a need for a broader range of services to meet the needs of fast-moving start-ups in this space, she founded BlockSparks OÜ early in 2018, as a specialist marketing communications service for blockchain and emergent technology businesses, and became a prolific writer and speaker in the industry with a personal interest in inclusivity and social impact. She now hosts the Crypto Confidence podcast, explaining the underlying ideas of blockchain and digital currencies to everyday listeners, with expert guests and diverse use cases.

After co-authoring *"Thinking Remote: Inspiration For Leaders Of Distributed Teams"* in 2019, *"Beyond The Chain"* represents Maya's first published work of fiction – a format which enabled her to bring together a number of ideas about bitcoin as a route to financial emancipation, as well as demystifying some fundamental cryptocurrency principles for a consumer audience.

She remains on the Costa Blanca with her husband and teenage daughters, where she runs BlockSparks as an e-resident of Estonia, and also consults for London-based remote leadership company Virtual Not Distant. When she's not writing and podcasting and learning about the fascinating and fast-moving trends of the future, she enjoys hiking, travel, and the culture and gastronomy of her chosen home, while reminding herself to unplug from time to time from the tech she is so passionate about to enjoy connecting with life in the real world.

ENDNOTES

1   Find detailed instructions for setting up your first account at a cryptocurrency exchange here: **https://www.blocksparks. io/help-me-buy-some-cryptocurrency/**

2   The Block Explorer is a direct view of the blockchain data – for bitcoin, or any other blockchain, it can be a confusing sight, and you don't need to refer to during everyday transactions, in fact you'd only look at it to ensure confirmation, or to troubleshoot something unexpected.

If Carrie had copy-pasted the transaction ID from Samar or her public key into the search bar on this page https:// live.blockcypher.com/btc/, Then she'd have seen just those details, instead of an endless string of lines of code. She'd be able to see the public address it was sent from, and watch as the confirmations from the mining pool took place, and her transaction was fully written to the blockchain – complete with timestamp and fees.

3   Monero is a cryptocoin which is focused, as Carrie had learned, on privacy and security. Unlike bitcoin, it is completely fungible and anonymous, that is every coin of monero is indistinguishable from any other – just like fiat currency coins.

4   Mining is the process which generates and validates cryptocurrency, in a proof-of-work consensus algorithm (such as those used by Bitcoin or Monero). It's what drives the network, and both creating new coins and confirming every transaction. It commits computing processing power and energy as the raw material, and while some coins can be mined on home computers it does place a lot of demand on their resources, and Bitcoin can only be mined using specialist chips now. You don't need to understand the mining process any more than Carrie does in order to make use of cryptocurrencies, but if you want to learn more here's an accessible guide **https://blockgeeks. com/what-is-bitcoin-mining-an-easy-guide/**

5   Private keys and public keys both look similar, being strings of alphanumeric code not readable by humans, but they're very different. You can think of a public key as similar to a mailbox on your front door, or an email address. You can safely share it with anyone who might want to send you something. Your private key though is the password to enter and read your email, or to open the mailbox to get your paper post – that code must remain completely secret, as anyone could use it to unlock you cryptoassets, and it must also remain utterly secure – you cannot get new keys cut at the hardware store or reset it like a password.

6   Multi-factor Authentication is sometimes abbreviated to MFA, and 2FA – two factor authentication is also in common use. Every factor adds additional security, but also adds hassle. Setting up at least 2FA on every login is a great start.

7   ICO stands for Initial Coin Offering, and it's essentially an unregulated crowdfunding exercise. The crypto boom of 2017 brought some huge raises, and funded some excellent projects – as well as many exit scams or complete failures: caveat emptor.

8   See: **https://coinmarketcap.com**

9   Unlike most everyday users, Ritu is advanced and involved enough to actually participate actively in the network, running a local copy of the bitcoin blockchain, to support its existence for everyone else. Carrie doesn't know or care whether he is running a full node or a lightweight node, but if you do, you can learn more here: **https://en.bitcoin.it/wiki/Full_node**

www.ingramcontent.com/pod-product-compliance
Lightning Source LLC
Chambersburg PA
CBHW020312160726
47992CB00004B/1502